Excitement sparked through Twigpaw's pelt. She'd have her warrior name at last! But the thought seemed to freeze in her mind. She glanced across the clearing to where Violetpaw and Hawkwing were settling down to eat beside SkyClan. *Is that what I really want? To become a ThunderClan warrior?* Perhaps she should be preparing for a life in SkyClan, as Violetpaw clearly was. After all, that was what her father wanted.

Is ThunderClan really my home now?

WARRIORS

THE PROPHECIES BEGIN

THE NEW PROPHECY

POWER OF THREE

OMEN OF THE STARS

DAWN OF THE CLANS

A VISION OF SHADOWS

EXPLORE THE WARRIORS WORLD

Warriors Field Guide: Secrets of the Clans
Warriors: Cats of the Clans
Warriors: Code of the Clans
Warriors: Battles of the Clans
Warriors: Enter the Clans
Warriors: The Ultimate Guide
Warriors: The Untold Stories
Warriors: Tales from the Clans
Warriors: Shadows of the Clans
Warriors: Legends of the Clans

MANGA

The Lost Warrior
Warrior's Refuge
Warrior's Return
The Rise of Scourge
Tigerstar and Sasha #1: Into the Woods
Tigerstar and Sasha #2: Escape from the Forest
Tigerstar and Sasha #3: Return to the Clans
Ravenpaw's Path #1: Shattered Peace
Ravenpaw's Path #2: A Clan in Need
Ravenpaw's Path #3: The Heart of a Warrior
SkyClan and the Stranger #1: The Rescue
SkyClan and the Stranger #2: Beyond the Code
SkyClan and the Stranger #3: After the Flood

NOVELLAS

Hollyleaf's Story
Mistystar's Omen
Cloudstar's Journey
Tigerclaw's Fury
Leafpool's Wish
Dovewing's Silence

Mapleshade's Vengeance
Goosefeather's Curse
Ravenpaw's Farewell
Spottedleaf's Heart
Pinestar's Choice
Thunderstar's Echo

Also by Erin Hunter

SEEKERS

RETURN TO THE WILD

MANGA

Toklo's Story
Kallik's Adventure

SURVIVORS

THE GATHERING DARKNESS

Survivors: Tales from the Packs

NOVELLAS

BRAVELANDS

A VISION OF SHADOWS

WARRIORS

DARKEST NIGHT

ERIN HUNTER

HARPER

*An Imprint of HarperCollins**Publishers***

Special thanks to Kate Cary

Darkest Night

Copyright © 2017 by Working Partners Limited

Series created by Working Partners Limited

Map art © 2017 by Dave Stevenson

Interior art © 2017 by Allen Douglas

www.harpercollinschildrens.com

Library of Congress Control Number: 2017943443

ISBN 978-0-06-238651-9

Typography by Ellice M. Lee

19 20 21 22   CG/BRR   10 9 8 7 6 5 4

❖

First paperback edition, 2018

ALLEGIANCES

THUNDERCLAN

LEADER **BRAMBLESTAR**—dark brown tabby tom with amber eyes

DEPUTY **SQUIRRELFLIGHT**—dark ginger she-cat with green eyes and one white paw

MEDICINE CATS **LEAFPOOL**—light brown tabby she-cat with amber eyes, white paws and chest

JAYFEATHER—gray tabby tom with blind blue eyes

ALDERHEART—dark ginger tom with amber eyes

WARRIORS (toms and she-cats without kits)

BRACKENFUR—golden-brown tabby tom

CLOUDTAIL—long-haired white tom with blue eyes

BRIGHTHEART—white she-cat with ginger patches

THORNCLAW—golden-brown tabby tom

WHITEWING—white she-cat with green eyes

BIRCHFALL—light brown tabby tom

BERRYNOSE—cream-colored tom with a stump for a tail

MOUSEWHISKER—gray-and-white tom

POPPYFROST—pale tortoiseshell-and-white she-cat

LIONBLAZE—golden tabby tom with amber eyes

ROSEPETAL—dark cream she-cat

BRIARLIGHT—dark brown she-cat, paralyzed in her hindquarters

LILYHEART—small, dark tabby she-cat with white patches, and blue eyes

BUMBLESTRIPE—very pale gray tom with black stripes

IVYPOOL—silver-and-white tabby she-cat with dark blue eyes

APPRENTICE, TWIGPAW (gray she-cat with green eyes)

DOVEWING—pale gray she-cat with green eyes

CHERRYFALL—ginger she-cat

MOLEWHISKER—brown-and-cream tom

SNOWBUSH—white, fluffy tom

AMBERMOON—pale ginger she-cat

DEWNOSE—gray-and-white tom

STORMCLOUD—gray tabby tom

HOLLYTUFT—black she-cat

FERNSONG—yellow tabby tom

SORRELSTRIPE—dark brown she-cat

LEAFSHADE—tortoiseshell she-cat

LARKSONG—black tom

HONEYFUR—white she-cat with yellow splotches

SPARKPELT—orange tabby she-cat

QUEENS (she-cats expecting or nursing kits)

DAISY—cream long-furred cat from the horseplace

CINDERHEART—gray tabby she-cat

BLOSSOMFALL—tortoiseshell-and-white she-cat with petal-shaped white patches (mother to Stemkit, a white-and-orange tom-kit; Eaglekit, a ginger she-kit; Plumkit, a black-and-ginger she-kit; and Shellkit)

ELDERS (former warriors and queens, now retired)

GRAYSTRIPE—long-haired gray tom

MILLIE—striped silver tabby she-cat with blue eyes

SHADOWCLAN

LEADER **ROWANSTAR**—ginger tom

DEPUTY **TIGERHEART**—dark brown tabby tom

MEDICINE CAT **PUDDLESHINE**—brown tom with white splotches

WARRIORS **TAWNYPELT**—tortoiseshell she-cat with green eyes

APPRENTICE, SNAKEPAW (honey-colored tabby she-cat)

JUNIPERCLAW—black tom

APPRENTICE, WHORLPAW (gray-and-white tom)

STRIKESTONE—brown tabby tom

STONEWING—white tom

GRASSHEART—pale brown tabby she-cat

SCORCHFUR—dark gray tom with slashed ears

APPRENTICE, FLOWERPAW

QUEENS   **SNOWBIRD**—pure white she-cat with green eyes (mother to Gullkit, a white she-kit; Conekit, a white-and-gray tom; and Frondkit, a gray tabby she-kit)

ELDERS   **OAKFUR**—small brown tom

RATSCAR—scarred, skinny dark brown tom

WINDCLAN

LEADER   **HARESTAR**—brown-and-white tom

DEPUTY   **CROWFEATHER**—dark gray tom

APPRENTICE, FERNPAW (gray tabby she-cat)

MEDICINE CAT   **KESTRELFLIGHT**—mottled gray tom with white splotches like kestrel feathers

WARRIORS   **NIGHTCLOUD**—black she-cat

APPRENTICE, BRINDLEPAW (mottled brown she-cat)

GORSETAIL—very pale gray-and-white she-cat with blue eyes

LEAFTAIL—dark tabby tom with amber eyes

EMBERFOOT—gray tom with two dark paws

APPRENTICE, SMOKEPAW (gray she-cat)

BREEZEPELT—black tom with amber eyes

LARKWING—pale brown tabby she-cat

SEDGEWHISKER—light brown tabby she-cat

SLIGHTFOOT—black tom with white flash on his chest

OATCLAW—pale brown tabby tom

FEATHERPELT—gray tabby she-cat

HOOTWHISKER—dark gray tom

HEATHERTAIL—light brown tabby she-cat
with blue eyes

ELDERS   WHITETAIL—small white she-cat

RIVERCLAN

LEADER   MISTYSTAR—gray she-cat with blue eyes

DEPUTY   REEDWHISKER—black tom

MEDICINE CATS   MOTHWING—dappled golden she-cat

WILLOWSHINE—gray tabby she-cat

WARRIORS   MINTFUR—light gray tabby tom
APPRENTICE, SOFTPAW (gray she-cat)

DUSKFUR—brown tabby she-cat
APPRENTICE, DAPPLEPAW (gray-and-white
tom)

MINNOWTAIL—dark gray she-cat
APPRENTICE, BREEZEPAW (brown-and-
white she-cat)

MALLOWNOSE—light brown tabby tom
APPRENTICE, HAREPAW (white tom)

CURLFEATHER—pale brown she-cat

PODLIGHT—gray-and-white tom

HERONWING—dark gray-and-black tom

SHIMMERPELT—silver she-cat
APPRENTICE, NIGHTPAW (dark gray she-cat
with blue eyes)

LIZARDTAIL—light brown tom

HAVENPELT—black-and-white she-cat

SNEEZECLOUD—gray-and-white tom

BRACKENPELT—tortoiseshell she-cat
APPRENTICE, GORSEPAW (white tom with gray ears)

JAYCLAW—gray tom

OWLNOSE—brown tabby tom

LAKEHEART—gray tabby she-cat

ICEWING—white she-cat with blue eyes

ELDERS   **MOSSPELT**—tortoiseshell-and-white she-cat

SKYCLAN

LEADER   **LEAFSTAR**—brown-and-cream tabby she-cat with amber eyes

DEPUTY   **HAWKWING**—dark gray tom with yellow eyes

WARRIORS   **SPARROWPELT**—dark brown tabby tom

MACGYVER—black-and-white tom
APPRENTICE, DEWPAW (sturdy gray tom)

PLUMWILLOW—dark gray she-cat

SAGENOSE—pale gray tom

HARRYBROOK—gray tom

BLOSSOMHEART—ginger-and-white she-cat
APPRENTICE, FINPAW (brown tom)

SANDYNOSE—stocky light brown tom with ginger legs

RABBITLEAP—brown tom
APPRENTICE, VIOLETPAW (black-and-white she-cat with yellow eyes)

BELLALEAF—pale orange she-cat with green eyes

    APPRENTICE, REEDPAW

QUEENS   **TINYCLOUD**—small white she-cat

ELDERS   **FALLOWFERN**—pale brown she-cat who has lost her hearing

GREENLEAF
TWOLEGPLACE

TWOLEG NEST

TWOLEG PATH

TWOLEG PATH

CLEARING

SHADOWCLAN
CAMP

SMALL
THUNDERPATH

HALFBRIDGE

GREENLEAF
TWOLEGPLACE

HALFBRIDGE

CAT VIEW

ISLAND

STREAM

RIVERCLAN
CAMP

HORSEPLACE

MOONPOOL

ABANDONED
TWOLEG NEST

OLD THUNDERPATH

THUNDERCLAN
CAMP

ANCIENT OAK

LAKE

WINDCLAN
CAMP

BROKEN
HALFBRIDGE

TWOLEGPLACE

THUNDERPATH

KEY
To The
CLANS

THUNDERCLAN

RIVERCLAN

SHADOWCLAN

WINDCLAN

STARCLAN

NORTH

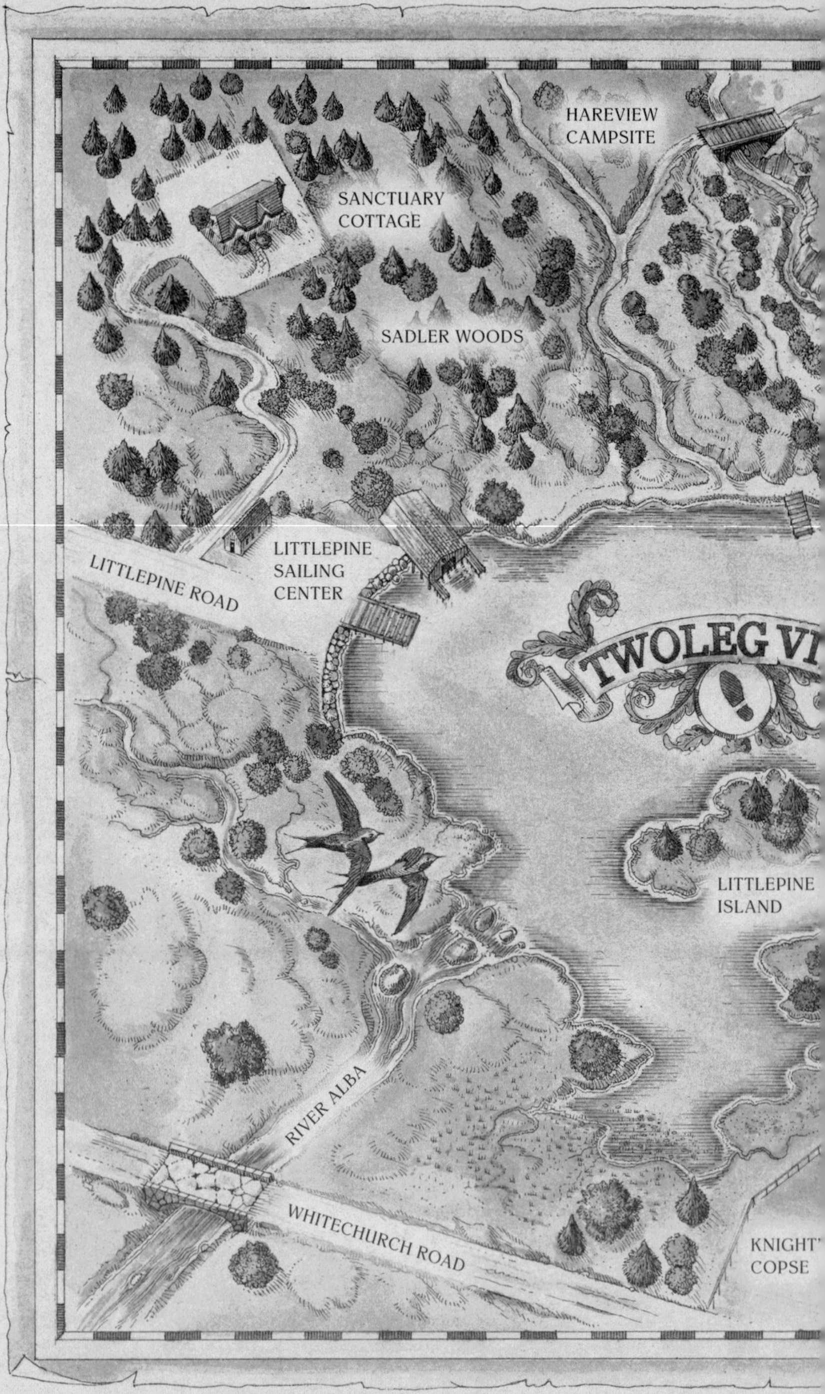
HAREVIEW CAMPSITE
SANCTUARY COTTAGE
SADLER WOODS
LITTLEPINE SAILING CENTER
LITTLEPINE ROAD
TWOLEG VI
LITTLEPINE ISLAND
RIVER ALBA
WHITECHURCH ROAD
KNIGHT'
COPSE

PROLOGUE
❧

The dying sun bronzed the rock outcrop where a tom sat, his yellow fur aflame as shadows lengthened behind him. It had been a good day. He'd caught enough prey to fill his belly and chased butterflies beside a stream where the water was clear and tasted of the mountains. Below him, there was a cleft in the rocks; high enough to be safe from prying foxes, and facing away from the wind, it would make a good place to spend the night.

He sat down, relishing the cool breeze in his fur. Its chill, which announced the coming of leaf-fall, excited him. Prey would be fattening itself for the long, cold days ahead. He licked his lips, anticipating the richer flavors and softer flesh. He was no longer afraid of the coming cold. His hunting skills improved every season. Only a very cruel leaf-bare would leave him hungry now.

He glanced down, spotting movement in the shadows below. A silver pelt. Familiar? "Who's there?" Green eyes glinted up at him, and he recognized them at once. "Needletail!" He purred as she climbed the rocks and stopped. "It's been ages since I've seen you. How are you?"

The she-cat paced around him, her pelt twitching.

The tom could see from her distracted gaze that Needletail was upset. He stood and gazed at her warmly, hoping he could soothe her. "What's wrong? Sit down and tell me about it."

She paused and stared at him, sadness in her eyes.

The tom's pelt prickled as he waited for her to speak.

"It's too terrible," she growled. The breeze ruffled her pelt.

The tom slid around her, smoothing her fur with his own. He felt her stiff posture soften. "Nothing can be that bad, surely?"

Needletail's unease seemed to give way to tiredness, and she slumped into a crouch.

He hunkered down beside her and followed her gaze to the distant horizon. She felt bony beside him; she'd grown thin. "What's wrong?" he asked gently.

"I've been so dumb," she mewed. "I trusted the wrong cat. Many suffered. I need to make it right." She turned her gaze to meet the tom's. "Will you help me?"

"I'll help you any way I can." He blinked at her eagerly, then paused. Suddenly, he could see through her glassy stare; shadows were buried in her eyes. Stiffening, he sat up and glanced along her silver pelt. A faint glow shone from within her. It was a glow he'd seen before, but not in Needletail. The fiery sunshine had disguised it, but now, as the shadows deepened into darkness, he could see the glow clearly. It lit her like swallowed moonlight. His heart ached with grief.

"Needletail," he breathed. "How did you die?"

CHAPTER 1

❧

"Hurry up, Twigpaw!" Ivypool's mew rang though the trees.

Hush! Twigpaw flicked her tail irritably. A mouse was snuffling through the freshly fallen leaves of an oak. She could see it in the shadow of a root. It froze as Ivypool's mew shattered the silence. Twigpaw didn't move, relaxing only when the mouse once more began rummaging through the leaves.

She leaped and felt the soft flesh of the mouse beneath her claws as she slammed her paws down. After giving a quick killing bite, she lifted its limp body between her teeth and turned to join the others.

Ivypool was hauling a thrush—an earlier catch—from beneath a clump of ferns. Sparkpelt paced behind Fernsong, and Cherryfall lounged in a patch of late-afternoon sun. As Twigpaw reached them, she tossed the mouse onto the pile of prey they had collected.

Lionblaze sat stiffly, his gaze probing the forest as though searching for danger.

"I don't know what you're looking for." Sparkpelt sniffed at him. "The rogues are gone and all the other Clan cats are in our camp."

3

"Not *all* the Clan cats," Ivypool pointed out.

"ShadowClan went home days ago," Fernsong added.

"But we've still got half of RiverClan and a whole *new* Clan cluttering up our dens." Sparkpelt fluffed out her fur. "I'm sick of sleeping under ferns so a RiverClan warrior can have my nest. In another moon, the ferns will have shriveled and I'll be sleeping in the cold."

"Reedwhisker needs your nest," Fernsong reminded her. "He's still recovering from being held captive by the rogues."

"And he won't be there much longer," Ivypool meowed. "Mistystar says that RiverClan has nearly finished rebuilding their camp. They'll be able to go home soon."

"What about SkyClan?" Sparkpelt challenged.

Lionblaze answered without moving his gaze from the distant trees. "SkyClan will be gone soon too."

"Where? They have nowhere to go." Cherryfall got to her paws.

"The Clan leaders will decide at the next Gathering," Lionblaze told her.

Sparkpelt's fur prickled along her spine. "What are they going to do? Invent new territory for SkyClan to live on?"

"There's not enough room around the lake for an extra Clan." Cherryfall glanced at Twigpaw.

Twigpaw shrank beneath her pelt. Was the ginger she-cat blaming her? *I found SkyClan and brought them here.* This fact, which had made her so proud initially, had begun to peck at her like a crow. The camp *was* overcrowded, and where *would* SkyClan live? *But my father is in SkyClan. I have a family now.*

Despite the happy thought, worry wormed in Twigpaw's belly. *Perhaps I was being selfish by bringing them to the lake. Perhaps there isn't room for another Clan.*

"Who's going to give up territory to make room for them?" Sparkpelt stared at Lionblaze as though the golden tom should have an answer.

He shrugged. "Let StarClan decide."

"StarClan wanted them back." Cherryfall pawed through the day's catch. "Let StarClan find them somewhere to live."

Fernsong shifted his paws. "At least the prey is running well," he meowed. "I just hope we have enough to feed everyone tonight."

"Bramblestar sent out five hunting parties today," Ivypool reminded him. "And RiverClan will bring prey with them when they return from working on their camp."

"*If* they return," Sparkpelt sniffed. "Last night Mistystar and her patrol didn't come back at all."

Twigpaw felt a twinge of irritation. "I thought you *wanted* them gone." Why was Sparkpelt being so crabby? She was usually so positive about everything. "You should be happy they didn't come back."

Sparkpelt flicked her tail dismissively. "Let's take our prey home." She snatched a shrew and a vole by their tails.

"Good idea." Ivypool picked up the thrush.

Twigpaw grabbed her mouse. *At least with her mouth full Sparkpelt won't be able to complain anymore.* Lionblaze, Cherryfall, and Fernsong gathered up the last of the prey, and together they headed back to the hollow.

At the camp entrance, Twigpaw waited for the rest of the patrol to duck through the thorn tunnel. The branches scraped her pelt as she followed them through. On the other side, cats crowded the clearing, chattering like a flock of starlings. Scents swirled around her. RiverClan and SkyClan scent mingled with the smell of her Clanmates. And the faint odor of ShadowClan still lingered on the bushes around the edge of the camp.

As usual, SkyClan's warriors lay around the apprentices' den, soaking up the last of the late-greenleaf sun before its rays disappeared behind the cliff top. Two of their apprentices, Dewpaw and Finpaw, practiced battle moves in the clearing, while Reedpaw jeered fondly at her brothers' clumsy leaps and rolls. Leaf-fall was coming fast; leaves drifted down from the trees at the top of the hollow, falling softly around them.

Twigpaw scanned SkyClan, looking for Hawkwing, Blossomheart, and Violetpaw. Her kin. When ShadowClan had returned to their own territory a few days ago, Rowanstar had allowed Violetpaw to remain behind so that she could spend time with their father and his sister. Twigpaw loved sharing the camp with kin at last, and when she couldn't see their pelts among the others, she wondered, with a prickle of anxiety, where they were. She couldn't let go of the fear that she might lose them again.

Leafstar stood near her Clan. Twigpaw caught her eye. The mottled brown-and-cream SkyClan leader must have seen worry in her gaze, because she nodded toward the medicine den. "Alderheart is checking on Hawkwing," she called over the murmur of voices. "Violetpaw went with him."

Twigpaw's pelt prickled with concern. "Is he okay?"

"Don't worry," Leafstar purred. "Alderheart's checked on all of us today. I think your medicine cat likes making us eat herbs."

Blossomheart, the SkyClan she-cat who Twigpaw had recently learned was her father's littermate, lifted her head. "He says it'll help us build up our strength, but I think he just likes to see the look on our faces as we swallow them."

Outside the nursery, Tinycloud shuddered. "I'm not swallowing any more herbs till I've kitted," she mewed indignantly. She glanced at her bulging belly. "There's hardly room for these kits in my belly, even without herbs."

Blossomfall lay beside her. "Your kits will come soon enough." As she spoke, Stemkit and Eaglekit scrambled over their mother and hurtled after Plumkit and Shellkit, who were darting among the other cats, squealing with delight as they played warrior and prey. Blossomfall purred loudly. "And as you know, once they do, you won't get any peace."

Feeling a pang in her stomach, Twigpaw hurried toward the fresh-kill pile. A group of RiverClan cats sat clustered below Highledge. Reedwhisker, Mintfur, Brackenpelt, and Icewing, who had been held captive by Darktail and his rogues, still looked thin and hollow-eyed after their ordeal. They had been starved in captivity, and their wounds had been left to fester. Now Lakeheart and Mallownose flanked them protectively while Willowshine licked another sticky poultice into Mintfur's scratches.

ThunderClan's patrols were back in camp, too. Berrynose and Poppyfrost were enjoying some prey beside the warriors' den, while Brightheart and Cloudtail shared tongues nearby. Jayfeather was outside the medicine den, helping Briarlight with her exercises. Birchfall stood at the center of the clearing, looking lost. He craned his neck, scanning the countless pelts as though looking for someone, then purred with delight as he caught sight of Whitewing and hurried to join her.

As Twigpaw picked her way between the cats sprawled around the clearing, Graystripe pushed his way out of the elders' den. Behind him, the honeysuckle walls bulged as cats moved inside. Mosspelt, the RiverClan elder, and two cats from SkyClan had made nests there. Graystripe shook out his fur. "Fresh air!" he rumbled, sounding relieved. "It's so stuffy in there, even the fleas are trying to get out."

His mew was swallowed by the chatter of the other cats. But from Highledge, Bramblestar caught the elder's eye and nodded sympathetically.

Finally, Twigpaw reached the fresh-kill pile and dropped her prey.

"Have you seen this?" Molewhisker was already there. "RiverClan brought back *frogs*." He was staring in disgust at the smooth, fat bodies among the furry forest prey.

Twigpaw wrinkled her nose. "I guess they like the taste."

"Just so long as they don't try to feed them to us," Mole-whisker sniffed.

Cherryfall dropped her rabbit onto the pile. "At least they caught *something*." She glanced pointedly at the SkyClan cats.

"*Some* of our visitors are still too weak to hunt."

Twigpaw bristled. "It's not their fault. They've been through a lot."

Ivypool brushed past and laid her catch on the ground. "Jayfeather said they're supposed to rest until they get their strength back."

Cherryfall grunted. "And who's going to help us get our strength back after we've finished feeding half the forest?"

As Lionblaze and Fernsong laid their prey beside the others', Lionblaze looked sternly at Cherryfall. "Complaining isn't going to help anyone."

"She's allowed to have an opinion." Molewhisker moved closer to the ginger she-cat and glared at Lionblaze. "Besides, are we even sure that SkyClan is a real Clan?"

Cherryfall flicked her tail in agreement. "They might just be another bunch of rogues."

Twigpaw stared at her. How could she *say* that?

She opened her mouth to defend her father's Clan, but Fernsong spoke first. "Bramblestar says they are one of the original Clans. Are you doubting your leader?" The pale yellow tabby tom blinked at Molewhisker.

"Then why hadn't we heard about SkyClan before? How come only Bramblestar knew about them?"

Ivypool flicked her tail crossly. "*StarClan* knew about them," she meowed. "Are you contradicting our ancestors?"

Twigpaw felt a rush of gratitude toward her mentor.

Ivypool went on. "It's not SkyClan's fault they returned to us at such a bad time."

"They *had* to return now," Lionblaze added. "It was part of the prophecy."

"But they didn't return because *StarClan* showed them the way." Cherryfall turned her gaze on Twigpaw. "Some cat *brought* them here because she wanted to find her father."

"That was part of StarClan's prophecy, too," Lionblaze retorted. "We found Twigpaw in the shadows so that she could clear the sky—"

Twigpaw couldn't listen to any more. Cherryfall's words were stinging like nettles. She turned away, hot with shame. Cherryfall was right. She *had* searched for SkyClan because she'd wanted to find her father. Her paws hadn't been guided by StarClan but by her own selfishness.

"Wait." Ivypool hurried after Twigpaw.

Twigpaw stopped, her pelt pricking with worry. "I didn't mean to spoil everything."

"You did a *huge* thing by bringing SkyClan here," Ivypool told her. "This is where they belong. StarClan wanted them to return, and you're the one who found them." She touched her nose to Twigpaw's head. "I am so proud of you. And"—she pulled back and looked Twigpaw in the eyes—"I'm sorry that I didn't support you when you wanted to find your kin."

Twigpaw looked at Ivypool gratefully. It did make her feel better to hear her mentor apologize. If ThunderClan had sent out a search party, Twigpaw wouldn't have had to go out on her own, against Bramblestar's orders. But more than that, it had hurt Twigpaw not to have her mentor's support on something so important to her. "Thank you." She closed her eyes. "But

I'm worried I may have caused more trouble for the Clans by bringing SkyClan here."

"If you have, it's trouble StarClan wants us to have." Twig-paw opened her eyes, and Ivypool met her gaze before she went on. "And it's far less trouble than we've seen in the past moons. Darktail is dead and his rogues are gone. The Clans must find their paws again, and we must find space for Sky-Clan. It may not be easy, but once it's finished, *all* the Clans will be stronger for it." Ivypool dipped her head. "I'm sorry. I wasn't thinking about you or SkyClan."

"What *were* you thinking about?"

Ivypool glanced around nervously. "Tigerheart and Dovewing were quick to volunteer to join the search." She lowered her voice. "I didn't think it was a good idea for them to travel together."

Twigpaw understood. While Tigerheart had been stay-ing in the ThunderClan camp, he and Dovewing had made more and more excuses to hunt and patrol together. They'd even shared prey. Twigpaw had seen the accusing glances exchanged by her Clanmates every time Dovewing and Tiger-heart brushed past each other on the way to the fresh-kill pile. Ivypool must be relieved that Tigerheart and the Shadow-Clan cats were gone. How could a relationship between her sister and another Clan's deputy lead to anything but trouble?

She nodded. "So you didn't want to stop me from finding my father?"

Ivypool blinked at her slowly. "Of course not. And I'm sorry you thought I did, and that my actions put you in danger."

"And you're not mad that I snuck off by myself?" Twigpaw pressed.

"I would have done the same." Ivypool's gaze was warm. "I'm glad you came back safely. ThunderClan is lucky to have you."

A purr swelled in Twigpaw's throat. She felt happy they'd cleared the air. Suddenly, Cherryfall's complaints didn't seem important. Once more she felt sure she'd done the right thing by bringing SkyClan home. "Thanks, Ivypool."

Ivypool nodded toward the medicine den. "I think Violetpaw wants you."

Twigpaw followed her gaze. Violetpaw was staring at her anxiously from beside the entrance. Was something wrong with Hawkwing? Twigpaw hurried toward her, heart beating in her throat. "What's happened?"

Jayfeather looked up as she passed him. "Nothing." He lifted one of Briarlight's crippled hind legs with his paws and began to ease it up and down slowly. "Alderheart's just decided that SkyClan needs twice as much attention as any other cats in this camp. Perhaps he's hoping Leafstar will make him *their* medicine cat."

"That's not fair!" Twigpaw stopped and stared at Jayfeather. "He's just being a good medicine cat. Like you taught him to be."

Jayfeather's blind blue gaze fixed on her, but he didn't say anything. Indeed, his eyes widened slightly, as though he was impressed that she'd stood up to him.

"Come inside," Violetpaw urged. Her gaze flitted around the busy camp. Twigpaw knew her sister wasn't comfortable in

ThunderClan. But she hadn't been comfortable in Shadow-Clan, either. Or with the rogues. She only seemed happy with Hawkwing by her side.

Twigpaw followed her into the medicine den. Inside, late sunshine glittered at the top of the small hollow, sparkling on the damp cliff face where water trickled down to a small pool. Beside it, Alderheart was checking Hawkwing's pelt. "The scratches have healed and you're looking better," the medicine cat told him.

"So I can hunt now?" Hawkwing looked eager.

"You should still rest for a few more days." Alderheart pawed a small pile of herbs toward the SkyClan deputy.

"Are you sure?" Hawkwing meowed impatiently. "I don't like being a burden on ThunderClan. I want to contribute to the fresh-kill pile."

"I'm sure." Alderheart sat back on his haunches. "And I'm sure a few mice and voles will be happy to live another day."

Hawkwing caught sight of Twigpaw. He purred. "How was the hunt?"

"Great." She crossed the medicine den and rubbed her cheek against his. "I caught a mouse and a shrew."

"I can't wait until I can be out there with you." His gaze flicked to Violetpaw. "I always dreamed I'd hunt beside my kits one day."

Violetpaw sat down and wrapped her paws over her tail, returning her father's gaze happily.

Twigpaw felt a twinge of guilt. Hawkwing had already said that he would be happy for her to join SkyClan. Was she supposed to? Were kin more important than the Clan that had raised her?

"You've both grown into such fine cats." Hawkwing turned to Alderheart. "I can't thank you enough for finding them and looking after them."

Alderheart glanced away self-consciously. "It was my privilege," he murmured. "And I'm glad SkyClan is back where it belongs. I've been searching for you ever since my first vision."

"It's good to be among the other Clans," Hawkwing meowed. "All we need now is our own territory so we don't have to rely on the kindness of others."

There's not enough room around the lake for an extra Clan. Cherryfall's words rang in Twigpaw's head. But there was plenty of room. It took a whole day to mark the borders of ThunderClan territory. She guessed the same was true of the other Clans' land. Surely they didn't need *that* much space? *Cherryfall's just being difficult.* She dismissed her Clanmate's words. "There's prey outside," she mewed. "Let's go and find something to eat."

"Eat your herbs first," Alderheart told Hawkwing.

Twigpaw headed for the entrance while Hawkwing lapped up the shredded leaves. As she ducked outside, an angry yowl pierced the air.

"What is Mosspelt supposed to eat?" Owlnose, a brown tabby RiverClan tom, was staring angrily at Cloudtail. The fresh-kill pile had dwindled, but there were still plenty of mice and voles there, along with Cherryfall's rabbit.

"There's more than enough left for Mosspelt," Cloudtail

answered sharply. "I don't know why you're making a fuss."

Owlnose glared at him. "Have you forgotten the warrior code? The weakest cats eat first." He glanced at the Thunder-Clan warriors eating prey around the edge of the clearing and then at Graystripe and Millie, who were tucking into a thrush. His angry glare seemed to silence the Clans. A hush descended over the hollow. "Why do your elders eat while ours goes hungry?"

Mosspelt was sitting outside the elders' den, eyes bleary.

Graystripe looked up from his meal, his ears pricking. "Has some cat gone hungry?"

"Mosspelt," Owlnose meowed indignantly.

"She was asleep," Graystripe told him. "Even RiverClan cats can't eat in their sleep, and I didn't want to wake her. There's nothing worse than being woken from a nap."

Owlnose scowled at him. "Going hungry is worse."

Millie sat up. "Mosspelt can share with us." With a flick of her tail, she beckoned the RiverClan elder toward the thrush.

Mosspelt headed toward it, her pelt prickling self-consciously.

Owlnose's fur bristled. "So all we get is ThunderClan leftovers now?"

"Perhaps if you spent more time hunting and less time complaining, there'd be enough for everyone." Molewhisker lifted his chin defiantly.

But there is enough for everyone. Twigpaw looked at the prey left on the fresh-kill pile. Why were the toms making such a fuss?

Hawkwing and Violetpaw padded from the medicine den.

"What are they arguing about?" Violetpaw whispered as Lakeheart and Brackenpelt joined Owlnose and glared at Molewhisker.

Twigpaw shifted her paws uneasily. "I think there are too many warriors in one camp."

The thorn barrier trembled and Mistystar padded in, Minnowtail, Breezepaw, Mallownose, and Podlight following at her heels. They stopped and stared in surprise. The camp was suddenly silent. "What's happening here?" the RiverClan leader demanded.

Bramblestar leaped from Highledge. "Just a disagreement," he explained. "It's nothing to worry about. Every cat will feel better once they've eaten."

Mistystar looked at Owlnose, Lakeheart, and Brackenpelt. "I hope you are showing respect. ThunderClan has been kind to us."

The warriors didn't meet her gaze.

Mistystar flicked her tail sharply. She turned to Bramblestar and dipped her head. "Thank you for your generosity. But I think it's time RiverClan returned to our camp."

Bramblestar flicked his muzzle toward Reedwhisker and Mintfur, the most injured of the RiverClan warriors. "Are you sure that's wise?"

Mistystar glanced at them. "Don't worry. Our injured cats will be cared for. Our medicine cats are as skilled as yours. And we've made good progress rebuilding the camp. We need to be home now to finish the work."

Bramblestar nodded. "Very well. Would you like me to

send a ThunderClan patrol with you? They could stay and help."

"Thank you, but no." Mistystar was firm.

"At least stay and eat with us." Bramblestar glanced at Mosspelt, who had only just taken her first bite of thrush.

All gazes were fixed on Mistystar. Twigpaw felt tightness in her chest and realized that she was holding her breath. She didn't want RiverClan to leave while tensions were still running high.

After a moment, Mistystar blinked softly. "Thank you, Bramblestar. We will."

Relieved, Twigpaw waited beside Violetpaw and Hawkwing while Bramblestar led the RiverClan leader to the fresh-kill pile and nosed Cherryfall's rabbit toward her.

Mistystar pushed it aside and picked out a shrew. "This will be enough."

When she had left, Twigpaw padded toward the pile. She passed a mouse to Hawkwing and a shrew to Violetpaw before picking a vole for herself.

"Where shall we eat?" Violetpaw glanced nervously around the crowded clearing.

"Over there." Twigpaw nodded toward an empty spot beside the SkyClan cats.

As Hawkwing and Violetpaw headed away, Ivypool called to her.

"Twigpaw!" Her mentor trotted happily toward her. "I've spoken to Bramblestar. We both agree it's time for your assessment."

My assessment! Excitement sparked through Twigpaw's pelt. She'd have her warrior name at last! But the thought seemed to freeze in her mind. She glanced across the clearing to where Violetpaw and Hawkwing were settling down to eat beside SkyClan. *Is that what I really want? To become a ThunderClan warrior?* Perhaps she should be preparing for a life in SkyClan, as Violetpaw clearly was. After all, that was what her father wanted.

Is ThunderClan really my home now?

CHAPTER 2

Alderheart ran his paw over Tinycloud's belly, happy to feel the fur now thick and smooth and her kits moving around inside. "They're stronger and so are you." He sat back and admired the SkyClan queen as she lay outside the ThunderClan nursery. Like the rest of her Clan, she'd gained weight during her stay in ThunderClan and was looking fitter. Her shoulders no longer stuck up like sparrows' wings. "Your kits will come soon."

Leafpool shifted beside him, looking the queen over. "I'm glad they waited until you were strong enough to kit them."

"I hope they'll wait until we've got our own camp." Tinycloud's eyes shone excitedly.

Alderheart purred. For the first time in moons, everything was going well. RiverClan had left three days ago; their camp must almost be rebuilt by now. ShadowClan was surely settling back into their old home. WindClan's borders were no longer closed, and SkyClan's warriors were strong enough to hunt and bring back prey.

Some ThunderClan cats were still grouching about the overcrowded camp, but SkyClan would soon have territory of their own. Finally, StarClan's prophecy would be properly fulfilled: SkyClan would be one of the Clans once more. Alderheart blinked warmly at Tinycloud. "Your kits will be the first SkyClan cats to be born beside the lake."

Leafpool caught his eye. A warning look. "Come on," she meowed briskly. "Jayfeather wanted us to help him clear out the herb store."

Had he said something wrong? "Shouldn't we discuss which of us is going to help with Tinycloud's kitting?" He hurried after the light brown tabby medicine cat as she crossed the clearing. "Don't forget, SkyClan doesn't have a medicine cat yet. One of us should be with her."

"We can decide that when the time comes." Leafpool kept walking.

"But what if she's in their new camp?" Alderheart protested. "Perhaps I should go with them when they move, until they find their own medicine cat."

Leafpool stopped outside the medicine den and faced him. "You shouldn't have told her that her kits would be born beside the lake."

Alderheart blinked in surprise. "But they will be, won't they? They're due any day."

"We're not sure yet if SkyClan is going to stay."

Leafpool's words hit him like a fierce gust of wind. "What are you talking about?"

"You've heard the cats grumbling, haven't you?" Leafpool lowered her voice, her gaze sweeping around the Thunder-Clan cats as they milled about the clearing. Molewhisker and

Thornclaw were comparing battle moves. Birchfall and Ivy-pool were sharing a mouse with Fernsong, and Sparkpelt was sitting on Highledge beside Squirrelflight. "I want SkyClan to make their home here as much as you do. But not everyone feels the same way."

Alderheart was confused. "Cats are just complaining because they have to share their nest and their fresh-kill. Once SkyClan has its own camp, they'll have nothing to complain about."

Leafpool leaned closer. "What makes you think cats who don't like to share their nests will want to share their *territory*? If SkyClan stays beside the lake, where will they live? They'll need land, and that land will have to come from the other Clans."

"*So?*" Alderheart refused to understand. He wasn't going to let the selfishness of others change the way he felt. "StarClan wants SkyClan here. They sent a prophecy that led them back to us. Why would any cat think that a piece of territory was more important than the wishes of StarClan?"

"Some cats may find it hard to believe that StarClan wants them to give up land they've fought so hard for," Leafpool warned him.

"No cat thinks land is more important than StarClan!"

"Are you sure about that?" Leafpool's gaze drifted toward Highledge.

Alderheart, puzzled, looked up to where Squirrelflight and Sparkpelt were talking. "Squirrelflight supported my search for SkyClan."

"What about Sparkpelt?" Leafpool meowed.

"She came with me on the first quest to find them!"

"But *finding* is not the same as *keeping*."

"What are you trying to say?" Alderheart couldn't believe his ears. "You think Sparkpelt doesn't want SkyClan to stay?"

"You'll have to ask her yourself." Leafpool shrugged.

As she spoke, Jayfeather appeared at the entrance of the medicine den. "Hurry up, you two! I want to sort the herbs before sunhigh. Leaf-fall won't wait. If we're running low, we need to start gathering before cold weather spoils them."

Leafpool glanced at Alderheart. "My son seems to have forgotten that I've been running the medicine den since before he was born."

Alderheart hardly heard her. He glanced anxiously at Sparkpelt. If *she* didn't believe SkyClan belonged beside the lake, who did?

Alderheart rushed to catch up to his littermate. "I hope Twigpaw's assessment goes well tomorrow," he said, falling into step beside her as she followed her Clanmates along the shore. "I think she's nervous." It was true—Twigpaw had seemed distracted in the days since Ivypool had told her she was going to be assessed. But Alderheart wondered if by bringing up Twigpaw, who had brought SkyClan back to the lake, he might get at Sparkpelt's feelings on the new Clan.

"She'll be fine," Sparkpelt purred. "This time tomorrow, she'll have her warrior name."

The moon, huge and yellow, hung in the crow-black sky. A

crisp wind gusted from the lake, lifting Alderheart's fur. The Gathering would start soon. Bramblestar and Squirrelflight led the way to the island. Leafpool followed with Ivypool, while Cherryfall and Molewhisker trailed behind. Thornclaw and Birchfall padded farther up the shore, shadowing the party beside Lilyheart, Honeyfur, and Twigpaw. SkyClan trailed behind, no more than shadows on the shore.

Alderheart wanted to ask Sparkpelt what she thought about SkyClan. Jayfeather had kept him busy gathering herbs all afternoon. This was the first chance he'd had to talk to her alone. Now he was struggling to find the words. Would he offend her by asking if she thought SkyClan didn't belong here? And what if she said it was true?

"What do you think the Clans will decide?" Pebbles crunched beneath his paws.

"About what?" Sparkpelt glanced at him.

"About SkyClan."

Sparkpelt turned her gaze back to Bramblestar. "Let's hope they decide to do the right thing."

"What is the right thing?" Alderheart tried to sound casual.

"The right thing is for the *real* Clans to carry on living the way they've always lived."

"The *real* Clans?"

"You know. Us and ShadowClan and RiverClan and WindClan. The Clans that have always lived beside the lake."

"Not SkyClan?" Alderheart fur prickled with alarm.

"This isn't their home. It never has been." Sparkpelt sounded matter-of-fact.

Alderheart swallowed. "Then what do you think should happen to them?" He was scared of her answer.

She glanced at him, her eyes sharp. "They should go back where they came from."

Alderheart could hardly believe his ears.

"Darktail has left the gorge now," she went on. "They can go back to their proper home."

"But what about StarClan?" Alderheart spluttered. "My visions? Don't they mean anything to you?"

"StarClan wanted us to find SkyClan and we did." The trees on the island were looming larger, casting moon shadows on the shore ahead. "Did they say anything about SkyClan moving onto our territory?"

Alderheart remembered the messages from StarClan, wishing again that his ancestors weren't so vague. They had urged him to find SkyClan, but Sparkpelt was right; they'd never clearly said what they must do once they had. "Not exactly. But I'm sure StarClan wants us to keep SkyClan close."

Sparkpelt glanced at him doubtfully. "And how will that help? You've seen what happens when strange cats move into our territory."

"SkyClan isn't *strange cats!*" Was she really comparing SkyClan to Darktail's rogues? "They're warriors. Just like us. They follow the same code. They share dreams with their ancestors."

"So which Clan is going to give up territory for them?" Sparkpelt challenged. "Do you really want more borders around the lake? Are you sure that will bring peace?"

She didn't give him a chance to answer, but quickened her

pace and caught up with Cherryfall and Molewhisker. Alderheart stared after her, his mouth dry. Had everything he'd worked for meant nothing? Were the Clans going to force SkyClan to leave?

Tiny waves slapped the shore. He could hear the wind in the trees on the island. *Please, StarClan. Don't let the others feel the same way as Sparkpelt.*

At the tree-bridge, which spanned the water between the shore and the island, he waited for his Clanmates to cross. Only Leafpool paused beside him. "Are you okay?"

He blinked at her despondently. "You were right. Sparkpelt wants SkyClan to leave."

Leafpool touched her nose to his ear. Her warm breath bathed him as she spoke. "Sparkpelt doesn't speak for every cat," she murmured. "But if the Clans do decide that SkyClan can't stay, you must accept it."

Alderheart bristled. "I could never do that!"

"We have no choice." Leafpool leaped onto the fallen tree and crossed the water. "Whatever happens, we must trust StarClan to guide the leaders' paws."

SkyClan was nearing the bridge. Alderheart jumped onto the fallen tree before they reached him, unable to face their hopeful gazes. He followed his own Clanmates through the long grass on the other side and emerged into the clearing beyond. WindClan, ShadowClan, and RiverClan had arrived, but only a soft murmur filled the clearing. The cats spoke to one another in muted mews, exchanging wary glances, each Clan keeping to themselves.

Alderheart's pelt prickled with worry. He'd expected to

find them more jubilant. After all, they'd killed Darktail and chased the rogues from their land. And SkyClan had been found. *The skies have been cleared,* Alderheart thought, remembering StarClan's prophecy. *Am I the only one who's happy about it?*

Leafpool beckoned him with a flick of her tail. She was already sitting beneath the Great Oak beside Willowshine, Mothwing, Puddleshine, and Kestrelflight, who sat, hunched and stiff, gazing uneasily at the Clans.

Alderheart hurried through the wide gap between River-Clan and ShadowClan. He was surprised to see how few ShadowClan cats had come. WindClan sat apart on the far side of the clearing. His own Clanmates had gathered near the medicine cats. He remembered, with a pang, his first Gathering, when apprentices from all the Clans had swapped stories and showned off the new hunting moves they had learned.

Now the apprentices sat in silence. Whorlpaw and Snakepaw sat like stones beside their ShadowClan mentors. Brindlepaw, Fernpaw and Smokepaw, the young WindClan cats, blinked at them, as though puzzled by their aloofness. Nightpaw, the dark gray RiverClan apprentice, glanced nervously at Breezepaw. But her denmate looked away, the wind ruffling her brown-and-white fur.

Alderheart's paws pricked. What was wrong with them? His gaze flitted farther around the clearing. Where were all the elders? They loved to come to Gatherings to share gossip and stories with one another. Tonight, Millie and Graystripe were the only elders here.

As he reached Leafpool's side, the SkyClan cats began to

emerge from the long grass. A hush fell over the clearing. Plumwillow and Blossomheart followed Leafstar and Hawkwing, their Clanmates on their heels. All of SkyClan had come, except Tinycloud, who'd stayed in camp, too close to kitting to make the journey.

Leafstar paused and lifted her chin, letting her Clanmates file past. Hawkwing scanned the gathered cats through narrowed eyes, then padded toward an empty space beside ThunderClan and with a flick of his tail beckoned Plumwillow to follow.

Blossomheart strolled after her. Dewpaw, Reedpaw, and Finpaw stayed close to their mentors' sides. The young cats stared at the other Clans, their eyes wide. Had they ever seen so many cats in one place? Violetpaw looked nervous as she slid from the long grass. She paused beside Hawkwing, her gaze flitting from her father to her ShadowClan Clanmates. Alderheart guessed she was wondering where to sit: with ShadowClan or SkyClan? Perhaps she'd choose ShadowClan. There were so few of them here.

She whispered something in her father's ear and he murmured back. Quickly, Violetpaw dropped her gaze and hurried to where Twigpaw was sitting beside Lionblaze. Alderheart felt a pang of sympathy for the young cat as SkyClan took their places beside Hawkwing. Rowanstar had given her permission to remain with ThunderClan for a while. But had she ever really known where she belonged?

Bramblestar padded forward and dipped his head to Harestar, Rowanstar, and Mistystar. One at a time, the Clan leaders leaped onto the long, low branch of the Great Oak.

Alderheart looked expectantly at Leafstar. Was she going to join them? He felt a twinge of disappointment when she padded beneath the tree and sat neatly among her Clanmates, curling her long brown tail over her paws.

The Clan deputies, Tigerheart, Squirrelflight, Reedwhisker—looking healthier now—and Crowfeather, took their place among the roots of the Great Oak. Hawkwing stayed beside Leafstar as the Clans drew closer, gathering beneath the tree. Hostile glances flashed in the darkness, focused on Rowanstar.

"Should Rowanstar even be up there?" Icewing's sharp yowl cut through the chilly air. The RiverClan she-cat was bristling with anger.

Lakeheart lashed her tail. "Right, is ShadowClan even a Clan anymore?"

"They chose *rogues* as their campmates," Podlight snarled.

"*I* didn't." Rowanstar stared back at the RiverClan warrior.

Podlight held his gaze. "But your Clan thought Darktail would be a better leader than you!"

"What sort of leader loses the faith of his Clan?" growled Crowfeather.

"If the rest of us have lost Clanmates, their blood is on your paws!"

Alderheart's breath caught in his throat as he realized that was Molewhisker's yowl.

"We suffered losses too," Rowanstar spat back.

Alderheart glanced at the ShadowClan cats. There were so few of them now. And yet they looked as surly as ever, chests puffed, pelts prickling. He wondered suddenly if they held their leader responsible for the deaths of their Clanmates. Tigerheart's gaze was unreadable as he sat beside the other deputies. Tawnypelt gazed up at Rowanstar with pity in her eyes. Of course *they* wouldn't judge Rowanstar; Tigerheart was his son, Tawnypelt his mate, and both had remained loyal to Rowanstar the whole time. But how did the others feel?

Their Clanmates shifted uneasily, avoiding one another's gaze and the gaze of the Clans. Alderheart felt their shame. They had chosen to follow a rogue. Their decision had almost destroyed their Clan. But if Rowanstar had been a better leader, would they ever have followed such a dreadful path?

Bramblestar's stern gaze swept over the gathered cats. "There is no use in blaming. What is important now is to remember that we came together to drive out the rogues. We would not let them destroy the Clans then, and we must not let them tear us apart now. Together we are strong. If the events of the past moons have taught us anything, they have taught us that."

The cats murmured indignantly, but no voice yowled out.

Bramblestar went on. "We come here tonight to remember our dead and to plan a way forward." He glanced at Leafstar encouragingly, shifting a little as though making room on the branch beside him. She gave a quick shake of her head as if to tell him not yet. Alderheart understood the SkyClan's leader's reluctance to face the Clans now. Pelts were still bristling.

"Rowanstar." Bramblestar dipped his head to the Shadow-Clan leader. "I am sorry for your lost Clanmates. Let us remember them here."

Rowanstar blinked at him gratefully. "Many disappeared under Darktail's rule," he began. "We don't know what has happened to them, but I fear the worst. We've lost Mistcloud, Birchbark, Cloverfoot, Lioneye, Slatefur, Berryheart, Rippletail, Sparrowtail . . ."

Alderheart felt shock freeze him as Rowanstar continued to list the names of his missing Clanmates. *So many!* He hadn't realized the full extent of their loss. No wonder there were so few ShadowClan cats at the Gathering.

"If only we knew what happened to them . . ." Rowanstar's mew trailed away.

"They probably went with the rogues!" Lakeheart snapped.

"No!" Rowanstar's eyes sparked with rage as he returned the RiverClan warrior's gaze. "It is true we lost some warriors to the rogues. Sleekwhisker, Yarrowleaf, and Spikefur chose to follow them, and ShadowClan will never forgive them. But the others were lost trying to *escape* Darktail."

"It's true!" Snowbird wailed. "I persuaded Berryheart and Beenose to go to ThunderClan so they'd be safe. But they never arrived!"

"Birchbark and Lioneye told me they were planning to leave the rogue camp," Puddleshine called out. "I haven't seen them since."

Violetpaw's eyes rounded with grief. "Needletail died standing up to Darktail. She saved me and her Clanmates!"

Rowanstar lifted his gaze to the Clans. "You judge us, but you don't realize how much we have suffered. If we made a mistake, then we have paid for it with our own blood."

"Our blood too!" Mistystar lashed her tail. "*Your* Clan chose its own path, Rowanstar. Our suffering was forced on us by your Clan's actions. We lost Clanmates because of you. Shadepelt, Foxnose, Petalfur, and Heronwing were killed fighting the rogues."

Rowanstar looked solemnly at the RiverClan leader. "I know," he meowed. "And I hope one day StarClan will forgive us. I do not expect you to."

"We will never forgive!" Icewing yowled.

Angry hisses rose again from RiverClan, spreading quickly to the other Clans.

"ShadowClan nearly destroyed us all!"

"Rowanstar has no right to be leader!"

What's happening? Fear lurched inside Alderheart. Were the Clans going to crumble just as they'd found the missing part of themselves?

Harestar stood and lifted his tail. "You blame Rowanstar and forget that it was Onestar who brought Darktail's vengeance to the Clans. Onestar was Darktail's father, and Onestar rejected him. But Darktail *chose* his path. He *chose* cruelty and murder. And Onestar died putting an end to that cruelty. We have *all* suffered. But we must listen to Bramblestar. He is right. Let us not blame. Let us remember the dead and the missing. Let us remember Onestar and his courage. He faced up to his past mistakes and he gave his last life to destroy Darktail, his own son."

His words seemed to sweep over the Clans like a cooling wind. The cats settled, their anger turning to solemnity.

As calm seeped like water through the clearing, Alderheart realized he was shaking. But hope sparked in his chest. Sense would prevail. He remembered Leafpool's words. *Trust StarClan to guide their paws.*

Mistystar faced the new WindClan leader. "You speak wisely, Harestar. WindClan chose well in making you their leader, and I'm glad StarClan blessed you with nine lives, for you will need them." She looked around at the Clans. "I wish you well. I wish you *all* well." Alderheart's paws pricked as her tone darkened suddenly. "But this is RiverClan's last Gathering for a while."

Harestar blinked in shock. "What do you mean?"

"We will stay on our land and rebuild what was destroyed by the rogues," Mistystar told him. Alderheart stared at her, his mouth dry. She seemed to have given her words much thought. Had RiverClan only come here to share this news? Why hadn't Mistystar spoken earlier? Had she wanted to see first what ShadowClan had to say? "But the Clans can make decisions without us for now. RiverClan needs time. We need peace, and we need to look inward to heal the wounds that have been inflicted on us. From tonight, I am closing our borders."

She leaped down from the branch and signaled to her Clan with a nod. They crowded forward, following her as she headed for the long grass.

"But we must decide about SkyClan!" Bramblestar called after her.

Mistystar glanced back. "Decide what you like. But I warn

you to think twice about letting more strange cats onto your land. You have seen what strangers bring."

"You can't go!" Rowanstar called. "Look what happened to the Clans when WindClan closed its borders. We must work together."

"We are not WindClan," Mistystar answered. "If there is trouble, you may send a patrol to ask for help. But for now, RiverClan follows its own path." She slid into the grass. Her Clanmates followed.

Alderheart stared after them, hardly believing his eyes as the grass closed over them like water. "They can't go."

Leafpool shifted beside him, her fur pricking. "Perhaps it's for the best."

Alderheart blinked at her. "How can you say that?"

She didn't answer. She was watching the Clans shift and murmur, their mews edged with disbelief.

"This isn't like RiverClan."

"RiverClan has gone crazy!"

Anxious mews rippled though the crowd.

Leafpool got to her paws. "Don't be alarmed." Her mew echoed over the clearing. "It makes sense for RiverClan to focus on rebuilding. They are like an injured cat, vulnerable and protective of their wounds. Let them have their peace. I know RiverClan. I know how resilient they are. Let them heal, and they will return to us a more powerful ally than before."

As the Clans' mews softened to murmurs, Bramblestar blinked gratefully at Leafpool and then turned to the gathered cats. "Without RiverClan, it is more important than ever that we work together. And we are fortunate that an old ally has returned to us." He nodded toward SkyClan. "Leafstar, please, join the other leaders where you belong."

As Leafstar got to her paws, the outraged yowl of Crowfeather rang through the air. "No!" Leafstar hesitated. "She doesn't belong there. What do we know about SkyClan?"

"We'd never heard of them until ThunderClan told us about them," Scorchfur called out from among the ShadowClan cats. "Why did Firestar, and then Bramblestar, keep this missing Clan a secret so long?"

"Typical ThunderClan!" Strikestone hissed.

The ShadowClan cats sounded suddenly confident.

Alderheart glanced at Sparkpelt. Her gaze was flitting excitedly from WindClan to ShadowClan. Would she join their outcry?

Bramblestar lashed his tail. "You all know of StarClan's prophecy. *StarClan* asked us to bring them back."

"StarClan only told us to *find* them," Scorchfur argued. "They didn't say we had to make them one of the Clans."

"They *are* one of the Clans!" Bramblestar's mew was taut with frustration.

"We only have your word for that!" Crowfeather snapped back.

And StarClan's! Alderheart wanted to shout out, but he held his tongue. Was it his place to speak for StarClan?

"StarClan sent a prophecy about SkyClan." Rowanstar raised his voice above the Clans. "We would be foolish to ignore it."

Harestar nodded. "Another Clan would make us stronger."

Crowfeather flattened his ears. "We were strong once, without them."

"Their home is here, with us!" Bramblestar beckoned to Leafstar with a sharp flick of his tail. "Climb up."

She scrambled awkwardly up the trunk and stood beside the ThunderClan leader. Her gaze was anxious as she surveyed the Clans below. "We want only to live peacefully among our fellow Clans," she meowed over the hisses. "Darktail was our enemy! He killed our Clanmates too!"

"How?" Juniperclaw demanded. "You only joined our last battle with the rogues. I don't remember hearing that any of you died."

"He invaded our home in the gorge and took over," Leafstar explained. "Eventually, he drove us from our camp."

"*Eventually?*" Juniperclaw's mew was suspicious.

"He lived with us for a while. Like ShadowClan, we didn't realize how evil he was until it was too late."

The world spun around Alderheart as an uneasy silence settled over the Clans. Alderheart could feel his Clanmates' distrust. *StarClan! Make them understand!* His breath stopped as Sparkpelt got to her paws. What was she going to say? He braced himself, fearing the worst.

"I know SkyClan has suffered much and lost many Clanmates," she began. Her voice shook, but there was determination in her mew, and the other cats quieted as she went on. Tigerheart, watching silently from the roots of the Great Oak, leaned forward and stared at her intently. "But why can't they return to their old home? Darktail is gone now, and so are his rogues. SkyClan's old home is safe again. I'm sure they were happy there once. They can be happy there again. We managed without them before. Why do we need them now?" She paused, her bright gaze holding the attention of the cats. "If they stay beside the lake, who is going to give up territory to give them a new home?"

Alderheart swallowed. He knew her words echoed the feelings of many cats. Why couldn't the Clans see there was more to life than territory?

Before the Clans could agree with Sparkpelt, Tigerheart leaped onto a root of the oak and looked up at his leader. "Rowanstar, may I speak?"

Rowanstar nodded, looking at his deputy with puzzlement.

"We have suffered because of Darktail's cruelty." Tigerheart padded along the root and stopped in a pool of moonlight. "He has left us weak and frightened. RiverClan has withdrawn to rebuild their shattered Clan. ShadowClan has lost so many warriors that it will take moons for us to become what we once were."

Rowanstar shifted uneasily on the branch above, but he let his deputy go on.

"There is no doubt that StarClan wanted us to find Sky-Clan. I believe StarClan had a reason. Not just to clear the sky of the darkness we have suffered, but because StarClan knew that the five Clans belong together. With an extra Clan beside the lake, we will find strength when we most need it."

"But who will give up territory for them?" Crowfeather's

ears twitched distrustfully.

"We could." Tigerheart turned his gaze on Rowanstar. "We have fewer mouths to feed now. And fewer warriors to patrol our borders. It makes sense to exchange some of our land for an ally."

Rowanstar looked thoughtful, as though weighing Tigerheart's words. The Clans watched him in silence. He turned to Leafstar. "Would you be our ally?"

"Yes," Leafstar told him. "We are Clan cats. We share the same ancestors. It would be an honor to stand beside you. And we'd always be grateful for any territory you gave us."

Alderheart held his breath as the cats of WindClan and ThunderClan exchanged glances.

Molewhisker's gaze flashed with suspicion. "You'd be allies to us all, right? Not just ShadowClan."

"Of course." Leafstar stared into the crowd. "We want to live among the Clans our ancestors hunted beside countless moons ago." She looked hopefully at Rowanstar. "Would you be willing to give us land?"

Rowanstar shifted his paws nervously. "You could have some of the land beside ThunderClan, with a narrow piece that opens onto the lake."

"*Our* land?" Scorchfur looked outraged.

Rowanstar straightened as though settling the decision in his mind. "Our land," he meowed firmly.

Tigerheart stared unblinking at Scorchfur. "Is that a problem?"

Scorchfur looked away, growling to himself.

Leafstar's eyes lit up. "Thank you!" Her mew was filled with joy.

"Then it's settled." Harestar flicked his tail.

Bramblestar nodded. "Leafstar, you should stay in our camp tonight, and tomorrow ShadowClan can help you mark out your new territory."

Alderheart felt limp with relief. A decision had been made. SkyClan was staying beside the lake. He sensed tension ebbing away as the Clans began to move, like stones freed from ice. ShadowClan had lost some of its territory, but perhaps the gratitude of a neighbor was worth more.

Bramblestar jumped down from the Great Oak. Rowanstar, Harestar, and Leafstar followed him. The Gathering was over. The Clans began to separate, each following their leader as they headed home.

Alderheart watched Twigpaw and Violetpaw move happily toward Hawkwing. Their father was staying.

"You see?" Leafpool looked relieved. "We *can* trust StarClan to guide our paws."

Mist hung in the hollow, lingering even as the sun rose above the cliff top. The browning trees shone like gold in the early morning light. Alderheart padded from the medicine den, fluffing his fur against the damp air. He glanced nervously at the camp entrance, wondering how Twigpaw's assessment was going.

Below Highledge, Squirrelflight was organizing the day's hunting patrols. Graystripe padded toward the elders' den, a stiff mouse in his jaws. Brackenfur sat next to Cinderheart and Lionblaze, lifting his face to the sun as though relishing its warmth. SkyClan milled restlessly at the edge of the clearing, their pelts rippling with excitement.

Violetpaw paced around Hawkwing, both cats watching the camp entrance. When the thorn barrier rustled, she whisked her tail. "They're back!" She raced across the clearing. Hawkwing hung back, but his eyes followed her eagerly.

Alderheart's paws pricked as Ivypool hurried into camp. Her dark blue eyes were shining with pride. Hope quickened his heart.

Violetpaw skidded to a halt in front of her.

Ivypool purred at the black-and-white apprentice. "She passed."

Twigpaw padded though the thorn tunnel, fur ruffled and breathless.

"You passed!" Violetpaw hopped around her sister.

Alderheart hurried to congratulate her. "Well done! You deserve it."

"Thanks." Twigpaw blinked at him.

Why didn't she look more excited?

"Let's go and tell Hawkwing." Violetpaw nosed Twigpaw across the clearing, but Hawkwing was already hurrying to meet them, his eyes curious and hopeful.

Alderheart turned to Ivypool, worry worming beneath his pelt. "Did she do okay?" He wondered whether her mentor would know why Twigpaw seemed so subdued.

Ivypool's whiskers twitched happily. "She did brilliantly.

I'm so proud of her. She deserves her warrior name." She headed up the tumble of rocks toward Bramblestar.

Alderheart frowned. Twigpaw was standing quietly while Hawkwing and Violetpaw spoke softly to her. Alderheart wondered if he saw disappointment in Hawkwing's eyes. *Was he still hoping she might join him in SkyClan?* But that wouldn't explain Twigpaw's lack of excitement. Perhaps she was tired, he reasoned. Or she could be nervous about the ceremony. After all, she would be going through it alone. Most apprentices received their names alongside their denmates, and sat beside them during the all-night vigil that followed.

SkyClan crowded around the entrance, caught in their own excitement as they prepared to leave for their new territory. Fallowfern and Plumwillow flanked Tinycloud protectively while Harrybrook sniffed the air and Rabbitleap paced beside them.

Macgyver flicked his ear nervously. "It may be a long walk to our new home."

"We're only crossing the border," Sandynose reminded him.

Macgyver glanced at Tinycloud. The queen looked exhausted already, as though struggling to carry the weight of her kits. "Let's hope those kits can wait until we've found a good spot for a camp before they decide to join us."

"They've waited this long," Sparrowpelt meowed proudly. "They can wait another few days."

Alderheart hurried toward the tabby tom. "When her kitting starts, send someone to fetch me or Leafpool." He was still worried about SkyClan starting their new life beside the lake without a medicine cat.

"I will," Sparrowpelt promised.

Leafstar stood beside the camp entrance and lifted her tail. "Are you ready?" She glanced at her Clanmates.

As they nodded, Bramblestar leaped down from Highledge. "Good luck." He dipped his head to Leafstar. "There will be a ShadowClan patrol at the border to meet you. Would you like an escort?"

"We can manage," she told him.

Alderheart's gaze flicked to Twigpaw. She was going to find it hard to say good-bye to her father and sister. He tried to think of words to comfort her, frowning as he realized that she didn't look sad at all. In fact she looked relieved, as though a weight had dropped from her shoulders.

As he met her gaze, she padded forward. "I have something to say." Avoiding the eyes of her Clanmates, she looked directly at Bramblestar.

Alderheart felt the chill of the mist reach into his fur. Suddenly he knew what she was going to do. He swallowed, his heart aching.

"Thank you for raising me and training me." Twigpaw dipped her head to the ThunderClan leader. "I shall always value what I have learned here. But I don't want to be a ThunderClan warrior. My place is in SkyClan"—she paused to look at Violetpaw and Hawkwing, her eyes glistening with emotion—"with my kin."

CHAPTER 3

Violetpaw was dreaming. Ferns trembled in a moonlit clearing. Black shadows, soft as fur, hid the forest. She knew this place. It was where Alderheart and Needletail had brought her and Twigpaw to meet when they were kits.

She heard a muffled squeak and the brush of fur against leaves. She purred quietly to herself. Didn't Twigpaw realize she was making more noise than anything in the forest? Stealthily she crossed the shallow dip in the forest floor, creeping on silent paws toward the ferns.

They quivered as she approached. She pricked her ears and heard her sister breathing. *ThunderClan cats are so bad at hide-and-seek.* She ducked low. She wasn't sure she had ever quite fit in at ShadowClan, but they'd taught her how to move as silently as moonlight.

She stopped at the ferns, her heart quickening. She could hear her sister trying hard to swallow a purr and not succeeding. She paused, relishing her triumph. In a moment she'd dive into the thick foliage and give Twigpaw a surprise that would make her squeak out loud.

A rush of gratitude swelled in her chest. *Thank you, Needletail, for bringing me here.* As she thought of her friend, Violetpaw stiffened. A silver tail was snaking between the trees.

She forgot her game. "Needletail!" She had to catch up to Needletail. It had been so long since she'd seen her. "Wait for me!" Haring into the darkness, she raced after the flash of silver. Needletail kept moving, her pelt flitting like starlight through the shadows. Leaves crunched beneath Violetpaw's pads. Wind ruffled her ears. "Needletail! Wait!" Why was Needletail running away? "I have to talk to you." She ran faster, but Needletail kept ahead. The lithe she-cat seemed to be moving effortlessly, while Violetpaw struggled to follow. Brambles snagged her fur. Roots caught her paws. Violetpaw felt her lungs burn with effort. She struggled on, her limbs heavy, the air seeming to thicken around her so that she felt as if she were struggling through water. Needletail kept darting ahead like a fish. "Please! Wait!"

At last, Needletail paused. Violetpaw glimpsed her green eyes as they flashed in the shadows.

"Why chase me now?" Needletail's mew was cold and mocking. "You made your choice."

Dread surged through Violetpaw, jolting her awake. "No, I didn't!"

A voice sounded beside her. "Violetpaw? Are you okay?"

Violetpaw was still half dreaming. Needletail's scent was heavy on the air. "I never wanted to lose you."

"Violetpaw. Wake up. You're dreaming."

"It was never a *choice*!" Her own mew surprised her. She lifted her head and opened her eyes. She was in the temporary den she'd made with Hawkwing and Twigpaw. She could feel the warmth of their bodies. Darkness swathed her. It was the middle of the night.

Hawkwing was blinking at her. "You were dreaming."

She dragged her thoughts from her dream and blinked back at him. Beside them, Twigpaw was snoring, lost in sleep.

Violetpaw realized she was with her whole family. *Twigpaw came with us to SkyClan.* The thought still surprised her. Twigpaw had always seemed so comfortable in ThunderClan.

"Are you okay?" Concern shadowed Hawkwing's round eyes. "Was it a bad dream?"

"Not a *bad* dream." Violetpaw shifted in her nest. She didn't want to explain. "Just weird."

He frowned. "Are you sure?"

"I'm sure." Violetpaw rested her muzzle on her paws and closed her eyes before he could ask any more. As she did, an image of Needletail flashed in her thoughts.

Panic spiked her pelt like burning splinters. Her friend was in the river. Darktail was holding her beneath the water. As Needletail struggled beneath his paws, the rogue stared blankly at Violetpaw. "Maybe you're right," he meowed. "Maybe I should give Needletail another chance. What do you think?"

"Oh, yes!" Violetpaw remembered the dumb relief she had felt. "Please give her another chance! I'll do anything you want!" It hadn't been enough! Grief twisted her heart. *If only I'd tried harder.*

Horror pulsed in her paws. She wanted to run, to let the

chilly night air wash the memory away. But she couldn't let Hawkwing see her pain. She hadn't told him the whole story about Needletail, and she wasn't sure she wanted to. *What if he wants nothing to do with me after he hears that I let her die?*

"Thanks." Violetpaw sniffed the mouse that Twigpaw had brought from the prey pile. It smelled stale. Hawkwing stretched beside her in the dawn light. He yawned.

Violetpaw felt a flash of guilt. "Sorry I woke you last night."

"It's okay." Hawkwing sat down, nodding thanks to Twigpaw, who had brought him a vole. "I went back to sleep pretty quickly."

"What happened?" Twigpaw dropped her own mouse and settled beside them. "Did you wake up last night?"

"Violetpaw had a bad dream," Hawkwing told her.

"Not a bad dream." Violetpaw repeated, trying to make herself believe it. "Just a weird one."

"You seemed pretty upset," Hawkwing meowed.

"It doesn't matter." Violetpaw wanted to change the subject.

Twigpaw took a bite of her mouse. "Violetpaw's always been sensitive," she mewed, chewing.

Around them, SkyClan had woken up. Fallowfern shared tongues with Bellaleaf. Blossomheart was showing Finpaw a hunting crouch, but she looked up and nodded when she saw Twigpaw and Violetpaw. Violetpaw nodded back quickly before focusing on her prey. She knew the she-cat was her kin, and she had been nothing but kind to her, but Violetpaw didn't quite feel comfortable around any cat but Twigpaw or Hawkwing.

Leafstar rummaged through the fresh-kill pile. It was still well stocked from yesterday.

Three sunrises had passed since they'd left the Thunder-Clan camp. In that time they'd made progress on building their own new camp. Leafstar had picked out the small clearing where the pine trees opened to let a narrow stream cut through. Cedar and juniper grew here, creating a curious oasis among the straight lines of pine. Violetpaw knew the spot well. Needletail had shown it to her many moons ago. Low branches, hung with dusty lichen, formed a natural dome for the grove. Soft green moss grew over the smooth rocks, which edged the stream. Ferns made natural walls, though Leafstar planned to reinforce them with bramble twines. The Sky-Clan leader had already chosen a low-growing juniper for the apprentices' den and a bramble for the warriors' den, though it would take some work to make them habitable. Another bramble thicket, growing where the stream flowed into the camp, would be the nursery. Macgyver and Sparrowpelt were working on it now, weaving in straggling tendrils to strengthen the walls. Tinycloud had already made a nest inside.

Leafstar's den was a hollow in the old cedar at the far end of camp. Its entrance was at the top of a tangle of roots. The space below, where the roots formed a natural cave, would make a good medicine den when the Clan had decided who its medicine cat would be.

Violetpaw bit into her mouse, stung by Twigpaw's words.

Violetpaw has always been sensitive. Her sister hadn't meant them meanly but it felt like a criticism. Violetpaw prickled with resentment. *You were raised among cats who wanted you around.* She glanced at Twigpaw, who was happily eating. *Maybe if you'd been the one chosen for ShadowClan, you'd be sensitive too.*

Twigpaw looked up from her meal. "What was your dream about?"

Violetpaw avoided her gaze. "Nothing really."

"Let her be," Hawkwing mewed softly.

"It had to be something if it woke you and Hawkwing up." Twigpaw took another bite of mouse and stared inquisitively at Violetpaw. "I want to know."

"It was about Needletail." Violetpaw stared at her mouse.

"Needletail was Violetpaw's friend," Twigpaw explained to Hawkwing. "Darktail killed her."

Violetpaw shuddered.

Hawkwing rested his tail over hers. "We've all lost someone." He gazed sympathetically into her eyes. "Please don't feel alone in your grief." He nodded toward Macgyver, raising his voice so the black-and-white tom could hear. "We've all suffered these past moons."

Macgyver turned from his work to meet the deputy's gaze. "That's true enough." He glanced at Blossomheart. The look seemed to flit around the camp, passing from one cat to another, making them pause and grow solemn as though awaking sad memories.

Leafstar straightened beside the fresh-kill pile. "We are not the Clan we used to be," she admitted. "But once we are settled, I will send a patrol back to the gorge to look for lost Clanmates who may still be alive." She spoke encouragingly. "We must not give up hope on all those who are lost."

"There must be more of us still alive," Blossomheart agreed.

Tinycloud padded toward the stream. "Once my kits are born, the Clan will seem more like its old self."

Hawkwing purred. "It will be good to have kits running around."

"Do you ever wonder what we looked like when we were kits?" Twigpaw looked at him brightly.

"Every day." Hawkwing's eyes glazed wistfully.

"Do you miss our mother?" Twigpaw asked.

Violetpaw glared at her. Were all ThunderClan cats so insensitive? Twigpaw seemed unaware of her stare. She blinked at her father, waiting for an answer.

"Yes." Hawkwing's mew was husky. Violetpaw winced, feeling his grief. "Pebbleshine was kind and warm. I loved her very much."

"Will you tell us about her?" Twigpaw asked.

"He will, when he's ready," Violetpaw mewed quickly.

Hawkwing glanced gratefully at Violetpaw. "It's okay, Violetpaw. I'm always happy to talk about your mother."

Violetpaw dropped her gaze. Did he really mean it? She was curious about the cat who had kitted them, then died before they'd opened their eyes. She wished she remembered, but Pebbleshine had no real shape in her thoughts. *I don't even remember her scent.*

Twigpaw jumped to her paws. "Tell us about her while

we're hunting." She glanced eagerly toward the fern tunnel that formed the camp entrance. "I have so many questions!"

Hawkwing purred fondly. "Let me finish my vole first." He glanced at Violetpaw. She was halfway through her mouse. "We'd better hurry up or Twigpaw will leave without us."

Twigpaw blinked at him, puzzled. "I'd *never* leave without you," she mewed earnestly.

"Of course not," Hawkwing soothed. "I was just teasing."

Violetpaw gulped down the rest of her mouse. *I hope hunting makes Twigpaw forget her questions.* When Hawkwing had finished his vole, they headed out of camp.

The land Rowanstar had given to SkyClan ran half the length of the ThunderClan border and reached like a paw down to the lake's edge. SkyClan had a small stretch of shore, though their land grew wider as it reached into the pine forest.

As Twigpaw trotted ahead, tail high, Violetpaw recalled how she had told Rowanstar that she wanted to leave Shadow-Clan and become a SkyClan cat. He had been standing on the lakeside while the SkyClan cats sniffed the water's edge and marked the borders of their new home.

"I understand." Rowanstar had looked at her, his gaze betraying little. She had wondered if he was sad to lose her or simply unsurprised by her decision.

"I want to be with my kin," she explained. "But I'll always be grateful to ShadowClan for taking me in." As she spoke, Violetpaw felt a flash of guilt. She *wasn't* grateful. She wished they'd never separated her from Twigpaw. But perhaps they'd meant well. Perhaps she'd just never gotten a chance to see the real ShadowClan—before the rogues came.

Rowanstar dipped his head. "I respect your decision."

He padded away, leaving Violetpaw alone in the chilly wind from the lake. He must be angry that she was abandoning the Clan when it was so short of cats. And yet she sensed that his disappointment was not too great. After all, she had left ShadowClan to live with the rogues. Perhaps, after all that had happened, he felt he would never be able to trust her.

"Are the ditches this way?" Twigpaw paused and glanced back at Violetpaw. The ditches were the best place for easy hunting. Prey liked to run along the gullies.

"No." Violetpaw hurried to catch up and nodded toward the rise. "They're over here." Twigpaw was still finding it hard to navigate the pine forest.

Twigpaw frowned. "All the trees look the same," she complained.

"You'll get used to it," Violetpaw promised. "When you've been here a bit longer you'll realize that pine trees are as different from one another as they are from oak and ash."

Twigpaw looked unconvinced. "Yeah, sure," she sniffed.

"Let Violetpaw lead the way," Hawkwing called from behind them. "You can learn from her."

Twigpaw's tail drooped as Violetpaw slid past her and started along the rise to where it began to dip. Violetpaw felt a twinge of guilt. *I can't help knowing this territory better than you.* She guessed that her sister felt self-conscious about still being a 'paw. After all, Twigpaw had passed her assessment back in ThunderClan. *I hope Leafstar gives her a warrior name soon. She's worked hard and she deserves it.* "The ditches are downslope," she told her. "Just remember to follow the way water flows."

"Okay. Thanks." Twigpaw fell in beside Hawkwing and changed the subject. "You were going to tell us about Pebble-shine."

Violetpaw glanced back at her father, trying to read his gaze. Did it still hurt to talk about his lost mate? She quickened her pace. Once they started hunting, Twigpaw would be too busy to ask questions.

Hawkwing swished his tail. "I'll tell you about one time she was training," he began. "Your mother had only been an apprentice for a moon, but it had already been far too long as far as she was concerned."

"I know how she felt." Twigpaw sighed.

Hawkwing went on. "She was desperate to impress her mentor, Billystorm. She woke before dawn every day and practiced warrior moves before he woke up. Billystorm would always emerge from his den to find her ambushing pinecones in the camp clearing or stalking crickets." Hawkwing purred fondly, as though relishing the memory. "One day, he set her a test. She was supposed to find a secret way out of the gorge, then catch a rabbit, then head back to camp. But Billystorm told her that, along the route, he would ambush her and try to take her rabbit. She was supposed to escape the ambush, take the rabbit, and race Billystorm back to camp." Hawkwing swished his tail. "She was so excited. This was her chance to really impress Billystorm. I remember how her fur ruffled along her spine as she searched the gorge for a secret way to climb out." His eyes darkened wistfully. "She seemed so young."

Violetpaw heard his mew catch in his throat. "You don't

have to tell us the story now," she called over her shoulder.

"Yes, you do!" Twigpaw mewed eagerly. "I want to know what happened."

"Pebbleshine did everything right. She climbed out of the gorge and caught a rabbit and, when Billystorm ambushed her, she fought him off using all the battle moves he'd taught her. But she forgot one important thing."

Hawkwing paused teasingly.

"Tell us!" Twigpaw demanded.

Hawkwing purred. "She left the rabbit where Billystorm had ambushed her. She'd been so desperate to beat him back to camp that she forgot all about it and raced home as fast as she could."

"Oh no!" Twigpaw gasped. "She must have been so disappointed."

"Wait and see."

Violetpaw pricked her ears. She was as keen as Twigpaw to hear what happened next.

Hawkwing flicked his tail. "Pebbleshine realized her mistake as soon as she reached the camp. She knew Billystorm couldn't be far behind. I was waiting at the entrance to see how she had done. When she saw me, she begged me to help. She was so out of breath she could hardly talk. She told me to distract Billystorm. She said I must run to a Twoleg nest nearby and climb a tree and wait there. I thought she had bees in her brains. How would climbing a tree distract Billystorm? But I did it. I ran to the nearest Twoleg nest and climbed the first tree I came to. Before long, I saw Billystorm racing toward me. His fur was standing on end. He stopped below the tree and called up to me." Hawkwing roughened his mew, clearly impersonating Billystorm. "'Hawkwing! Are you okay? Pebblepaw told me she thought she'd seen a dog chasing you.'"

"She *lied*?" Twigpaw sounded horrified.

"Not exactly. She only said that she'd *thought* she'd seen a dog chasing me. And there was a dog barking nearby. I *could* have been chased. Your mother was smart. Her story distracted Billystorm long enough for her to race back and fetch her rabbit and get back to camp before him."

Twigpaw whisked her tail happily. "Was Billystorm impressed?"

"Yes. He let her pick the first prey from the pile that night." Hawkwing's eyes shone affectionately. "And when he found out she'd used me as a decoy, he said it was quick thinking and a sign of a good warrior. Pebbleshine purred about it for days."

Violetpaw glanced back at him. Talking about Pebbleshine seemed to have made him happy, even though she was dead. Was that how it was when you lost someone you loved? Her thoughts drifted to Needletail. Even *thinking* of her friend made Violetpaw's chest tighten with grief. *I could never talk about Needletail happily. Not after what happened.*

She carried on walking, her paws suddenly heavy.

A pelt brushed her side. Hawkwing fell in beside her. "I hope you don't mind me talking about Pebbleshine," he meowed softly. "I know you must miss her."

"I don't really remember her." Violetpaw guiltily avoided his gaze.

"You were very young when you lost her." His mew was soft.

"Don't you find it hard to talk about her?" Violetpaw asked.

"I *like* to remember her," Hawkwing meowed. "And it's easier now that I have found you both." He looked back at Twigpaw, raising his voice. "She was the kindest, sweetest cat I've ever known, and I miss her every day. But missing her doesn't have to feel so sad anymore because I have part of her with me."

"Do we remind you of her?" Twigpaw called from behind.

Violetpaw felt a rush of irritation. Couldn't Twigpaw ever let a moment pass in silence without filling it with questions?

Hawkwing stopped and looked at Twigpaw. "*You* remind me of her very much," he meowed fondly.

Twigpaw puffed out her chest happily.

"Thank you for finding SkyClan. It's the sort of thing your mother would have done. She was brave and adventurous too."

Violetpaw swallowed back jealousy. *Aren't I brave and adventurous?*

Hawkwing touched his nose to Violetpaw's ear. "*You're* more like me," he purred. "Your mother would have loved you both very much, just as I do."

Violetpaw held his gaze, saying nothing. The grief in her heart seemed to melt into warmth. Purring, she rubbed her muzzle along Hawkwing's jaw, and then Twigpaw's. She suddenly was happier than she could have ever imagined possible.

For the first time in her life, Violetpaw felt like she belonged.

CHAPTER 4

❧

Twigpaw glanced nervously at the towering pines. A fierce wind was hollering through the branches, rocking the trees. She missed ThunderClan territory, where the trees seemed sturdier, their ancient roots thick and twisted deep into the earth. Here in the pine forest, she felt as if a tree could topple anytime.

"Twigpaw! Stop staring at the trees and help," Finpaw called. The brown-and-ginger apprentice blinked at her.

Leafstar had sent Twigpaw with Finpaw and Dewpaw to find twigs to build the camp, while Reedpaw had stayed behind to pick burrs from the moss they'd gathered yesterday. Finpaw had already collected a pile of sticks. His brother was a little farther off, reaching beneath a bramble bush.

Twigpaw padded toward them, still craning her neck to watch the swirling treetops. "Aren't you scared a tree might fall down?"

Dewpaw wriggled out from the bramble, his brown tabby fur ruffled. "Why should they? They've been here as long as StarClan."

"But it's so windy." Twigpaw had to raise her voice against the swish of the branches. She squeaked with alarm as a small twig tumbled down and landed on her back.

Finpaw's whiskers twitched with amusement. "I thought you were used to living in a forest."

"ThunderClan's forest is different." Twigpaw fluffed out her fur, pretending not to be embarrassed. "When the wind blows there, you can hardly tell. The trees protect us from the wind; they don't whirl about like reeds."

"ShadowClan seems happy in the pine forest," Finpaw reminded her.

"At least the wind means there are plenty of twigs to gather," Dewpaw added.

Twigpaw scanned the forest. Falling twigs caught her eye everywhere, and the forest floor was sprinkled with thin stems that would be perfect for weaving into den walls. She pawed one toward her, then turned to pick up the one that had bounced off her back. She tried not to notice the irritation that wormed in her belly. Why had she been sent out on an apprentice errand? She'd passed her assessment. If she'd stayed in ThunderClan, she'd have her warrior name by now. She'd be building dens, not gathering supplies.

She pushed the thought away. *You chose to join SkyClan,* she reminded herself. *You wanted to be with Violetpaw and Hawkwing.* And yet she was finding it strange to have new Clanmates. The SkyClan cats were kind, but she was used to the order and routine of the ThunderClan camp. Leafstar seemed more like an ordinary warrior than a leader. She worked and hunted and patrolled alongside her Clanmates as though she were no different. Hawkwing, even though he was deputy, let the cats organize their own hunting patrols. Occasionally he would suggest that it was time to patrol the border, but he let cats volunteer rather than ordering them to go.

It's just because they are finding their paws in a new home, she decided.

But that didn't explain SkyClan's fondness for kittypets. Twigpaw had been shocked to learn that SkyClan used to have kittypets as part of their Clan, and that they used to come and go, living with the Clan *and* their Twolegs. SkyClan had called these cats "daylight warriors." Twigpaw couldn't understand how you could be a warrior only part of the time. You were either a warrior or you weren't. At least Macgyver had made the decision to stay with the Clan for good. So he was *almost* a real warrior. But like Millie back in ThunderClan, he'd kept his kittypet name.

And there are so few SkyClan cats. Twigpaw frowned. There were almost as many apprentices as there were warriors. And it was strange to have no elders at all. Twigpaw remembered, with a pang, Graystripe and Millie. They had seemed like the steadying roots of ThunderClan, always ready with a reassuring word or teasing complaint that made everything feel okay.

She had thought being with Violetpaw and Hawkwing would cure her homesickness, but the longer she spent with them, the more she realized how *alike* the two of them were. They practically shared thoughts. Sometimes, talking to them felt like talking to one cat. It made her feel like an outsider. *I'm supposed to be the one with the special bond with Hawkwing. I rescued Sky-Clan.* She was ashamed of the thought, but she couldn't help thinking it. *You do have a bond with Hawkwing,* she told herself. *It's just not the same as Violetpaw's.*

She realized that Finpaw was staring at her. "Are all ThunderClan cats such dreamers?" he mewed.

She blinked at him, sensing that she'd been lost in her thoughts. "Sorry." She reached for another twig and dragged it onto her tiny pile. Pine needles caught under her claws. "I'm still getting used to being in a new home. Don't you find it strange?"

"Everything has felt strange for so long, it feels almost normal now," Finpaw told her.

"Do you miss the gorge?" she asked.

Finpaw shrugged. "I never lived there."

Dewpaw padded over, a bundle of twigs bunched between his jaws. He dropped them beside Finpaw's. "We were born beside another lake after they'd left the gorge," he explained. "SkyClan lived there for a season."

Twigpaw pricked her ears. "So you've never seen the gorge?"

"Never," Finpaw told her. There was a wistful look in his yellow eyes.

"But you wish you had?" she wondered.

Finpaw looked away. "The other cats talk about it so much," he mewed. "I kind of wish I knew what they were talking about."

Twigpaw's heart pricked with sympathy. "Me too." She'd thought she was the only one who felt left out when the Sky-Clan warriors started reminiscing about their old life.

Finpaw blinked at her warmly. "Next time they start talking about their old life, we can remember the exciting day we spent collecting twigs." He winked at her. Then he nodded at her meager pile. "We should collect a few more and head back to camp."

Dewpaw scanned the forest floor, whisking his tail as his gaze reached a patch of scattered sticks. "I'll fetch those."

"We'll look under this bush." Finpaw headed toward a spreading juniper. "There might be some snagged in the branches."

Twigpaw hurried past him. She wanted to make up for gathering so few. She dived under the bush and wriggled on her belly. A few sticks were caught around the central stem. She dug her claws into them and dragged them out. As she emerged, something slithered beside her. "Snake!" With a squeal, she leaped backward, her fur on end.

Finpaw purred loudly. "That's not a snake." He lifted a twisted root with his paw and blinked at Twigpaw. "You're so jumpy!"

Twigpaw shook out her fur, trying not to let him see her paws shaking. "All this wind is making me nervous," she mewed hotly.

It was still tearing at the trees, roaring louder now. The forest floor echoed with the creaking of trunks.

"Let's take these twigs back to camp," Finpaw suggested. He called to Dewpaw. "We're heading back now."

"Coming!" Dewpaw grabbed his pile between his jaws and headed toward them.

As he neared, a gust of wind slammed the trees around them. A crack rang though the air. Heart lurching, Twigpaw looked up. A massive branch hurtled at them. It was falling directly toward Finpaw.

"Look out!" She grabbed Finpaw's scruff in her claws and dragged him toward her. Pine needles sprayed her face as the branch hit the ground with a sickening thud. Dust and bark showered around them.

"Finpaw!"

The apprentice lay beside her, his eyes wide with shock.

"Finpaw!" Twigpaw shook the needles from her fur and leaned over him.

"His tail!" Dewpaw reached them, pelt bristling.

Twigpaw followed the gray cat's gaze. He was staring at Finpaw's tail. It was trapped beneath the branch.

"We have to move it!" Twigpaw leaped for the branch and tried to roll it away. The weight of it shocked her.

"It's too big." Dewpaw stared along the length of the branch. It was wider than a cat's belly and as long as an entire tree trunk.

"Finpaw!" Twigpaw darted back to his head and stared into his eyes. They were bright with pain. "Can you speak?"

"Yes," Finpaw gasped.

"We're going to get help." Twigpaw's thoughts were racing. SkyClan had no medicine cat. She needed Alderheart. But ThunderClan's camp was too far. Finpaw needed help *now*. She looked at Dewpaw. "Run back to camp and fetch help. With more paws, we might be able to move the branch. I'll head for ShadowClan's camp to get Puddleshine."

Dewpaw stared at her, ears flat with terror. "We can't leave

Finpaw here alone. What if he—"

Twigpaw cut him off. "It's not far to camp. You'll be back in the blink of an eye. Finpaw will be okay." She glanced at Finpaw. "You'll be okay," she promised. "We'll be back before you know it. Just hang on." She searched Finpaw's stricken gaze.

"Hurry," he croaked.

Twigpaw turned back to Dewpaw. "Run as fast as you can!" But the gray apprentice was already pelting between the trees.

She ran for the ShadowClan border. The forest floor flashed beneath her paws. The springy mat of pine needles seemed to push her on, faster and faster. She hit the scent line, breathing fast, and kept running. *Please let me be running the right way.* She'd been to ShadowClan's camp before, to visit Violetpaw. But that had been at night. Still, she knew she was heading away from the lake. The sun was above her, the wind behind. Her heart leaped as she recognized a rotting tree stump, and the ShadowClan scents began to grow stronger. She kept running, her paws burning, and scanned the forest ahead. Were those brambles looming between the trunks? She raced toward them, relief washing her pelt as she recognized the high wall of the ShadowClan camp. She rounded it and skidded through the entrance.

Skidding to a halt in the clearing, she faced the shocked ShadowClan cats.

"What are you doing?" Scorchfur glared at her.

Juniperclaw blinked in surprise. "How dare you—"

"Twigpaw?" Puddleshine poked his head out of his den.

"What's wrong? Are Tinycloud's kits coming?"

Twigpaw shook her head, fighting for breath. She gasped in a lungful of air and blurted, "Finpaw!"

Puddleshine hurried from his den.

"A branch fell," Twigpaw puffed. "His tail's trapped."

Puddleshine blinked at her, then turned back to his den. "Wait there." He slid inside.

Juniperclaw and Scorchfur stared at her in silence.

A moment later, Puddleshine emerged, a leaf wrap between his jaws. Herbs were rolled inside it and dangled out either end.

Twigpaw nodded quickly to Rowanstar, who was watching round-eyed from the end of the clearing, then rushed out of the camp.

Running, she led Puddleshine back to Finpaw. As she approached, she saw pelts moving around the branch. "They're trying to move it." She ran faster, relieved when she spotted Hawkwing among the other SkyClan warriors.

Plumwillow was crouched beside Finpaw's head. "Don't worry, Finpaw. We'll have this branch moved in no time."

Reaching them, Twigpaw saw the warriors straining against the branch. Hawkwing, Sandynose, Fallowfern, and Rabbitleap pressed their shoulders to the bark and heaved. Blossomheart and Macgyver had worked a smaller branch underneath and were trying to lever the fallen branch clear. Their paws slithered on the pine needles, and Sandynose grunted with effort. But the branch didn't budge.

Puddleshine slid past them and crouched beside Finpaw's

tail. He examined it, then leaned close to Finpaw's head. He ran a paw over his head and spine. "Are you hurt anywhere else?"

Finpaw didn't answer. His eyes were glazed over.

"He's in shock," Puddleshine meowed. "We need to get him warm."

Plumwillow pressed close to her kit, her eyes glittering with fear.

"It's not going to budge." Hawkwing stared frantically at the branch.

"Can we pull his tail out?" Macgyver asked.

Puddleshine shook his head. "It's pinned too tight."

Twigpaw felt sick.

"I need to cut him clear," Puddleshine meowed starkly. "Find me a sharp stone."

"*Cut?*" Plumwillow stared at the ShadowClan medicine cat with alarm. "Are you sure?"

Puddleshine lowered his voice. "If he stays here much longer, he will die of shock. He's hardly conscious. Cutting it now is our only option."

Plumwillow seemed to freeze, her gaze fixed on the medicine cat.

Sandynose padded to her side. He looked at Puddleshine. "Is it the only way to save him?"

Puddleshine nodded.

"Then do it," Sandynose meowed.

Puddleshine looked at Plumwillow, as though asking for her permission. The dark gray she-cat nodded.

As Macgyver dropped a sharp stone beside him, Puddleshine leaned closer to Finpaw's tail. With a flick of his own tail, he waved the warriors away.

Trembling, Twigpaw hurried to her father's side. "Will Finpaw be okay?"

"We don't know yet." He touched his muzzle to her cheek. He felt strong and warm, and she sheltered against him. "Let's get you back to camp."

Twigpaw glanced toward Finpaw. He was a small, limp shape, half hidden by Puddleshine. "I don't want to leave him," she whispered. Finpaw felt like the first friend she'd made in SkyClan. What if he died?

"Puddleshine will do his best," Hawkwing promised. "And Sandynose and Plumwillow are with him. You feel cold. I think you should be in your nest. You're probably quite shocked too."

Twigpaw suddenly realized her sister was missing. "Where's Violetpaw?"

"Rabbitleap took her hunting with Leafstar." Hawkwing gently nudged Twigpaw forward. "She may be back by now. Let's go and see."

Twigpaw glanced over her shoulder, her belly tightening as she heard Finpaw gasp with pain.

Hawkwing guided her away quickly.

Violetpaw met them at the camp entrance. "Where has everyone gone?" she asked. Rabbitleap was standing beside the stream, looking around the deserted camp.

"They're trying to help Finpaw. He's had an accident," Hawkwing told Violetpaw.

Rabbitleap hurried over. "Is it bad?"

"His tail is trapped beneath a branch," Hawkwing explained. "Puddleshine is with him now."

Rabbitleap flicked his tail anxiously. "I wish Echosong were still with us."

"Or Frecklewish," Hawkwing meowed.

As he spoke, Leafstar ducked through the fern tunnel. "I smell fear-scent. What's happened?"

Twigpaw was still trembling. She felt cold to the bone.

"Rabbitleap can tell you," Hawkwing mewed softly. "I want to get Twigpaw to her nest."

"Is she okay?" Leafstar looked worried.

Violetpaw's eyes widened. "Did Twigpaw get hurt too?"

Twigpaw gazed at them blankly, her mind spinning. Finpaw was suffering! Why were they wasting time worrying about *her*?

"She's just a little shocked and cold." Hawkwing led Twigpaw to the temporary apprentices' den, and ushered her inside.

As Twigpaw curled into her nest, Violetpaw hooked a wad of moss from her own nest and gave it to Hawkwing. "This will help her warm up."

Hawkwing draped it over Twigpaw, tucking it in at the edges. Gratefully, Twigpaw snuggled deep into her nest.

Fur brushed the branches near the den entrance as Leafstar slid inside. "How is she?"

"She'll be fine," Hawkwing reassured her.

"Who are Echosong and Frecklewish?" Violetpaw asked suddenly.

Leafstar blinked at her. "They were our medicine cats once.

Echosong died on the journey here. Frecklewish disappeared before we left the gorge."

Hawkwing lapped the top of Twigpaw's head with his tongue, and finally Twigpaw closed her eyes.

Leafstar's voice seemed far away. "We don't even know if Frecklewish is still alive."

"Maybe we could find out," Hawkwing meowed. "Isn't it time we sent a patrol back to the gorge to look for our lost Clanmates?"

"Can I go?" Violetpaw asked eagerly.

"It's too soon to decide who will go," Leafstar meowed thoughtfully. "But you're right, Hawkwing. It's time we sent one."

Twigpaw felt herself drifting into sleep. A patrol? To the gorge? *If Violetpaw's going, I should join too. It might be dangerous.*

But what about Finpaw? As dreams began to swirl around her, Twigpaw clung to one thought.

I don't want to leave him until I know he's all right.

CHAPTER 5
❧

Alderheart narrowed his eyes against the sunshine as he padded from the medicine den. Crisp, brown leaves littered the clearing. A soft wind lifted his fur.

"And don't forget borage!" Jayfeather called after him. "We need more borage. But not today. Remind me tomorrow." The blind medicine cat had been fussing over herbs since sunup, worrying about getting new supplies picked and dried before the rain came.

Alderheart had promised Jayfeather he'd gather comfrey today, but he hadn't eaten yet and his belly was rumbling. He padded to the fresh-kill pile, a little disappointed that none of the hunting parties had returned yet. A stiff mouse and a cold sparrow were left from yesterday. He glanced around the camp to check that no one else was heading for the pile. He didn't want to deprive any of his Clanmates of a meal.

Out of habit, he looked toward the apprentices' den first. Even though a half-moon had passed since Twigpaw had left with SkyClan, Alderheart expected her to pop out, with bright eyes, excited about the day's training. He tried to imagine her in SkyClan. She was probably a warrior by now.

Wistfully, he hoped that Leafstar had given her a name worthy of her spirit. He missed her questions and enthusiasm and endless ideas.

"Hi, Alderheart." Leafpool's cheerful mew jerked him from his thoughts. She was padding beside Briarlight as the crippled cat dragged herself around the edge of the clearing. "We're doing laps today. I think Briarlight's getting faster."

"I'm not getting faster." Briarlight puffed beside her, her forepaws holding her up while her useless hind legs splayed out behind her. "You're getting slower."

Leafpool meowed with amusement. Then she turned toward Alderheart and nodded at the pitiful fresh-kill pile. "Why don't you wait until the hunting patrols return?"

Alderheart rolled the mouse closer. "I hate to waste prey."

"Waste it while you can." Briarlight paused to catch her breath. "Leaf-bare's coming. You'll have plenty of time to eat stale prey then."

"Thanks." Alderheart sighed. "But I'm so hungry, this old mouse will probably still taste sweet."

Briarlight began her slow progress around the clearing once more.

Leafpool trotted after her. "Just one more lap," she encouraged. "Let's see if you can get around without stopping this time."

"You're the one who keeps stopping," Briarlight retorted. "Do you have to speak to every cat in camp?"

As Alderheart leaned down to pick up the mouse, Squirrelflight's mew rang across the clearing. She stood on

Highledge, where Bramblestar was sniffing the air. "Cloudtail, Thornclaw, Poppyfrost. I want you to come on border patrol with me." As she leaped down the tumble of rocks, the three warriors hurried to meet her. They followed her to the entrance.

Poppyfrost's pale tortoiseshell-and-white fur was prickling. "We have *three* borders to patrol now," she complained. "ShadowClan, RiverClan, *and* SkyClan."

"It's still exactly the same border," Squirrelflight reminded her.

"But with different cats on the other side, we have to check for different scents," Thornclaw pointed out.

"You'll get used to it," Squirrelflight meowed briskly.

Cloudtail fluffed out his fur. "At least we don't have to pay much attention to the RiverClan border now that they've cut themselves off."

Squirrelflight looked at him. "We should pay more attention to it for that very reason," she told him. "If their scent marks grow stale, we should worry."

"Why?" Cloudtail shrugged. "Maybe keeping themselves to themselves means not bothering with borders."

Thornclaw flicked his tail. "Squirrelflight is right. As long as they're marking their borders regularly, we know they're still behaving like a real Clan."

Poppyfrost's gaze sparked with alarm. "Do you think they might stop being a Clan?"

"I've given up trying to predict what any Clan will do," Squirrelflight replied, ducking through the entrance tunnel.

Thornclaw and Poppyfrost exchanged glances, then followed, Cloudtail at their heels.

Alderheart stared after them. His belly tightened with worry. They'd just found one Clan. They mustn't lose another.

Lilyheart padded to the fresh-kill pile. "You look worried." She blinked at him, concerned.

"There has been too much change recently," he mewed distractedly.

Lilyheart brushed past him and pawed the sparrow from the pile. "I still can't believe Twigpaw left."

Alderheart heard sadness in her mew. "You must miss her."

"Don't you?" She met his gaze.

Melancholy settled over him like mist as he imagined Twigpaw trotting out of the medicine den, Jayfeather grumbling behind her. "Very much."

"It's hard to raise a kit only to watch her leave," Lilyheart sighed. "And she was such a bright young cat."

Stones clattered behind them as Bramblestar scrambled down the rock tumble. He stopped at the bottom and shook his head before crossing the clearing to where Brackenfur and Lionblaze were sitting with Cherryfall and Molewhisker. As the ThunderClan leader greeted the warriors, Alderheart nodded to Lilyheart and picked up his mouse. He headed toward a clump of ferns where sunshine was pooling. It looked like a warm spot to eat.

He passed Millie and Graystripe, who were playing with Blossomfall's kits outside the elders' den while Blossomfall dozed beside Daisy in the sunshine near the nursery.

Plumkit hauled her way up Graystripe's side and clung to his shoulders. "Give me a badger ride," she demanded. Her black-and-ginger pelt twitched with excitement.

"Me too!" Stemkit scrambled up beside his sister.

"I want a badger ride!"

"So do I!"

Eaglekit and Shellkit began wailing.

Millie purred at them affectionately. "I think there's room for you all." She nipped Eaglekit by her ginger scruff and plopped her down behind Plumkit, then placed Stemkit beside her.

Graystripe pretended to stagger. "You weigh more than owls!"

The kits squealed with delight and clung on desperately as Graystripe swayed one way, then the other.

"I can't carry this much weight," he puffed.

Millie nudged his shoulder with her muzzle. "Of course you can," she told him. "You're still the strongest cat in Thunder-Clan."

"Okay." Graystripe sighed dramatically and began to lumber around the clearing, lurching with each step so that the kits squealed with fear as he swung them this way, then that.

Millie caught Alderheart's eyes as he passed. "Silly old fool," she mewed fondly, nodding toward Graystripe.

Alderheart's chest swelled with affection, and he dipped his head to Millie, unable to speak because of the mouse between his jaws. What a shame Twigpaw was missing this. *But she'll have Tinycloud's kits to watch soon,* he reminded himself.

He padded around Dewnose and Ambermoon, who were sweeping leaves into the sunniest part of the clearing with their paws. Once dried, the leaves would make a perfect lining for nests, to help keep out the leaf-bare chill.

Sparkpelt and Larksong lingered nearby, and Dewnose glared at them sternly as he swept. "I thought you two were meant to be helping us."

Sparkpelt eyed him with amusement. "I *would* help if Larksong didn't keep distracting me." She glanced teasingly at Larksong.

The gray-and-white tom looked at his paws, self-conscious.

Alderheart's pelt prickled with annoyance. Sparkpelt was flirting. How could she be such a featherbrain? She'd always been so ambitious about being the best warrior in ThunderClan. Why was she wasting her time acting like a dandelion-headed apprentice? Alderheart stalked past her. He still hadn't forgiven her for speaking out against SkyClan at the last Gathering.

He settled a few tail-lengths from them, where the sun was chasing away the shadow of Highledge. Ivypool and Fernsong lay close by, stretching in the warmth.

As Alderheart bit into his mouse and started chewing, he heard Ivypool sigh.

"I'm not ready to have kits yet," she told Fernsong.

From the corner of his eye, Alderheart noticed disappointment flash in the yellow tom's eyes.

"Kits mean endless moons in the nursery." Ivypool went on. "Daisy's getting too old to look after another litter, and I want to be out in the forest hunting and patrolling, not stuck in camp all the time."

"Why do *you* have to be in the nursery with them?" Fernsong asked.

Ivypool sat up. "What do you mean? I have to nurse them, don't I? Who else can do that?"

"But the nursing is over soon enough," Fernsong went on. "Then you'd be able to go back to your warrior duties."

"And leave our kits to raise themselves until they're six moons old?" Ivypool sounded shocked.

"Of course not," Fernsong explained. "Once the kits are eating prey, I can move into the nursery. I can move in *before* that, if you like, so that you can go on patrols between feedings."

"*You?*" Ivypool stared at him. "But you're a tom! Toms don't live in the nursery."

"Why not?" Fernsong blinked at her affectionately. "Apart from food, all kits need is love and some cat to play with. I can't think of a better way to spend my days." As he spoke, Graystripe thumped past, the kits clinging to his back with excited squeaks and purring so loudly that Alderheart could hardly hear himself chew.

Ivypool watched them pass, and then leaned down and nuzzled Fernsong's ear. "I'll think about it," she murmured. "Maybe after leaf-bare is over."

As Alderheart took another bite of mouse, the thorn barrier rustled. He looked up to see Bumblestripe escorting Violetpaw and Hawkwing into the camp. His heart leaped. Was

Twigpaw with them? He got to his paws and headed toward them. "What are you doing here?" He glanced behind them as he neared, hoping to see Twigpaw follow them through the entrance tunnel. But there was no sign of her. "Have you come alone?"

"Yes," Hawkwing told him.

"I found them at the border," Bumblestripe reported. "They want to speak with Bramblestar."

But Alderheart wasn't listening to the gray tabby tom. "Why didn't you bring Twigpaw?" Disappointment jabbed his belly.

"She's busy with her training," Hawkwing explained.

"Sandynose is her mentor," Violetpaw told him happily.

"She's still an apprentice?" Alderheart stared at the Sky-Clan deputy. "But she passed her assessment."

"Her *ThunderClan* assessment," Hawkwing meowed pointedly. "Leafstar thinks Twigpaw and Violetpaw"—he glanced fondly at Violetpaw before going on—"need to learn to hunt and fight like SkyClan cats."

Alderheart's pelt prickled with irritation. *SkyClan got driven from their home and ended up nearly dying. Twigpaw saved them.* He glared at Hawkwing. *She should be training you.*

Paw steps sounded behind Alderheart as Bramblestar joined them. Molewhisker, Lionblaze, Brackenfur, and Cherryfall crowded behind the ThunderClan leader, their ears pricked with curiosity.

Bramblestar dipped his head to Hawkwing. "What brings you here?"

"Leafstar has decided it's time we sent a patrol to the gorge to search for our lost Clanmates," Hawkwing told him. "We were hoping you could spare a few warriors. We could use help finding our way back, and we know you've sent a few patrols there already. We hoped you'd know the way."

Bramblestar sat down. "Some of us know the route," he mewed thoughtfully. "But I've sent enough parties to the gorge. And with leaf-bare coming, my warriors should be concentrating on filling the fresh-kill pile, not searching for more mouths to feed."

"It's *because* leaf-bare is coming that we want to go," Hawkwing pressed. "Would you want your Clanmates to be lost and alone during the cruelest moons?"

Molewhisker padded forward. "It can't do much harm to send a patrol with them," he ventured. "I know the way. So do Cherryfall and Sparkpelt."

Alderheart leaned forward. "And me!"

Bramblestar shook his head. "I'm sorry, Alderheart. Jayfeather needs you here to help him stock his herb store."

Disappointment dropped like a stone in Alderheart's belly.

"I could go," Molewhisker volunteered.

Alderheart looked at the brown-and-cream tom, puzzled. Why was he so keen to help a Clan that he hadn't even wanted around half a moon ago?

"It would be an honor to show them the way to the gorge." Molewhisker dipped his head, glancing at Cherryfall.

Alderheart bristled. Was Molewhisker hoping that if he showed the SkyClan cats the route to the gorge, they might go back for good?

"Very well." Bramblestar's mew cut into Alderheart's

thoughts. "SkyClan would be stronger if it could find its lost Clanmates, and a strong Clan is a good ally." He nodded to Hawkwing. "I will send a ThunderClan cat to guide your patrol. Just let me know when you are leaving, and my cats will be ready."

"Thank you." Hawkwing dipped his head graciously.

Violetpaw's eyes shone. "Thanks," she mewed happily. She glanced at Hawkwing. "Let's go back and tell Leafstar."

Hawkwing headed for the entrance.

"Say hi to Twigpaw from me!" Alderheart called after them.

"We will!" Violetpaw and Hawkwing chimed together.

Alderheart watched them disappear through the thorn tunnel. Violetpaw and her father seemed so close. He hoped Twigpaw's bond with her father was just as strong. And yet, if it was, why wasn't she here with them? *I'm just worrying.* He pushed the thought away and tried to imagine her practicing hunting techniques while Sandynose gave her orders. Unease pricked his belly. Twigpaw was such an independent cat. She'd done more than enough to earn her warrior name. Could she really be happy being a SkyClan apprentice?

Alderheart leaned over the rim of the hollow, straining to see along the path. The stream shimmered in the chilly moonlight, but there was no sign of Mothwing and Willowshine.

"Are they coming?" Leafpool called from beside the Moonpool.

"It doesn't look like it," he mewed back, disappointed.

Jayfeather shifted impatiently beside the pool. "Let's not

waste any more time waiting for them. They've clearly decided to stay away."

"They were probably ordered to stay away," Kestrelflight meowed. "That's what Onestar did to me when he cut ties with the Clans."

Alderheart tore his gaze from the path to the hollow and headed toward the pool. The smooth stone felt so cold beneath his paws that he could hardly feel the dimples made from countless moons of paw steps.

Kestrelflight was looking at the medicine cats apologetically. "You know I *wanted* to come when WindClan closed the borders, right?"

Leafpool blinked at him sympathetically. "Of course."

Puddleshine shifted his paws. "Did StarClan share dreams with you when you couldn't come here?"

Kestrelflight looked at his paws. "No," he admitted. "I think they were angry at me for staying away. But I had to stay with my Clan, didn't I?" He glanced at the others.

"Of course you did," Leafpool agreed.

"Let's stop *worrying* about StarClan and start *sharing* with them," Jayfeather snapped. "I'm cold."

The clear night sky sparkled overhead. A cool breeze whipped around the hollow, sending ripples across the Moonpool.

As Alderheart stopped beside Leafpool, Puddleshine cleared his throat. "There's something we need to discuss first," he meowed.

Kestrelflight pricked his ears.

Alderheart leaned closer, wondering what was making the ShadowClan medicine cat look so worried.

"It's SkyClan," Puddleshine told them. "They have no medicine cat. A few days ago, I was called out to help them."

"Tinycloud?" Anxiety flashed beneath Alderheart's pelt.

Puddleshine shook his head. "A branch fell on Finpaw's tail. I had to cut him free."

"*Cut* him free?" Leafpool looked shocked. "Is he okay?"

"He will be," Puddleshine told her. "I've been visiting the SkyClan camp daily and dressing the wound. I managed to make a clean cut, and there's no infection."

"You did well." Leafpool looked proud of her ex-apprentice.

"I did my best, and StarClan guided my paws," Puddleshine mewed modestly. "But it's dangerous for them not to have their own medicine cat, and I don't have time to check on them every day. Tinycloud's kits are very overdue. A medicine cat should be in the camp. Her kitting will be hard."

Jayfeather swished his tail over the stone. "One of us will have to stay with them, like we did with you"—he nodded toward Puddleshine—"when ShadowClan had no medicine cat. Do any of SkyClan's apprentices seem able to communicate with StarClan?"

"Well . . . I'm not sure. Twigpaw did want to be a medicine cat once," Alderheart mewed wistfully.

"Hanging around the medicine den getting under other cats' paws isn't the same as being a medicine cat," Jayfeather mewed sharply.

Leafpool ignored him. "SkyClan is planning to send a

patrol to the gorge to look for lost Clanmates," she told them. "Perhaps they'll find a Clanmate who's got some training in herbs."

Puddleshine still looked worried. "They need someone now. Tinycloud's kits will be at risk if they aren't born soon."

"I'll go." Alderheart realized with a rush that if he went to SkyClan, he'd see Twigpaw again. He'd be able to see how she was settling into her new home.

"Don't be mouse-brained," Jayfeather mewed impatiently. "Bramblestar just told you that you have to stay in camp to help me with my herb store."

Alderheart glared at the blind medicine cat. Why did his hearing have to be so sharp?

"Besides," Jayfeather went on, "Leafpool trained Shadow-Clan's medicine cat. She's used to working with other Clans. She should go."

Leafpool dipped her head. "I'd be happy to do it."

Frustration tightened Alderheart's belly. Why did it seem like everyone was trying to stop him from seeing Twigpaw? He'd rescued her. He'd watched her grow up. Surely he had some right to see how she was doing?

Kestrelflight moved closer to the water. "Let's begin." The others followed his lead, crouching close to the edge.

Still upset, Alderheart hunched beside Leafpool and stretched his head forward. Closing his eyes, he touched his nose to the pool.

The ground under him seemed to drop away. He felt the familiar falling sensation in his belly and relaxed into it, let himself swirl down as countless stars rushed to meet him. Then, suddenly, he felt grass beneath his paws. Sunshine warmed his pelt and he opened his eyes to see the sunny meadows of StarClan's hunting grounds. He was surprised to see the other medicine cats lined beside him. They sat up, blinking at one another in the sunlight. Alderheart tensed. *A shared vision!* It must be important.

"Where are they?" Puddleshine whispered, glancing around. The hilltop where they stood was deserted.

In the distance, Alderheart could see cats stalking, stretching in the sunshine, or gathered in groups.

Leafpool got to her paws. "Let's go to them."

"There is no need." A deep mew took Alderheart by surprise. He recognized it and turned.

Firestar was padding toward them, his star-specked fur sparkling even in the bright daylight. Others followed him, and Alderheart stretched to see which StarClan cats had come to greet them. He recognized the lithe shapes of Wind-Clan cats, the light tread of ShadowClan warriors, and the thick, glossy pelts of RiverClan cats. ThunderClan cats were among them, as sleek and tough-looking as they had been in life. The cats he did not recognize must, he guessed, be Sky-Clan's ancestors. He saw Purdy and broke into a purr. He hoped he knew how much he was missed.

"Where are Willowshine and Mothwing?" A large River-Clan tom with a twisted jaw slid in front of Firestar and scanned the medicine cats with dismay. *Crookedstar?* Alderheart guessed it was RiverClan's old leader.

Leafpool dipped her head to him. "They would be here if they could, I'm sure," she mewed apologetically.

Crookedstar glanced at Firestar. "It is worse than we thought."

Firestar nodded. "You must bring RiverClan back to the Clans," he told Leafpool.

Leafpool exchanged an anxious look with Kestrelflight.

Kestrelflight shrugged. "Once a leader has made up her mind, it is hard even for a medicine cat to change it." He looked at Firestar. "They will come back in their own time, just as we did."

Firestar's emerald gaze was dark with worry. "There may not be time for that."

Before he could explain, Leafpool gasped. A slender black she-cat was staring at her. "Hollyleaf!"

Alderheart knew of Leafpool's daughter; the Clan told vague stories of how they thought she'd died in a tunnel, though her body was never found. Jayfeather and Lionblaze hardly spoke of their dead littermate, and when they did, there was a strange tension in their words. But there was no tension in Leafpool. She gazed on her kit, her eyes brimming with affection.

Hollyleaf blinked lovingly at her mother. There seemed a curious calm about the black warrior as she padded slowly forward. She reached Leafpool and they touched cheeks with such gentle solemnity that Alderheart felt his throat tighten.

"Are you happy here?" Alderheart heard Leafpool whisper.

"I am at peace," Hollyleaf answered.

Kestrelflight's mew snatched Alderheart's attention away. "Onestar." The WindClan medicine cat dipped his head low as he caught sight of his leader. "It is good to see you."

"And you." Onestar lifted his head. He looked so different from the thin, anxious cat Alderheart had seen last. He was young and strong again, starlight showing in his eyes.

As Kestrelflight threaded his way among his WindClan ancestors, Firestar sat down. His gaze was placid but his tail-tip flicked impatiently, as though he was resigned to the greetings that must be made, but anxious to speak. What did he want to say?

Puddleshine touched noses with ShadowClan cats. "Kink-fur! How are you?"

Kinkfur shook out her long gray fur. "It's good to be free of aches and pains at last."

Beside her, Crowfrost looked healthy, his black-and-white pelt sleek. Alderheart's breath quickened. Which other ShadowClan cats were here? Was Needletail among them? He scanned the crowd hopefully, looking for her silver pelt. But he couldn't see her. There was no sign of any of Shadow-Clan's missing Clanmates, either. Were they still alive, or were they still finding their way to StarClan?

Firestar got to his paws and padded to the hilltop. "I real-ize it is good to see old friends," he called. "But we have words to share." As he spoke, a small, soft-furred, silver-gray tabby joined him.

Echosong! Alderheart recognized SkyClan's dead medicine cat from his visions. He pushed his way to the front of the gathered cats. Firestar was eyeing them impatiently, clearly waiting to speak. Leafpool and Jayfeather joined Alderheart, Kestrelflight and Puddleshine at their side.

Firestar went on. "We are glad you have made room beside the lake for SkyClan."

Delight surged in Alderheart's belly. He'd been right. Sky-Clan *was* meant to stay beside the other Clans.

Firestar turned to Echosong, dipping his head respectfully.

She blinked at him and turned to the medicine cats. "Sky-Clan is where it belongs, but there are still challenges ahead for all the Clans. What you decide now will change your path forever. Remember only this." She paused, her green eyes grave. "The dark sky must not herald a storm."

Alderheart's fur lifted along his spine. *The dark sky must not herald a storm.* Despite the warm sunshine, he felt a chill pierce his pelt and shivered at her words. What did she mean? He looked at Jayfeather, hoping to see understanding in his blue gaze. But the ThunderClan medicine cat was fading before his eyes. All around him the grass and sky and cats were dissolving into a shimmering haze. He felt himself fall, his heart rushing into his mouth as darkness engulfed him.

The smooth cold stone of the Moonpool hollow shocked his paws. He opened his eyes. The Moonpool seemed to shiver. The reflected stars glimmered on its surface. "What did Echosong mean?"

The other medicine cats sat up. They looked at each other, puzzled.

"Another prophecy." Jayfeather got to his paws and flicked

his tail irritably. "Let's not waste time trying to make sense of it here. We'll pass it on to our leaders and let them decide what must be done."

"No!" Alderheart stiffened. "We must try to understand. If it was left to our leaders, we never would have found Sky-Clan."

Leafpool blinked at him. "We need to think about it, certainly. And discuss it once we've thought. Perhaps there will be another sign to guide us. But it won't come tonight."

The others nodded in agreement. There was nothing Alderheart could do but follow them toward the rim of the hollow, anxiety worming beneath his pelt. He had been hoping to see Needletail, but there had been no hint of her. If she wasn't with StarClan, where was she? Overhead, the half-moon shone silently while the wind moaned around the hollow.

I hope she is at peace, wherever she is.

CHAPTER 6

❧

Violetpaw wrinkled her nose. She could still feel the bitterness of the traveling herbs on her tongue. She swiped it around her lips, hoping to get rid of the taste.

Hawkwing's whiskers twitched. "You didn't like the herbs?"

"No." Violetpaw shuddered.

They were standing near the camp entrance, waiting to leave. Blossomheart and Rabbitleap, Violetpaw's mentor, crouched beside them, sharing a mouse while Molewhisker paced beside the stream.

Rabbitleap looked up. "Have you eaten?" he asked Violetpaw.

"Only the traveling herbs." Violetpaw had been too nervous to eat anything else. She'd never traveled so far beyond Clan territory before.

"It's a long journey," Rabbitleap reminded her. "I don't know when we'll be able to stop and hunt."

"The traveling herbs will stop her getting hungry for a while." Hawkwing said, watching the nursery. Tinycloud's kitting had started before dawn. Leafpool was with her.

The ThunderClan medicine cat had arrived two days ago,

just after half-moon. She had been tending to Finpaw, who was recovering from his accident but was still confined to his nest. The stock of herbs that Leafpool had brought with her had been safely stored in the hollow beneath the cedar tree, and she'd made her nest there. She'd moved Finpaw there too, so she could watch over him. Molewhisker had joined her in the SkyClan camp yesterday after Macgyver had gone to fetch him from ThunderClan.

Now it was nearly time to leave for the gorge, and Violet-paw was so nervous that she felt as though frogs were jumping inside her belly. She wished Twigpaw were coming with them, but Twigpaw had asked to stay behind to help finish building the new camp. Violetpaw could see her tail now, sticking out from beneath the juniper bush where she was hollowing out the space for the apprentices' den.

"How far is it to the gorge?" Violetpaw asked Hawkwing, trying not to imagine the dogs and Twolegs and unfamiliar land that lay between here and there.

Molewhisker answered. "It may take a quarter moon." Blue sky showed through the branches above the camp. "But the weather is with us."

Blossomheart swallowed the last of her share of the mouse and sat up. "Leaf-fall weather can be changeable." She licked her paw and ran it over her face.

"A little rain won't hurt us," Hawkwing meowed.

As he spoke, Leafpool's face appeared at the nursery entrance. She slid out, blinking happily at Sparrowpelt, who was pacing anxiously outside. Leafstar was with him, and both cats lifted their tails excitedly as Leafpool shared the news.

"You have three newborn kits," the medicine cat announced happily. "A tom and two she-kits." She dipped her head to Sparrowpelt. "You can go and see them if you like."

"Thank you!" Purring loudly, the brown tabby tom squeezed through the entrance.

"Is Tinycloud okay?" Leafstar asked when he'd gone.

"She's tired," Leafpool told her. "But she did fine. Perhaps Sparrowpelt could sleep in the nursery for a few days to keep her company? A new litter can be daunting."

"Of course." Leafstar glanced toward the party preparing to leave.

As Leafpool turned back toward the nursery, the SkyClan leader headed toward her deputy. "May StarClan guide your paws," she meowed.

Hawkwing flicked his tail. "With Molewhisker's help."

Leafstar blinked at the ThunderClan tom. "Are you sure you know the way?"

He nodded.

Violetpaw looked around the camp. Even though SkyClan had been here only a short while, it felt like home. She would miss the sound of the stream and the swishing branches of the pine forest.

Hawkwing seemed to sense her unease. He swept his tail along her spine. "We'll be home soon, hopefully with some more of our Clanmates." He purred. "There are so many cats I want you to meet."

Leafstar caught his eye. "I hope you find them."

"We will find as many as we can," Hawkwing promised. "Soon we will be a bustling Clan again."

Wistfully, Leafstar held his gaze. "We will never be as we once were."

The juniper bush shivered as Twigpaw scrambled from underneath. She raced across the camp, leaping the stream and stopping beside her sister. "Are you leaving now?" She rubbed her muzzle along Violetpaw's jaw.

Violetpaw pressed against her. "I wish you were coming with me."

"I'll be here when you get back." Twigpaw blinked at her brightly. "You're going to have such an exciting time."

Violetpaw shifted her paws nervously. "I hope so."

"You *will*!" Twigpaw insisted. "Some cats never get to leave the forest. You'll remember this journey forever, and you'll always be known as one of the cats who helped reunite Sky-Clan."

Twigpaw was always so positive. Sometimes Violetpaw wished she were more like her. But then she glanced at Hawkwing; being more like Twigpaw would mean being less like him, and she *liked* being like Hawkwing. One day she'd be as brave as him too.

"We should leave," Molewhisker meowed, glancing at the sky once more. "I'd like to get to the Thunderpath before sunhigh."

The Thunderpath? Violetpaw swallowed.

Rabbitleap stretched and padded toward the entrance. Blossomheart followed.

"Good luck!" Leafstar called as Molewhisker headed after them.

Hawkwing touched his nose to Twigpaw's head. "Take care of SkyClan while we're away."

Leafstar purred. "I'm sure she will."

Twigpaw turned to Violetpaw, her gaze suddenly dark. "You'll be careful, won't you?"

"Of course." Violetpaw touched Twigpaw's muzzle with her own. She breathed in the soothing scent of her sister, and then padded after Hawkwing as he followed Rabbitleap, Blossomheart, and Molewhisker out of camp.

As her paws scuffed the needle-strewn forest floor, the frogs in her belly grew still. Suddenly she felt ready for the journey ahead. *We're going to find our lost Clanmates.*

Two sunrises later, as the sun reached its peak in the wide, blue sky, Violetpaw smelled the acrid scent of another Thunderpath. They'd crossed many, but the smell of this one was stronger. The sound of growling stirred her ear fur. It came from beyond the trees, as though a pack of huge dogs were arguing over prey. She glanced at her father, wondering if they should stop, but he kept walking. Molewhisker too. Rabbitleap and Blossomheart glanced at each other.

She followed them to the edge of the forest and padded out onto grass. Blinking in the bright sunshine, she saw a wide verge sloping toward a Thunderpath. This one was much wider than the ones they had crossed already, and instead of being deserted as those had been, it had monsters roaring along it in both directions, with barely a gap between them.

Violetpaw stopped, her heart skipping a beat. She thought of Pebbleshine with a sickening jolt. Her mother had been killed on a Thunderpath. "We can't cross that!"

Hawkwing turned and paused. His eyes were round and dark. "We have to."

Molewhisker padded back to Violetpaw. "This is the most dangerous Thunderpath we'll have to cross," he promised. "Once we've crossed it, we'll be safe."

Will we? Violetpaw tried to stop herself from trembling. On the other side, home would seem beyond reach.

Rabbitleap met Violetpaw's gaze. "You are fast and smart. I've seen you hunt and I've watched you practice battle moves. You have all the skills you need to make this crossing."

"But how will we ever get back?" Violetpaw suddenly felt very small.

"If we can cross it once, then we can cross it again," Hawkwing told her.

"You can do this." Rabbitleap nudged her gently forward.

Violetpaw dug her claws into the grass. "Pebbleshine was killed on a Thunderpath like this," she croaked.

Hawkwing looked at her, grief sharpening his gaze. "She was unlucky," he meowed thickly. "But I'm with you. I won't let the same thing happen to you."

Reluctantly, Violetpaw began to pad toward the Thunderpath. Every hair in her pelt told her to retreat, but she forced herself on, reassured as Molewhisker and her Clanmates fell in beside her. Together they approached the edge.

Monster after monster hurtled past. Sour air blasted her face. Grit sprayed her paws.

Molewhisker raised his voice. "Wait for a big enough gap."

Violetpaw wondered if a gap would ever come. The monsters chased after one another like foxes chasing rabbits.

"When I say go"—Hawkwing lifted his chin—"run as fast as you can."

Blossomheart and Rabbitleap nodded. Violetpaw stared at her father, her mouth dry with terror. A huge monster thundered past. The hot wind from its flanks nearly knocked her off her paws. She clung to the filthy grass and waited, her heart pounding in her ears as the monsters streamed past.

At last, a gap appeared. To one side, a distant green monster trundled toward them, spattered with mud. To the other, the Thunderpath curved toward an empty rise. The way between was clear.

"Run!" Hawkwing's yowl made Violetpaw jump. Blossomheart shot forward, Rabbitleap at her heels. Molewhisker raced past them, his tail skimming the stone. Hawkwing shoved Violetpaw forward. "Hurry!"

She ran, eyes narrowed, terror sparking in her belly. The hot stone burned her pads. The green monster rolled closer, as though in no hurry. The rise was still clear. *We're going to make it!*

As exhilaration surged beneath Violetpaw's pelt, a howl rose behind the green monster. A smaller monster had edged out and was hurtling toward her. It let out a desperate wail, as though running for its life. Terror choked Violetpaw's thoughts. Her paws froze beneath her, and she skidded to a halt. Ahead of her, Molewhisker, Hawkwing, Rabbitleap, and Blossomheart dived onto the safety of the green embankment.

Rooted by panic, Violetpaw stared at the small monster. It roared past the green one, neck and neck with it now. In a moment it would pass it and plow straight over Violetpaw. She knew she should move, but she was frozen with terror. *StarClan, help me!*

The small monster's paws squealed on the stone as the Twoleg inside stared in horror at Violetpaw. The monster let out a wail, as though warning her to move. It swerved suddenly, the Twoleg's eyes bulging as it dived in front of the green monster, veering so close that its flank caught the green monster's nose. Violetpaw stared, as though watching a nightmare from a long way away. Hypnotized, she heard the thump of their thick hides collide. The small monster spun out across the Thunderpath and came to a juddering halt on the far side.

Teeth grabbed her scruff, and Hawkwing's fear-scent bathed her as her paws half lifted from the stone. With a grunt, her father dragged her clear. He dropped her on the embankment beside her Clanmates. Blinking dumbly, she gazed at them.

"What in StarClan were you doing!" Hawkwing glared at her. "You just stood there while it—" His mew stopped short. Grief glittered in his gaze. He thrust his muzzle against her neck, his breath hot and quick. "You could have been killed."

Stiff with shock, Violetpaw looked back at the small monster, silent now on the far side of the Thunderpath. The big green monster had stopped and a Twoleg had jumped out. It ran to the small monster, where another Twoleg had climbed free. The Twolegs yelped at each other for a few moments, and then the Twoleg from the small monster pointed at Violetpaw. As its gaze fixed on her, panic flashed fresh inside her.

"Run!" she shrieked.

She pelted away from the Thunderpath, glancing behind to see the others chasing after her. She kept running, slithering beneath a fence and tearing over a wide stretch of earth, until the sounds of the Thunderpath dimmed behind her.

She stopped, her lungs burning. Hawkwing slowed to a halt beside her, and Molewhisker, Rabbitleap, and Blossomheart pulled up a few tail-lengths ahead. Their flanks heaved as they stared at one another with wide, round eyes.

"I'm sorry," Violetpaw puffed. Her fur was still on end. "I froze."

"You're safe now," Rabbitleap grunted between breaths. "That's all that matters."

"I didn't know monsters attacked each other!" Blossomheart was trembling. "Why do Twolegs go near them?"

"Who knows why Twolegs do anything." Molewhisker shook out his fur. "Let's go. We've still got a long way to travel."

Hawkwing looked at Violetpaw, concern shadowing his eyes. "Are you okay?"

She nodded, swallowing back fear. "Thanks for saving me."

"I will always save you if I can." Hawkwing blinked at her. "I just wish I had been around to save your mother."

* * *

Violetpaw was in the starlit woods again. Was it another dream?

Needletail's mew sounded from the darkness. "You made your choice."

Violetpaw strained to see her friend's pelt between the trees. "Wait! Please wait! I can't lose you."

Silver flashed in the shadows, weaving between the black trunks. Once more Violetpaw saw Needletail's green gaze flash at her accusingly.

"I thought you *wanted* to lose me."

Violetpaw jerked awake, her heart twisting with grief. She blinked in the darkness of the crevice where the patrol had sheltered for the night. Her Clanmates, plus Molewhisker, were curled around her, squashed into the narrow gap between two boulders, sheltered from the chilly wind.

Her heart was thumping hard. She needed fresh air and to walk off the anxiety itching beneath her pelt. Hardly breathing, she got to her paws and delicately picked her way around the sleeping cats. Molewhisker stretched out his legs, pushing against Rabbitleap, who snorted, wriggled, and fell still as Hawkwing snored softly beside him. At the entrance, Violetpaw hopped out into the fresh wind.

Outside, the moon glowed through thin cloud. The boulders opened onto a sandy clearing in an oak forest. They'd trekked through it most of the afternoon, stopping to hunt and then rest once the sun began to set behind the trees. Violetpaw drew in a deep breath of air, letting it soothe her. A light breeze made the leaves rattle overhead. Somewhere in the distance, a fox screeched. An owl answered as if telling it to be quiet.

Violetpaw padded cautiously between the trees. If she couldn't sleep, she might as well hunt. Her Clanmates would be pleased to wake to fresh-kill. Opening her mouth, she tasted the air. Among the musty scents of fallen leaves, she smelled mouse.

Violetpaw slowed, scanning the shadows for movement. Something glowed between the trees. She blinked, wondering if she was imagining the hazy light ahead, and padded closer. Curiosity pricked her pelt. Was it a patch of moonlight on the forest floor? But the moon was hidden, and starlight wouldn't be strong enough to make such a bright pool. She widened her eyes, straining to see.

A familiar scent touched her nose. *Needletail?* As she neared the glow, she saw the shape of a cat. She recognized it at once. It *was* Needletail! *Am I still dreaming?* She curled her claws into the fallen leaves. They crunched. The breeze in her fur felt real. *I am awake!* She was sure of it.

She hurried toward Needletail. Could the ShadowClan warrior have survived Darktail's attempt to kill her? *I didn't see her die.* All she remembered from when she fled was that the rogues had heavily outnumbered Needletail. "What are you doing here?"

Needletail didn't answer. She only stared. Her pelt looked as though she were lit from inside.

"What happened to you?" Violetpaw's thoughts whirled. "Are you dead?"

Needletail snorted. "Of course I'm dead. Do you think Darktail had a change of heart after you got away?"

"But there are no stars in your pelt. . . ." Violetpaw's mew trailed away. Wasn't Needletail with StarClan? Her belly tightened. Had she come from the *Dark Forest*? She swallowed. The young warrior had betrayed her Clan, but StarClan must have known that it was a mistake. They must have seen her give her life to save her Clanmate. She didn't deserve to go to the Dark Forest.

Needletail turned and began to walk away.

Violetpaw followed. "Am I dreaming you?"

Needletail didn't answer. She kept walking, the pale light from her fur showing the way between the trees.

"Where are you going?" Violetpaw glanced around as Needletail led her deeper into the forest. She was aware of her sleeping Clanmates, farther behind her with each step. "Do you want me to come with you?"

Violetpaw's mew echoed through the forest. The fox screeched again. Movement caught her eye and she looked up. An owl glided silently between the trees. Violetpaw's heart quickened.

"Needletail!" Violetpaw stopped. Where was Needletail going? Why was she so silent? But as she spoke, the faint light disappeared. Needletail was gone.

Violetpaw stiffened, suddenly aware that she was alone in a strange forest.

She turned back, breathing rapidly. What if the owl decided she was prey? What if the fox picked up her scent?

She had to get back to her Clanmates.

Why did you lead me so far away, Needletail? She shivered. Had her friend wanted to separate her from Hawkwing and the others? *Is she angry with me?* She sped up, hurrying back along the path she had come. Quickly she lost her scent trail. Had she gone the wrong way? She looked around. The trees looked the same in the dark. The strange scents of the unfamiliar forest confused her. What if she was heading farther away from the cleft in the rock? She froze, unsure what to do. *I should stay here,* she decided. *When dawn comes it will be easier to find my way back.*

She looked around for cover. A hollow between arching tree trunks would give her shelter for the night. She fluffed out her fur, determined not to be afraid. *I can hunt and I can fight,* she told herself. *I will be safe until dawn.*

Paw steps made her freeze. Leaves crunched nearby. Something was heading her way. She unsheathed her claws, blood thumping in her ears.

"Violetpaw?"

She recognized her father's mew. Relief washed her pelt like a cool breeze.

"Hawkwing." She raced toward the sound, joy bursting in her chest as she saw his familiar pelt in the starlight.

"What are you doing out here?" He hurried to meet her.

"I couldn't sleep," she told him. "So I thought I'd hunt. But I got lost." She could never tell him about Needletail. She didn't want to tell him about how her friend died, and she didn't know if she could explain what had just happened.

"We're not far from the boulders," Hawkwing reassured

her. "Let's go back. You should get some more sleep. We've got a lot of traveling to do tomorrow."

Violetpaw nodded and let him lead her between the trees, but she couldn't resist glancing over her shoulder. *Where did you go, Needletail?* Another thought pricked her mind. *And why did you come?* Did Needletail want something? And, if she did, what could it be?

CHAPTER 7

♣

Outside the camp wall, Twigpaw pulled up another fern frond. Earth showered her paws as she shook out the roots and laid it on the pile beside her. She would soon have enough to line every nest in the apprentices' den. She shivered and fluffed out her fur. The clear sky had brought colder weather. She hoped Violetpaw and Hawkwing had found somewhere sheltered to spend the night.

At least they would come home to cozy dens. The juniper bush was rainproof at last, and Twigpaw had helped Fallowfern and Sandynose weave the bramble walls of the warriors' den so thickly that no draft could get through. While Fallowfern and Sandynose had turned their attention to the clump of ferns that would become the elders' den, Twigpaw had begun to build nests for Violetpaw, Reedpaw, Dewpaw, and herself. She hadn't started Finpaw's nest yet. He was still recovering in the medicine den.

Leafpool had told her that Finpaw was healing well but his spirits were low. Plumwillow had sat with him until he'd sent her away, and now he refused to have any visitors. Twigpaw had asked to see him, but Leafpool told her that he probably needed time to come to terms with losing part of his tail.

Paw steps pattered behind her. "Look at all the moss I've collected." Dewpaw dumped a heap beside her. "Reedpaw's followed the stream to find more. We are going to have the softest nests in the whole camp."

"Perhaps we should take some to Finpaw," Twigpaw suggested.

Dewpaw rolled his eyes. "Don't make him too comfortable or he'll never move out of the medicine den."

"He doesn't *want* to be there," Twigpaw mewed defensively.

"Really?" Dewpaw sniffed. "I got the idea that he's sort of enjoying feeling sorry for himself."

Dewpaw sounded unsympathetic, but Twigpaw could see worry in the gray tom's eyes. "Did he refuse to see you again today?" she asked gently.

"Yes." Dewpaw sat down heavily. "I know it's terrible that he lost part of his tail. I don't know how I'd feel in the same situation. But he still has half of it, and being sad won't help."

"Leafpool says he needs time."

"I need my brother." Dewpaw looked despondently at the moss he'd gathered. "We should be sharing a den. It took us so long to become apprentices—we were so excited when it finally happened." He glanced beseechingly at Twigpaw. "Would *you* go and see him?"

Twigpaw looked away, her pelt suddenly hot. "He won't want to see me either."

"Of course he will," Dewpaw mewed eagerly. "If it weren't for you, he might have died. You pulled him clear of the branch."

"Not entirely clear," Twigpaw mewed guilty.

"Clear enough." Dewpaw leaned closer. "He won't be able to send you away."

"You mean he *has* to see me to be polite."

"Exactly." Dewpaw leaned back on his haunches. "I bet you can cheer him up."

Twigpaw pulled up another fern, avoiding Dewpaw's gaze. "Do you think so?" she asked shyly.

Dewpaw narrowed his eyes. "You *like* him, don't you?"

"No!" Twigpaw shriveled inside her pelt. "He's just a friend, that's all."

"*We're* friends." Dewpaw poked her. "But your fur doesn't twitch when you talk about me."

Twigpaw poked him back. "My fur does not twitch!"

Dewpaw changed the subject. "I hope some of those are for *my* nest." He nodded at the pile of ferns.

"Of course." Twigpaw blinked at him gratefully. She didn't like being teased about Finpaw. "Let's take them into the den, then I'll see if Finpaw will let me visit."

"Great." Dewpaw got to his paws. "By the time you return from the medicine den, I'll have our nests finished. We can start on Finpaw's nest. When he moves in and Violetpaw gets back, it'll be like a real apprentices' den. Especially if they bring back more SkyClan cats." He paused. "Perhaps we should make extra nests, just in case they find some apprentices." He grabbed his pile of moss between his jaws and headed toward the camp entrance.

Twigpaw bundled the fern fronds together and began to drag them after him. Her thoughts wandered. Dewpaw,

Reedpaw, and Finpaw had been so lucky, growing up together. If only ShadowClan had let Violetpaw stay in ThunderClan. *Perhaps she would have ended up more like me.* Twigpaw pushed the thought away. Sighing, she heaved the fronds to the entrance of the juniper bush.

"Twigpaw!" Dewpaw called from inside. "Reedpaw's back."

Reedpaw poked her head out of the den. "I found so much moss!" Her eyes shone. "It's a bit damp, but it will dry out soon."

Lost in thought, Twigpaw stared blankly at the small tabby she-cat. Would the journey to the gorge make Hawkwing and Violetpaw even closer?

Dewpaw pushed his way out of the den and began to rummage through Twigpaw's pile of ferns. "Perhaps we should spread out the moss in the sunshine so it can dry while we're weaving these." He paused as he saw Twigpaw's face. "What's wrong?"

"Nothing." She shook out her fur. She was being dumb. So what if Hawkwing and Violetpaw were close? SkyClan was a great home. She was living with kin at last. And Dewpaw was great. Reedpaw was friendly. And there was Finpaw. She glanced toward the medicine den, her heart quickening. "I'll go and see him now," she told Dewpaw.

"Say hi from me."

As Dewpaw disappeared back inside the juniper bush, Twigpaw marched to the hollow beneath the cedar and stopped outside. "Leafpool?"

No cat replied. Twigpaw tasted the air. Leafpool's scent

was stale. She must be out gathering herbs or hunting. "Finpaw?" She mewed softly through the lichen, which Leafpool had draped over the entrance.

Ferns rustled inside.

"Are you awake?" she called softly.

"I am now." Finpaw sounded grumpy.

"Can I come in?"

"I don't want any visitors."

Twigpaw sniffed. She'd hung out with Alderheart long enough to know that no cat was cured by loneliness. "I'm coming in anyway." She pushed though the lichen.

Finpaw lay in his nest, his stunted tail sticking over the edge. It was wrapped in moss and cobweb, and smelled of marigold. Twigpaw was relieved to see how much of it was left. She blinked at Finpaw. His fur was sleek and his nose and ears were clean. Apart from his injured tail and the shadows in his eyes, he looked fine. "You look well."

Finpaw avoided her gaze. "I'm half a tail away from being well."

Twigpaw sat beside him, her chest aching with sympathy. But she kept any trace of pity from her voice. "In ThunderClan, we had a cat with a broken spine. She's the most cheerful cat in the Clan."

"Good for her," Finpaw muttered.

"What do you need a whole tail for anyway?" Twigpaw persisted.

"Um . . . to *balance*?" Finpaw snapped.

"Only mouse-brains need a tail to help them balance."

"Then I must be a mouse-brain."

"You really don't want visitors, do you?" Twigpaw swallowed back frustration. "I hope you're not this mean to Leafpool."

Finpaw didn't answer.

Twigpaw looked at the young tom, his face turned away. She wanted to cheer him up. She'd been thinking about him ever since his accident. It was heartbreaking to see that his spirit had been as crushed as his tail. He'd been so cheerful and open. Now he was as snarly as a fox. "If only I'd been able to pull you clear," she mewed without thinking. Sadness flooded her chest. Perhaps if she'd tugged harder when the branch was falling, she could have saved him from this.

Finpaw blinked at her, alarmed. "*You're* not supposed to be sad," he mewed urgently.

Twigpaw was confused. "Why not?"

Finpaw raised himself up on his front paws. "Because you're never sad. That's why I like you."

Twigpaw didn't know what to say. She looked at her paws. "Dewpaw says hello. He's helping me make nests in the apprentices' den. He wants you to move there as soon as you can." She glanced at him shyly. "I want you there too. I was the only apprentice in ThunderClan. Sharing a den will be fun."

"Fun?" Finpaw seemed to brighten. "Have you heard Dewpaw *snore*?"

"He *snores*?" Twigpaw played along.

"He could outsnore a badger." Finpaw assured her. "Reedpaw says he could wake a hibernating bear."

"Perhaps I should gather some extra moss," she mewed. "To stuff in my ears."

Finpaw's whiskers twitched with amusement.

Twigpaw pricked her ears happily. "You're going to be fine."

He glanced at his tail. "Leafpool keeps telling me that I'm lucky I only lost half of it."

Twigpaw caught his eye. "What happened to the other half?"

"Puddleshine said he was going to bury it."

"Bury it?" Surprise twitched through Twigpaw.

Finpaw gave her a mischievous look. "Perhaps we should find its grave and sit vigil." There was a purr in his mew.

"We could mark it with a stone and visit every leaf-fall to pay our respects."

"Here lies Finpaw's tail," Finpaw mewed solemnly. "It died protecting its Clan."

"Perhaps it's in StarClan right now, lying in the sunshine," Twigpaw joked.

"There must be other tails there. I hope it's made friends," Finpaw mewed.

Twigpaw nudged his shoulder fondly with her nose. "You've got bees in your brain."

"You started it."

As he nudged her back, the lichen swished and Leafpool padded through the entrance. She blinked happily at Twigpaw. "I see you've decided to have visitors after all," she mewed to Finpaw.

"Twigpaw barged in." Finpaw mewed.

"I promised Dewpaw I'd see how he was." Twigpaw didn't admit how much she'd wanted to see Finpaw.

"You'll have to leave in a moment," Leafpool told her. "I'm going to dress his wound."

"Can't she stay?" Finpaw begged. "If I have someone to talk to, it'll take my mind off it."

"Does it hurt?" Twigpaw asked.

"Kind of," Finpaw murmured.

"Okay," Leafpool agreed. "I'll be back in a moment. I just want to soak these leaves in the stream." She grabbed a pile of herbs and headed out of the den.

Finpaw shifted in his nest, making himself comfortable. "Are you missing Violetpaw and Hawkwing?"

"Yeah." Twigpaw wrapped her tail over her paws. "It feels strange being in a new camp without them. Kind of like I'm in the wrong place."

"I think everyone feels a bit out of place at the moment. But Sandynose says it'll start to feel like home soon." Finpaw's eyes rounded with curiosity. "Leafpool says that you and Violetpaw were raised by different Clans. I didn't know that. You seem so close."

"We *are* close," Twigpaw told him. "And now we get to live together, now that we've found Hawkwing."

"I like Hawkwing." Finpaw's gaze grew distant as though he were thinking. "He's reassuring."

"Yeah."

"Sandynose was missing when we were born, so Hawkwing kind of helped take care of us."

"Sandynose went missing?" Twigpaw hadn't heard about this.

"We thought we'd never meet our real father. But we had Hawkwing. He was nice."

Twigpaw blinked at him sympathetically.

Finpaw looked thoughtful. "You're quite like him."

"Violetpaw's more like him than me."

"Yes," Finpaw agreed. "But you and Hawkwing are more like Clan cats than Violetpaw. Sometimes she seems uncomfortable in her own fur and unsure of herself. You have the same confidence as Hawkwing. And you're brave and loyal like he is. And kind."

"I am?" She looked at him.

"Sure."

As Twigpaw's fur tingled at the compliment, Leafpool nosed her way into the den. Wet leaves dripped from her jaws. She draped them over the edge of the nest, beside Finpaw's tail. "I'll get the dressing changed as quickly as I can." She promised. "But I need to make sure the wound's clean before I dress it again."

"I'll distract him," Twigpaw leaned closer to Finpaw, trying not to look at his tail as Leafpool began to peel away the cobwebs.

Finpaw winced.

"What games do kits play in SkyClan?" Twigpaw asked quickly.

"Hide-and-seek, warrior and prey, hide the beechnut . . ."

"I played those too." Twigpaw felt pleased that all Clan kits

were the same, wherever they'd been born. "But in Thunder-
Clan we played hide the pebble. And Violetpaw probably
played hide the pinecone in ShadowClan."

Leafpool moved to her herb store and pulled out a long
strand of cobweb.

"Did you ever have a chance to play with Violetpaw?" Finpaw asked.

"We played lots before we were separated. But afterward,
we couldn't." Twigpaw longed to tell him about sneaking out
of camp with Alderheart to meet Needletail and Violetpaw,
but she was aware of Leafpool, who was wrapping a fresh
dressing around Finpaw's tail. She didn't want to get Alderheart in trouble.

Finpaw shifted in his nest. "When she gets back, we can
play hide the pinecone with her and Dewpaw and Reedpaw,"
Finpaw mewed.

"Aren't we a bit old?"

"Of course not!"

As Finpaw purred, Leafpool sat back on her haunches. "I've
finished," she told him.

"Already?" He looked around at his tail, surprised. "That
hardly hurt at all."

"It's healing well," Leafpool told him.

"And I had good company." Finpaw blinked warmly at
Twigpaw.

She felt heat beneath her pelt, and blinked back self-consciously.

"You're well enough to start getting some exercise."

Leafpool brushed the herb scraps away with her tail.

Twigpaw's tail twitched excitedly. "I could show you the forest! The Sky Oak and the old Twoleg nest . . ." As she spoke, she realized that she wasn't in ThunderClan anymore. She didn't know SkyClan territory any better than Finpaw did. "Or we could explore together," she corrected herself quickly.

Finpaw's yellow eyes shone. "That would be great."

Leafpool licked green herb pulp from her paw. "You shouldn't leave camp for a few days," she advised. "Not until your wound has healed properly."

"That's okay," Twigpaw mewed brightly. "There's plenty to do in camp. I think I saw a fish in the stream yesterday. It was just a small one, but it would be fun to catch."

Leafpool wrinkled her nose. "You sound like a RiverClan cat."

"We're not going to *eat* it," Twigpaw purred.

"We'll throw it back," Finpaw agreed.

Leafpool shook her head. "You'll have to *catch* it first."

Twigpaw glanced at Finpaw. Her heart seemed to skip as he held her gaze. She wondered if he could possibly be as excited as she was at the thought of spending time together.

CHAPTER 8

❧

As Alderheart stomped out of camp and headed for the lake, Jay-feather hurried to catch up with him. "I know StarClan's prophecies are frustrating," the blind tom mewed. "I've had to deal with plenty. But this one will become clear eventually, just as the others have."

"Doesn't it worry you that Bramblestar won't do *anything*?" Alderheart glanced at him. "The last prophecy told us to find SkyClan. We only sent out one patrol. We'd never have found them if Twigpaw hadn't disobeyed Bramblestar and gone out alone. And now Bramblestar wants to ignore this prophecy."

Actually, what Bramblestar had said was, "If there were something I *could* do, then I would. But it would be foolish to act before we fully understand StarClan's message." Alder-heart's pelt prickled with frustration, and he wasn't sure who he was more upset with: Bramblestar or StarClan. Why *did* StarClan have to be so obscure?

"Our duty is to share messages from StarClan with our leader," Jayfeather reminded him now. "And to advise him. But he is the leader and he must make the decisions."

"Even if he's wrong?" Alderheart's paws itched with anger.

"He's Clan leader," Jayfeather meowed. "If he went into a panic every time some cat came to him with a worry, he'd spend more time running in circles than solving the problems he *can* solve."

Alderheart didn't respond. What was the point? Jayfeather was obviously going to defend Bramblestar whatever happened. Perhaps Kestrelflight and Puddleshine would have something more helpful to say. The day before, Alderheart and Jayfeather had sent messengers to each camp to arrange this meeting.

As he broke from the trees, he could see them waiting on the shore. They stood beside the new SkyClan border, within two tail-lengths of the water, looking toward the forest.

Puddleshine lifted his tail as he caught sight of Alderheart and Jayfeather.

"They've seen us." Alderheart raced ahead of Jayfeather. He leaped onto the pebbles, stumbling as they shifted beneath him. "What did Harestar and Rowanstar say about the prophecy?" He scrambled to a halt in front of them.

Puddleshine eyed him anxiously. "Rowanstar is worried that the dark sky means SkyClan. He's decided to concentrate patrols on the SkyClan border."

Alderheart's pelt pricked uneasily. "But StarClan was pleased we made room for SkyClan beside the lake. They can't be the dark sky!"

Kestrelflight flicked his ears. "Even if they are, the prophecy says that the dark sky *mustn't* herald a storm, and extra patrols will mean extra tension."

Alderheart frowned. "Do you think Rowanstar might cause the storm StarClan is warning us about?"

Jayfeather reached them. "Rowanstar doesn't have enough cats to cause a storm. He barely has enough to cause a mild breeze." He turned his muzzle to Alderheart. "I thought you'd be pleased that he's taking the prophecy seriously."

Puddleshine looked puzzled. "Why wouldn't he?"

Alderheart shifted his paws. "Bramblestar doesn't seem concerned by the prophecy," he explained. "He thinks we should wait and see."

"Harestar says that we've seen nothing but dark skies in the past few moons," Kestrelflight meowed. "He fears the prophecy is warning us that the situation might get worse. He's stepped up patrols too."

"More tension," Puddleshine mewed darkly.

"At least they're *doing* something." Alderheart felt a fresh prickle of irritation with his father.

"Yes, and half the Clans are on edge now," Jayfeather mewed sarcastically. "I'm sure that will help." He looked a little way up the shore, toward SkyClan's stretch of forest. "I can't scent Leafpool."

"Perhaps we should go into SkyClan's camp," Alderheart suggested, "and tell her we're heading out?"

Jayfeather gave a mew of agreement, and led the medicine cats toward SkyClan's camp.

Alderheart followed him. "I still don't understand why StarClan would give us a prophecy if they thought it wouldn't help."

"StarClan doesn't know everything," Jayfeather murmured.

Puddleshine caught up to them. "They must. They're StarClan!"

"You haven't known them as long as I have." Jayfeather flicked his tail.

Kestrelflight seemed lost in his own thoughts. "I wonder if StarClan has shared the prophecy with Mothwing and Willowshine."

"You said they didn't share with you when Onestar cut WindClan off from the Clans," Alderheart reminded him.

Kestrelflight shrugged. "Maybe they blamed me for not helping enough. The Clans were in crisis then, but things are calmer now."

Jayfeather grunted. "There's no point in guessing whether RiverClan knows about the prophecy. We will find out when we get there. But if we go to SkyClan to get Leafpool, we can see what Leafstar thinks."

Alderheart slid into the lead. He knew the route to SkyClan's camp. He'd carried herbs there for Leafpool, hoping for a chance to speak with Twigpaw. But Twigpaw had been out training with Sandynose. Would he see her this time? He had not spoken to her since she'd moved to SkyClan. He was eager to know how she'd settled into her new home, and secretly he hoped she missed him and ThunderClan a little.

He climbed the short, steep bank from the shore to the forest and padded between the trees, the other medicine cats following. He was pleased to be out of the wind. His leaf-bare pelt hadn't grown in yet, and he felt the chill keenly. He followed the scent line until he recognized the place where he'd crossed it with Leafpool. It smelled as though Molewhisker had come this way too. He wondered how the expedition to the gorge was going, his heart lurching as a thought sparked in his mind. What if Twigpaw had gone with Violetpaw and Hawkwing? She'd be away from camp when they reached it.

Of course she's gone with them. She left ThunderClan to be near them. Prickling with frustration, he led the way between the towering pines. He wove around a sprawling bramble and climbed a rise where boulders clustered at the top. The path between them led downhill, and before long he saw the cedar grove that marked the SkyClan camp. Following the fern wall, he found the entrance and ducked inside.

"Alderheart." Leafstar stood beside a low-spreading juniper with Plumwillow and Bellaleaf. She blinked at the medicine cat in surprise.

"Forgive us for barging in like this," Alderheart began.

Jayfeather pushed past him and stopped in front of the SkyClan leader. He dipped his head. "Has Leafpool shared StarClan's prophecy with you?"

"She has." Leafstar's gaze flicked from Jayfeather to Kestrelflight and Puddleshine.

Jayfeather sat down and gazed sightlessly at Leafstar. "May I ask your thoughts?"

"On the prophecy?" Leafstar's tail twitched. She turned her muzzle to the new dens where cats were busy weaving branches. "We are building a new home. I've had little time to think about prophecies. We are a very busy Clan right now."

Alderheart leaned forward. "But you must have considered it."

"'The dark sky must not herald a storm.'"

As Leafstar quoted Echosong's warning, Leafpool slid out of the hollow beneath an old cedar. She padded toward them. "Jayfeather!" She greeted her son warmly.

Jayfeather touched his muzzle to hers. "Did you forget about our meeting?"

"Oh!" Her eyes widened with alarm. "Oh, I'm so sorry, all of you. Things have been so busy here . . . it just completely slipped my mind."

A prophecy slipped your mind? Alderheart thought indignantly. *Is* every *cat too distracted to take this message seriously?*

But Jayfeather didn't seem bothered. "Well, it's not as though you haven't had enough to do here," he said cheerfully. "How are Tinycloud's kits?"

"They were born just before the patrol left for the gorge," Leafpool purred. "Two she-kits and a tom."

Alderheart kneaded the ground impatiently. He was pleased to hear about Tinycloud's kits, but there were more important things to discuss. "What about the prophecy? Have you had any thoughts about what it might mean?"

"I haven't. I've tried to think it through, but . . . well, we've been so busy." Leafpool echoed Leafstar's answer apologetically.

Kestrelflight padded forward. "Harestar has stepped up patrols."

"So has Rowanstar," Puddleshine told her.

Leafstar pricked her ears. "Does he have enough warriors?"

"He's only patrolling your border," Jayfeather told her bluntly. "He thinks the dark sky means SkyClan, of course. ShadowClan never did have much imagination."

Puddleshine glanced sharply at the blind medicine cat. "Are you surprised Rowanstar's being cautious?" he snapped. "After everything we've been through?"

Leafstar's ears twitched. "We can't change what the other Clans do. For now, we must take care of ourselves, and that means finishing our camp and finding our lost Clanmates so that we can be a real Clan again."

Alderheart felt a pang of sympathy for the Clan leader. Until SkyClan had found their paws in their new home, they could do little except keep going.

Movement caught his eye. A brown-and-ginger tom with a short tail, still raw at the tip, shot out from the ferns. *Finpaw.* He was pleased to see that the tom was recovering from his accident.

Twigpaw bounced after the apprentice, her whiskers twitching happily as she knocked a pinecone ahead of her. "I found it!"

"Only because I told you where it was."

Twigpaw! Happiness rippled through Alderheart's pelt. It was a relief to see that she seemed at home here.

Her eyes shone as she spotted him. "Alderheart!" Racing across the camp, she cleared the stream with one jump and skidded to a halt beside him. "How are you?"

"I'm fine." Alderheart purred. "Are you settling in okay?"

"Yeah." She glanced back at Finpaw. "It's great."

"You must be getting your warrior name soon."

Twigpaw's pelt ruffled self-consciously. "I don't know. I guess I'll have to wait. But the other apprentices are great."

Alderheart frowned. How strange that Leafstar was keeping her an apprentice. "I imagine you're bored with training," he meowed. "I'm surprised you're not with Hawkwing's patrol. Didn't you want to go?"

Leafstar answered for her. "Twigpaw wanted to help her Clan build their camp." The SkyClan leader flashed Alderheart a stern look.

He shifted his paws. Clearly the SkyClan leader didn't want him stirring up discontent.

Finpaw called across the camp. "Hurry up, Twigpaw! It's your turn to hide the pinecone."

Twigpaw looked anxiously from Finpaw to Alderheart. "I'll see you soon, okay?" she mewed to Alderheart.

He blinked at her. "Sure." Did she want to end their meeting so quickly? Wasn't she as eager to talk as he was? Disappointment pricked his belly. She must be settling into SkyClan better than he'd imagined.

She turned and hurried away, leaping the stream and grabbing the pinecone between her jaws before disappearing among the ferns.

Alderheart watched her go. He was glad to see her happy, but he had secretly hoped she was missing ThunderClan more.

Jayfeather whisked his tail. "Thank you for your time,

Leafstar." He nodded to his mother. "Do you still want to come with us to RiverClan? Remember, we're going to tell Mistystar about the prophecy."

Leafpool narrowed her eyes. "Do you think you'll be allowed to cross the border?"

"We have to try," Jayfeather answered. "Remember what she said at the Gathering: 'if there is trouble, you may send a patrol to ask for help.' Well, we're asking for help."

Leafpool glanced at a half-finished nest outside the apprentices' den, and then at her medicine den, where herbs were drying outside. "I appreciate your coming, but if you four can handle it, then I'd better stay here. There's so much to do, and with four cats gone, there aren't enough paws to do everything."

"Of course." Jayfeather nodded curtly. He headed for the entrance, letting Puddleshine guide him out of the unfamiliar camp.

Alderheart hurried after them, Kestrelflight at his heels. "Do you think RiverClan will stop us from seeing Mistystar?"

"If I could predict the future, we wouldn't need StarClan to guide us." Jayfeather ducked through the fern tunnel that led into the forest. The browning fronds slicked his fur.

The medicine cats headed back to the shore, skirting the water where it crossed ShadowClan's shore before heading into the marshy reed beds of RiverClan territory.

Jayfeather took the lead. Alderheart guessed that his whiskers guided him along the meandering route between the rushes, for his paws seemed to find the driest paths and the wind was always behind them. Alderheart tasted the air. The musky fish-scent of RiverClan was strong. The camp must be close. He was eager to meet Willowshine and Mothwing. Their absence from the half-moon meeting had felt strange. The bond between medicine cats felt almost stronger than the bond between Clanmates. They shared knowledge and visions warriors would never experience. Their connection with StarClan tied them to one another almost like kin.

He lifted his muzzle, peering through a clump of bulrushes. Their heads bobbed around him like birds. A heron stalked through shallow water a few tail-lengths away. Its feathers rustled as it lifted suddenly and wheeled into the air.

Jayfeather halted. "Wait." With a flick of his tail, he signaled them to stop. Ahead, the reeds swished as a cat pushed through. Duskfur hopped onto the path ahead of them. Sneezecloud and Shimmerpelt followed. The RiverClan cats glared at them with open hostility.

"What are you doing here?" Duskfur's greeting was a snarl.

Alderheart's pelt prickled uneasily. Why was she being so hostile?

Jayfeather ignored the she-cat's aggression. "We've come to see Mistystar." He faced them unblinking. "We have news from StarClan."

"What news?" Duskfur tipped her head, a sneer on her face.

Jayfeather's tail twitched. "If StarClan wanted to share with warriors, they would."

Shimmerpelt thrust her muzzle forward. "The border is closed!"

"Is it closed to StarClan too?" Jayfeather shot back.

Sneezecloud looked past the medicine cats, scanning the path behind them. "I don't see any StarClan cats with you."

Puddleshine stepped forward and stood beside Jayfeather. "They sent us."

"We have to speak with Mistystar," Alderheart chimed.

"Or Willowshine," Kestrelflight added.

"Mothwing will want to speak with us," Jayfeather meowed evenly.

Duskfur narrowed her eyes. "My orders are to stop any cat from crossing into our territory. RiverClan is rebuilding. We don't need any distractions."

Alderheart sighed. "That isn't what Mistystar said at the Gathering."

Duskfur glared at him. "It's what she's saying now," she insisted. Her gaze flicked to the far edge of the reed bed. "You shouldn't be so far inside our border."

Shimmerpelt flattened her ears. "There's no way we're letting you reach the camp."

"Then bring Willowshine or Mothwing here." Jayfeather's pelt bristled. "We need to share StarClan's news."

"If you won't tell us what it is," Duskfur growled, "then I guess we'll have to wait for StarClan to bring the news themselves."

Sneezecloud showed his teeth. "If it's important, they'll let us know."

Alderheart's chest was tight with fear. It was bad enough that Bramblestar wouldn't act. Mistystar wouldn't even hear them out.

Kestrelflight curled his claws into the soft earth. "Perhaps they only want to share with cats who behave like a real Clan."

Sneezecloud hissed. "How dare a WindClan cat judge RiverClan after what Onestar did! Cats *died* when he closed WindClan's borders. He deprived them of herbs that could save them, all because he couldn't face the fact that he'd fathered Darktail."

Kestrelflight's hackles lifted. "This has nothing to do with Onestar. He's dead. Harestar is our leader now."

"So you're a *real* Clan again?" Shimmerpelt curled her lip.

"We've learned what happens when you reject the other Clans," Kestrelflight meowed pointedly.

Duskfur padded closer, ears flat. "Are you going to leave or do we need to drive you away?"

Jayfeather lifted his chin. "Will you tell Mistystar we came? Or do you think she might not want to hear that you have been making decisions for her?"

A menacing growl rumbled in Duskfur's throat.

"Come on." Alderheart slid in front of Jayfeather and guided him away. "This is in StarClan's paws now."

He glanced over his shoulder as he led Jayfeather, Kestrelflight, and Puddleshine back toward the shore. Duskfur paced back and forth, her brown tabby pelt bristling as the RiverClan patrol glowered at them. He felt sick. He hadn't expected *hostility* here.

Alderheart trudged back through the reed beds. Worry weighed like a stone in his belly. The Clans had taken so long to obey StarClan's command to embrace what lay in the shadows that it had almost destroyed them. They couldn't let the same thing happen this time.

And yet RiverClan refused to hear this prophecy. Rowanstar had interpreted it as a warning about SkyClan. Harestar had stepped up patrols. Leafstar was too busy, and Bramblestar was too weary of StarClan's visions to care. The prophecy seemed only to have shone a light on the rifts between the Clans. *We must work together to figure this out.* Alderheart's thoughts were spinning. How could he make them understand when they were too wrapped up in their own problems to think clearly?

CHAPTER 9

❧

Violetpaw's legs still ached from yesterday as she padded beside
Hawkwing. The sun hadn't risen yet, but the sky showed
pink beyond the distant forest. They had been starting
early like this for days. Hawkwing and Blossomheart had
grown more and more excited as they neared their destina-
tion. They had told stories of a "farm cat" named Barley,
and of their mother, Cherrytail, and Cloudmist, their sister. Violetpaw had felt warm from her nose to her tail-tip at
the news that she had yet more kin. She felt as though she
knew them already. She hadn't realized how much Hawkwing had missed his mother and sister until she'd heard the
throb in his purr as he talked about growing up with them
in the gorge. But she was nervous about meeting them. She'd
known Twigpaw her whole life, and even their relationship
hadn't always been easy. She'd always felt closer to Needletail than any cat. What if Cloudmist and Cherrytail didn't
like her? Would she feel as attached to them as she had been
to Needletail? Her thoughts flitted back to Needletail often,
and she'd been sleeping badly, waking at the smallest gust
of wind or rustle in the undergrowth, hoping for another

dream about her friend, wondering if Needletail's spirit had returned again.

Hawkwing seemed to have sensed her distraction over the past few days and, though he hadn't pressed her, she could tell he was worried about her. He always seemed to have one eye on her and one eye on the path ahead. She wished she could confide in him about the guilt that twisted her heart every time she remembered her friend. But how could she tell him that she'd left Needletail to be killed by Darktail? He might never look at her the same way again.

"It's not far." He spoke to her now, nodding to the meadows, which stretched toward the rosy dawn sky. They'd spent the night sheltering in the square mouth of a cave cut deep into a wide cliff, and they'd woken early. Stars still showed as they'd scrambled down the steep slope and crossed the stretch of stone to where rough grass softened into pasture.

Molewhisker had wanted to follow the sun to where it rose, but Hawkwing had recognized the distant moorland and remembered a route that would take them to the last place he'd seen his mother and sister. As the stars began to fade, they crossed a deserted Thunderpath and climbed past swaths of gorse. Now fields stretched ahead of them as the sun lifted above the treetops.

Molewhisker and Blossomheart competed for the lead as they followed the edge of another meadow. Rabbitleap padded behind them, his pelt still ruffled from sleep.

Violetpaw shivered. Each day, the wind had grown colder and she had grown more tired. She longed to rest in a sheltered clearing where sunlight fell in warm pools. Wearily, she stared at her paws.

Hawkwing brushed against her. "We're nearly there. Look."

She lifted her head and gazed at the stubbly field beyond a fence. Molewhisker, Blossomheart, and Rabbitleap were already crossing it. Short, dirty yellow stalks poked out of the brown earth in rows, like prickles on a hedgehog. Shattered stems littered the ground between.

"Last time I was here, the stalks were green and tall." Hawkwing squeezed beneath the fence.

Violetpaw wriggled after him. "I wonder what ate them?" She glanced around nervously. Any creature that could bite through such thick stalks must be huge.

Hawking hurried after the others. "Whatever it was is gone now."

Violetpaw saw white shapes moving in the next field. As big as bushes, they floated like small clouds over the ground. Were they dangerous? She wondered warily if they had eaten the stalks. As she padded closer, she could hear grass tearing as they grazed. They stared ahead, chewing blankly, clearly unaware that their thick coats were filthy and matted.

"What are they?" she breathed, her nose wrinkling at their musky smell.

"Sheep." Hawkwing glanced at her. "They won't hurt you."

"Don't they ever wash?" Muddy lumps hung from their pelts. She didn't want to go any closer. Such strange, stinky creatures would have amused Needletail. She wouldn't have worried about approaching them. She'd have run right up to one and poked its thick, curly pelt just to see what it felt like.

As they skirted the sheep field, Molewhisker paused and looked back toward Hawkwing. For the first time, the ThunderClan tom looked unsure of himself. "Where do we go now?"

Hawkwing trotted past him, his tail high. He opened his mouth as though savoring familiar scents. "We head for Barley's barn." He nodded toward the large Twoleg nest looming beyond the sheep field.

"Is it safe?" Violetpaw's pelt prickled with anxiety.

Hawkwing pointed his muzzle to a smaller Twoleg nest farther away. "The Twolegs live over there. This is where Barley lives. It's safe here."

He quickened his pace, crossing a wide, dirt path onto a stretch of stone that led to the barn. Violetpaw saw Molewhisker glance doubtfully at Blossomheart.

"You'll like Barley," Blossomheart promised him.

As she spoke, a happy yowl echoed over the stone. "Hawkwing? Is that you?" A black-and-white tom was staring at Hawkwing.

Hawkwing broke into a run. "Barley!" He moved toward the tom, purring loudly. Violetpaw followed Blossomheart and Hawkwing to meet Barley, feeling suddenly nervous.

Barley broke away from Hawkwing and wove around Blossomheart. "It's good to see you again." He stopped and stared at Violetpaw. "Hawkwing! Is this your kit?"

Hawkwing lifted his chin proudly. "One of them. This is Violetpaw. Twigpaw stayed in camp. How did you know she's mine?"

Barley's whiskers twitched happily. "You have the same eyes," he mewed. "And the same thoughtful expression."

Violetpaw's chest swelled with pride.

Something moved near the corner of the barn. A tortoise-shell-and-white she-cat was squeezing out through a gap in the wood. She padded, blinking, into the sunshine. "Barley?" She tipped her head. "What's going on?" Her eyes widened as she spotted the visitors. Joy sparked like fire in their green depths. "Hawkwing!"

"Cherrytail!" Hawkwing hurried to meet his mother, his tail fluffed with joy. He rubbed muzzles with her roughly, a purr rumbling in his throat. Then he paused and drew back. His eyes clouded with unease. "Where's Cloudmist? Is she okay?"

Violetpaw heard fear in his mew. He had lost so many cats; he clearly worried about losing another.

"She's fine!" Cherrytail popped her head back through the gap in the wood and called. "Cloudmist! Hawkwing has come at last!"

As she ducked out, a white she-cat pushed past her, her ears pricked with excitement.

"What are you doing here?" She rubbed her cheek against Hawkwing's. "What happened to all of you? Where is everyone? Did you find the hunting lands Echosong dreamed of?"

"There's so much to tell you—" Hawkwing didn't have time to finish. Cherrytail's ecstatic gaze had flitted to Blossomheart.

"It's so good to see you!" She raced to greet her other kit, then blinked happily at Hawkwing.

Hawkwing had clearly decided explanations could wait, despite Cherrytail's barrage of questions. The cats were too excited. The stone beneath Violetpaw's pads seemed to echo with purring. She hung back beside Molewhisker while her Clanmates greeted one another.

Cherrytail caught her eye. "Who's this?" she asked eagerly.

Barley puffed out his chest. "Hawkwing has kits now. This is Violetpaw."

"Kits?" Cherrytail's eyes shone. "They must be Pebbleshine's! Do you have littermates?"

"I have a sister called Twigpaw." Violetpaw was suddenly nervous. She didn't like being the center of attention. "But she stayed at home." *I wish you were here,* she wailed silently to her sister, wondering how to explain why Twigpaw hadn't come. Everyone liked Twigpaw. She always knew exactly what to say. Violetpaw stared at Cherrytail, desperately searching for words.

"Come and meet Violetpaw!" Cherrytail beckoned Cloudmist with her tail.

The white she-cat hurried over, her yellow eyes wide. "I didn't know Pebbleshine was expecting kits!" She turned to Hawkwing. "Where is she?"

"Did she stay behind with Twigpaw?" Cherrytail asked.

Violetpaw stiffened. She looked at her father. Grief sharpened his gaze.

Cherrytail read his expression at once. "Hawkwing?" Concern edged her mew. "Did something happen?"

Hawkwing seemed to shrink inside his pelt. "Pebbleshine

got separated from us on the journey," he murmured. "We climbed onto a monster to steal prey, and it ran away with her. She couldn't jump off in time. The monster carried her off, and she had Twigpaw and Violetpaw alone beside a Thunderpath. Then she disappeared. I wish . . ." He broke off, his mew thick.

Claws jabbed Violetpaw's heart and she heard herself mumbling, "We think she was killed on the Thunderpath."

"Oh, you poor things!" Cherrytail rubbed her muzzle against Violetpaw's cheek.

Hawkwing blinked the grief from his eyes. "She and Twigpaw had hardly opened their eyes when Pebbleshine disappeared."

Cloudmist's eyes were round. "How did they survive?"

"They were found by Clan cats." Hawkwing looked fondly at Violetpaw.

"You found the other Clans!" Cherrytail blinked at him eagerly.

"They found us." Hawkwing shifted his paws. "Eventually. We wandered so far and so long. And we lost so many cats on the way." His yellow eyes looked suddenly haunted. Violetpaw pressed against him, her heart aching for his grief.

Cherrytail's gaze darkened. "Leafstar?"

"She's well. But Echosong died."

"No!" Cherrytail's eyes glittered with sorrow. "How?"

Blossomheart padded forward, touched her muzzle to her mother's cheek. "There's so much to tell. So many deaths. Let us tell it slowly."

Hawkwing nodded. "First, let's share good news."

"We have our own territory among the old Clans beside their lake," Blossomheart told her.

Rabbitleap joined in. "Macgyver and Sandynose are there. And Tinycloud has had a new litter of kits. . . ."

As her mentor listed their Clanmates, Violetpaw stared at Cherrytail and Cloudmist. For so long she'd believed Twig-paw was her only kin. And now she had more kin than she could ever have imagined. She looked at their tortoiseshell-and-white pelts and saw nothing of herself in them. Was she like them at all?

". . . and Plumwillow had her kits along the journey. They're apprentices in the new camp now . . ."

As Rabbitleap went on, Barley whispered in Violetpaw's ear. "Have you eaten today?"

Violetpaw shook her head.

Barley nodded at Molewhisker. "You don't look familiar. Are you a new member of SkyClan?"

"I'm ThunderClan," Molewhisker explained. "I came with the patrol to show them the way."

Barley's eyes flashed warmly. "How'd you like to help me hunt while they share their news? You look like you'd make a good ratter."

Molewhisker blinked happily at the farm cat. "I'll do my best."

Violetpaw watched them head toward the barn before turning her attention back to Hawkwing. She suddenly didn't mind being shy. Everyone was talking so fast that there wasn't a chance for her to speak. But they kept glancing at her with an acceptance she'd never seen in any cat besides Twigpaw and Hawkwing. She purred quietly to herself, relishing the feeling of belonging.

Outside the barn, the sun had lifted high into the sky. Inside, its bright rays flashed through holes in the high roof. Violetpaw lay on the warm, sheltered ground, stretched in a pool of sunlight, her belly full.

Between them, Molewhisker and Barley had caught enough fat, juicy rats to feed them all. It was the best meal Violetpaw had eaten in days. She half-closed her eyes, enjoying the warmth and comfort.

Barley dozed a few tail-lengths away. Molewhisker was exploring the shadows at the back of the barn. Cloudmist sat nearby, washing her face with a paw, while Blossomheart lay in the shadows beside Cherrytail. Their fluffy pelts looked so similar in the half-light that Violetpaw could hardly tell them apart.

Hawkwing finished off the rat Molewhisker had brought him and, licking his lips, blinked at his mother. "We didn't just come to visit," he mewed softly.

Cherrytail got to her paws, nodding as though she knew what he was about to say. "You want us to return to the lake with you," she guessed.

Hawking gazed at her solemnly. "We've found the place Echosong saw in her vision. You should be there with us."

Cloudmist shifted her paws. "I'm not sure. We have a good

life here, Hawkwing. We have plenty of fresh-kill and clean water."

"And it's safe." Shadows showed in Cherrytail's eyes, as though memories of danger still haunted her.

"You will be safe beside the lake," Hawkwing promised. "You only decided to stay here because you were injured—"

"And because it's closer to Sharpclaw." Cherrytail's eyes glistened with grief.

Violetpaw knew from Hawkwing's stories that Sharpclaw was his father and Cherrytail's beloved mate. Darktail had killed him in the battle for the gorge. It had been a huge blow to them all.

Hawkwing held his mother's gaze. "You can't live for the past and hide from the future."

"Your Clan needs you. We need you," Blossomheart urged.

Rabbitleap flicked his tail. "We need to reunite the Clan. We're heading for the gorge to look for more of our lost Clanmates. We're hardly enough cats to make a Clan beside the lake. We don't even have a medicine cat."

Cherrytail looked away.

Cloudmist got to her paws. "It's not easy to start over again," she mewed. "Especially having known so much pain."

Hawkwing dropped his gaze. "I understand that it's hard," he meowed softly. "But promise me you'll think about it."

"I suppose we should. After all, we said we'd rejoin you someday." Cherrytail sat down and curled her tail around her. "But leaving here would be a great loss."

Violetpaw saw hurt in her father's eyes before he quickly

blinked it away. "We'll stop here on our way back from the gorge," Hawkwing told his mother. "You can tell me your decision then."

Barley got to his paws and stretched. "Stay tonight," he meowed. "You all look tired; a good night's sleep and more food will do you good."

"Thank you," Hawkwing dipped his head. "We will."

Violetpaw felt a surge of gratitude to the farm cat. The barn was cozy and she might be able to sleep deeply enough to dream. If Needletail wasn't going to appear in the forest again, perhaps she would visit her dreams. Violetpaw wanted a chance to tell her that, even though she had found Cherry-tail and Cloudmist, Needletail would always be more like kin to her than any cat.

But at that thought, Violetpaw's heart quickened. Was there a reason Needletail hadn't visited for so long?

Are you still angry with me, Needletail?

CHAPTER 10

Movement flashed at the corner of Twigpaw's eye. A mouse was threading its way between the shriveling fronds of a fern a few tail-lengths away.

"Are you listening?" Sandynose's sharp mew jerked her attention back. He was staring up at a pine tree.

"I'm listening," Twigpaw answered, one eye still on the mouse.

Mist hung between the trees, muffling the sounds of the forest. High above the forest, thick clouds covered the sky. Twigpaw fluffed out her fur against the damp.

Sandynose's tail twitched irritably. "Can you see the bird?"

Twigpaw dragged her gaze from the mouse, which was nibbling a pinecone, and followed her mentor's gaze. A sparrow was flitting from branch to branch, pecking at cones that clustered at the tips. "I can see it."

"I want you to climb the tree and catch it," Sandynose instructed.

"There's a mouse over there." Twigpaw nodded at it. "It's meatier than a sparrow and much easier to catch."

Ivypool would have approved of her practical thinking.

But Sandynose glared at her. "When I tell you to catch a bird, I mean catch a *bird*. If I want you to catch a mouse, I'll say mouse. You're a SkyClan cat now. Any cat can catch prey on the forest floor. Only SkyClan can hunt in the trees."

Twigpaw thought of the bustling ThunderClan camp with a pang of longing. They seemed to be thriving on forest-floor prey. She blinked at Sandynose. Why couldn't he be more like his son? Finpaw was *fun*.

And he likes me.

"Twigpaw!" Sandynose growled at her as her thoughts wandered again.

"Sorry." Twigpaw gazed at him, pressing back irritation.

"Climb the tree!"

Claws itching with frustration, Twigpaw hooked them into the soft bark of the pine.

"Dig your claws in deep," Sandynose meowed.

I know that, Twigpaw fumed.

"Make sure three paws always have a grip on the trunk."

Why is he treating me like a kit? She understood Leafstar's wish for her to gain a little experience as a SkyClan apprentice before she received her warrior name, but Sandynose knew that she'd passed her ThunderClan assessment. And yet he acted like she'd just left the nursery.

She hauled herself up. The lowest branches of a pine were so spindly. She'd have to climb farther to reach a branch she could stand on. She wondered if Finpaw liked climbing trees. He looked strong enough to climb to the top of the Sky Oak in ThunderClan territory. Her thoughts wandered. Even though he was still an apprentice, his shoulders were as broad as a warrior's. He was going to be a handsome tom. He already *was* handsome. And so funny and kind.

"Twigpaw!" Sandynose yowled below her. "Are you going to hang there all day like a woodpecker?"

She realized that she'd stopped. Her claws burned from the strain. Pushing hard with her hind paws, she propelled herself upward and scrambled onto the first thick branch she reached.

The sparrow had fluttered higher. Twigpaw sighed. If she'd been allowed to catch the mouse, they could be heading back to camp now with prey for their Clanmates. Did Tinycloud really care whether she ate sparrow or mouse? She had three kits to nurse. Surely any prey was better than waiting?

Twigpaw scrambled onto the next branch, then the next, following them around as they spiraled higher up the tree. The sparrow hopped along a bough overhead. Twigpaw paused to trace out a route through the spiky twigs that would let her creep close to it without being seen.

"Have you caught it yet?" Sandynose's mew rang from the ground.

Alarmed, the sparrow hopped higher.

Hush! Anger burned through her pelt. Gritting her teeth, she hauled herself onto the next branch, climbing until, at last, she was level with the sparrow.

It skipped around a cluster of pinecones at the tip of the branch, digging its beak deep into the gaps. Twigpaw ducked low and drew herself along the bark. She moved each paw slowly, keeping them tucked in tight. As long as the sparrow didn't look up, she'd be close enough to leap in a few more breaths. *Slowly.* Her thoughts stilled as she focused on her prey. Energy bunched in her hind paws. She drew in a long, slow breath, and then she leaped. Reaching forward, she swiped for the sparrow. Her paws brushed its feathers. As she uncurled her claws to hook it, the branch cracked beneath her.

With a yelp, she felt herself falling. The branch tumbled away, and air rushed around her. Heart lurching, she wailed. Hard wood hit her flank as she thudded against the branch below, and she twisted, trying to grip it with her claws, but she was already slithering down to the next one. It knocked the side of her head with such force that for a moment she saw stars. Pain scorched through her as she fell and landed with a thud on the ground.

"Twigpaw!" Sandynose's alarmed cry sounded far away. "Are you okay?"

She struggled to free herself from the fog that was trying to drag her down like water. Her head throbbed. Her chest ached. She drew in a shuddering breath and blinked open her eyes.

Sandynose swam above her. The trees behind him seemed to sway.

"Are you hurt?" he asked, his eyes wide with panic.

She hauled herself to her paws, scanning her body, feeling for injuries. Her legs held her. Her body hurt, but she could breathe, and her mind was clearing. She shook out her fur. "I'm okay," she gasped, still winded.

"Let's get you back to camp," Sandynose mewed. "Leafpool should check you over."

* * *

The medicine den felt warm, screened from the mist and damp of the forest.

Twigpaw sat in its shade as Leafpool ran her paws over her spine and legs. "Nothing is broken."

Sandynose shifted anxiously inside the entrance. "Will she be okay?"

"She was lucky." Leafpool eyed the tom reproachfully. "There are easier ways to catch prey, you know."

"I feel fine," Twigpaw told her quickly. Sandynose was probably already mad at her for being so clumsy. The walk back to camp had revived her, and she felt clearheaded again. The only signs she'd had a fall were a few bruises beneath her pelt and stiffness, which was already easing.

"No dizziness?" Leafpool touched her nose to a spot behind Twigpaw's ear.

"No."

"There's a little swelling here."

"I guess I hit my head. But I hit so many other parts on the way down, I'm not sure." She glanced guiltily at Sandynose. "I guess I'm not much of a SkyClan cat."

"You're not hurt," he told her. "That's all that matters."

"You should rest here for a day or two," Leafpool advised. "So I can keep an eye on you."

The lichen behind Sandynose trembled as Finpaw stuck his head through. "What happened to Twigpaw? I saw Sandynose bring her here."

"She fell out of a tree," Leafpool told him.

His eyes widened and he blinked at Twigpaw in alarm. "Are you okay?"

"I'm fine." Her heart lifted at the sight of him. How much warmer his yellow gaze was than his father's.

"Will you sit with her while I collect herbs?" Leafpool asked the young tom. "I want to get some borage before this mist makes it too damp. I'll be downstream, where it flows down to the lakeshore. Fetch me if Twigpaw seems unwell."

Sandynose's ears twitched. "I can sit with her," he offered stiffly.

Leafpool swished her tail dismissively. "It'd be better for her to have someone her own age. She's had a shock and needs distraction."

Twigpaw's heart swelled with gratitude to her old Clan-mate. Had Leafpool guessed that spending the afternoon here with her mentor would be worse than falling out of the tree?

Leafpool nosed Sandynose out of the den, leaving Twigpaw alone with Finpaw.

"Why were you up a tree?" Finpaw sat beside her.

"Sandynose wants me to learn how to hunt like a SkyClan cat," Twigpaw told him.

Finpaw rolled his eyes. "He's obsessed with making every cat act like they are still in the gorge. He told me yesterday he was going to find a cliff so I could practice rock-climbing like a gorge cat. Doesn't he realize we're lake cats now? It would be better to learn how to swim."

Twigpaw shuddered. "Let's leave swimming to RiverClan."

"But still," Finpaw went on. "Pine trees are useless for climbing. They're so tall and spindly, and there's so much prey down here on the forest floor."

Twigpaw wanted to agree, but she felt a tug of loyalty to

her mentor. And she knew that, even though Finpaw might criticize his father, he loved and respected Sandynose. "I guess change is hard for older cats," she mewed. "In ThunderClan, the elders were always complaining about young cats and their silly ideas. I tried to show Graystripe a new hunting move once and he just sniffed and said, 'A mouse is a mouse. You don't need new ways to catch them.'"

Finpaw purred with amusement. "I'm glad we don't have elders. I mean, Fallowfern is officially an elder, but she's not old; she's just deaf. But it's hard enough listening to the *warriors* reminiscing about how good it used to be before the rogues came. If elders joined in, they'd never talk about anything else."

"I don't know why they can't just look forward instead of backward," Twigpaw agreed. "It's so great that SkyClan is beside the lake now. You're going to love it here." She felt a twinge of homesickness. "I wish I could show you around ThunderClan territory. It's so pretty and there are so many places to play." She paused, remembering suddenly the small clearing where Alderheart and Needletail had brought her and Violetpaw to play together when they were kits. "I know a place here, on SkyClan territory," she mewed excitedly. "At least, I *think* it's on SkyClan territory now. I used to play with Violetpaw there."

"I thought you said you couldn't play with her after she left."

Twigpaw winked at him. "It's a secret. I didn't want Leafpool to know."

"Can we go and find it?" Finpaw's pelt ruffled eagerly.

"Now?" Twigpaw's paws itched at the thought. "You're confined to camp until your tail is fully healed and I'm meant to be resting."

Finpaw flicked his half tail toward her. The wound was almost healed. "I'm only waiting for the fur to grow back," he mewed. "And you said you feel fine."

"I do." Twigpaw's head ached a little, but she was sure fresh air would be better for it than sitting in a stuffy den.

"Let's go, then." Finpaw got to his paws. "We know where Leafpool is, so we can avoid her, and we'll be back before she's finished collecting herbs."

"What about Sandynose?"

Finpaw stuck his head out of the den quickly, then turned back to Twigpaw. "There's no sign of him. The only cat in camp is Fallowfern, and she's sleeping."

"She probably doesn't even know that we're meant to stay in camp." Twigpaw stood and stretched. Her aches were gone and she could hardly feel her bruises. She felt sure that her headache would be gone, too, by the time they found the clearing.

Finpaw slid out of the den first and glanced around the camp as Twigpaw followed. Fallowfern dozed beside the bramble nursery, sheltered from the damp air by the overhanging fronds of the bracken behind her. She snored as Finpaw and Twigpaw crept to the camp entrance.

"It's all clear," Finpaw breathed, peeping out.

Quickly they darted from the camp and raced along the

rise to the cover of a patch of ferns. They ducked down behind them while Twigpaw scanned the forest. She tried to remember where the clearing had been. She knew it must be between the ThunderClan camp and the ShadowClan camp, so she began to lead the way toward the ditches. That would take them in the right direction.

"Why didn't you want Leafpool to know you used to play with Violetpaw?" Finpaw asked as he followed her.

Twigpaw glanced back at him. "Alderheart and Needletail used to take us there in secret. It was the only way we could see each other after ShadowClan and ThunderClan separated us."

"You must have missed her."

"She was the only kin I knew." Twigpaw realized, with a flash of guilt, that she had enjoyed being the only kin Violetpaw could rely on. Now Violetpaw had Hawkwing and a whole Clan to belong to. *She doesn't need me anymore.* She paused. *But I need them, surely?*

"Are you missing her now?" Finpaw asked.

"Sure." *But it's nice having you all to myself.* She avoided his gaze, relieved when she recognized the curving slope ahead. Brambles edged the base and she climbed it, quickening her step as she remembered where it led. "This way."

She scrambled down the other side and hopped the fallen tree she had hidden behind the first time they'd come. The forest opened around her, and she gazed up at the sky. The clouds were darkening. Rain was on the way.

"We mustn't stay long." A tom's mew sounded behind the

clump of ferns ahead of her. Twigpaw stiffened. Someone was already here. "I'm supposed to be checking on Scorchfur's patrol."

A she-cat answered. "I promised Squirrelflight I'd bring back prey. I need to hunt before I go home."

"Quick! Hide!" Pushing Finpaw back, Twigpaw ducked behind the fallen tree.

"What—"

Twigpaw cut him off. "Hush. Someone's here. We can't be seen out of camp."

"Who is it?" Finpaw peeked over the bark.

"Don't let them see you!" Twigpaw tugged his fur with her paw.

"They're behind the ferns," Finpaw whispered. "They won't see us, and we're downwind."

Twigpaw tasted the air. She could smell the other cats. ShadowClan scent mingled with ThunderClan. She popped her head up beside Finpaw's and strained to make out the pelts through the shriveling ferns.

Dovewing! She recognized the pale gray ThunderClan warrior at once. Her paws felt suddenly cold. Ivypool's words rang in her mind. *I didn't think it was a good idea for them to travel together.* With a sinking feeling she saw the dark tabby fur of ShadowClan's deputy showing between the browning leaves. Dovewing and Tigerheart were meeting, and she guessed by their hushed, anxious voices that they were meeting in secret.

She pricked her ears.

Tigerheart sounded worried. "It's bad timing, Dovewing.

Our warriors are losing respect for Rowanstar. And they keep looking at me, like I'm supposed to take his place."

"Is that what you want?" Dovewing's eyes shone with fear.

The ferns rustled as Tigerheart shifted his paws. "Shadow-Clan is weaker than it's ever been. They need a leader they can believe in."

"And that leader has to be *you*?"

"I don't know." Tigerheart avoided her gaze. "I'm trying to support Rowanstar, but that might not be enough."

"What about me?" Dovewing's mew caught in her throat. "What about *us*?"

Tigerheart looked at her, desperation glittering in his gaze. "I love you, Dovewing. I will *always* love you. We can sort this out, I promise."

Twigpaw ducked down, her pelt bristling anxiously. "We can't stay here."

Finpaw stared at her puzzled. "Why?"

Twigpaw turned away. She'd already heard too much. "This isn't our problem."

Finpaw hurried after her. "That was Tigerheart, wasn't it? Why was he with Dovewing?"

Isn't it obvious? Twigpaw flashed him a look. "Just don't say anything, okay?"

He blinked at her. "I never saw a thing."

"Thanks." She wished she'd never seen them. Should she tell Ivypool? Perhaps it was nothing. Perhaps they were just friends. Why upset Ivypool over this? She wasn't even a Clanmate anymore. *But she was your mentor. She'd want to know.*

Twigpaw blocked the thought. *It's none of my business. I'm SkyClan now.* Her loyalty was to her new Clanmates, not her old ones.

"Hurry up." She trotted into the lead. "We're meant to be having fun! Let's find a live frog to hide in Dewpaw's nest before he gets home from training." She broke into a run.

Finpaw followed, wobbling as his short tail unbalanced him. "You can carry it home!" he called. "I don't want to get the taste of frog on my tongue."

"Don't you like frog?" Twigpaw looked over her shoulder. "Perhaps I should hide it in *your* nest."

"I dare you!" Finpaw broke into a purr as he ran after her.

"Never dare a SkyClan cat!" Suddenly Twigpaw didn't care about Dovewing or Ivypool or Tigerheart. She was a *SkyClan* cat. And having a friend in her new Clan seemed more important than anything.

CHAPTER 11

Alderheart padded along ThunderClan's shore until the pebbles gave way to boulders. Early morning light sparkled on the water. Soft clouds drifted across the pale blue sky, and a mild breeze blew from the distant moor. Here, mallow grew in clumps. He bounded along the smooth, flat rocks until he reached a cluster of paw-shaped leaves. A few wilting flowers nodded among them, and he picked them first, pleased that he'd found some before cold weather killed them off. He tore off a leaf and rolled the petals in it, wedging in a crevice until he was ready to head home.

Movement caught his eye near the halfbridge. A cat slid from beneath it and hurried toward him.

Willowshine! His heart leaped as he recognized the River-Clan medicine cat's gray pelt. He hadn't seen a RiverClan cat since Duskfur had turned him and the other medicine cats away. She was heading straight toward him, and as she neared, he could see that her gaze was fixed on him. She looked anxious. He hurried to meet her, keeping close to the water as he crossed SkyClan's shore. Had something happened to River-Clan?

"Are you okay?" he called as he neared her.

She glanced nervously across the lake toward RiverClan territory.

Alderheart guessed she wasn't supposed to be here. He flicked his tail toward the woods at the top of the shore, and headed that way, glancing back to make sure Willowshine was following. He slid into the cover of the trees, ducking down behind a screen of bracken.

Willowshine reached him, breathless. "I had to come," she panted. "StarClan sent me a message."

Alderheart blinked at her anxiously. "What was it?"

"When I was looking for a fresh supply of marigold yesterday, I had a vision."

"While you were awake?" Alderheart was surprised. StarClan usually only shared *dreams* with medicine cats. This must have been important. Did it have something to do with the prophecy?

"It was sunny, and I'd just left the reed beds and was climbing the slope toward some herbs that prefer drier soil. Then the sky darkened."

Alderheart's breath caught in his throat. *It must be the prophecy!*

She went on. "I looked up and saw that the blue sky had been covered by thick clouds. They were dark, as though a storm was about to break. The air around me seemed to shimmer, and the air grew darker and darker. I was so frightened. Then a cat rushed past me. I felt the wind from its fur on my pelt. It raced down the slope, and as it disappeared into the reed beds, everything turned black as though the sun had disappeared." The medicine cat was shaking. "Then, in a blink, it was light again. The sky was blue. The sun was shining. I wondered if I'd been dreaming."

Alderheart stared at her expectantly. Was this StarClan's way of sharing the prophecy with her?

"The weird thing is"—Willowshine frowned, her bright green eyes clouding—"the picture that stuck in my mind was the cat's hind paw."

"Why?" Alderheart leaned forward eagerly.

"It had six toes." She shifted her paws nervously. "And then a voice sounded in my mind. 'To fend off a storm, you will need an extra claw.'"

Alderheart's thoughts raced. What could it mean? *An extra claw* . . . Most cats had five claws on each paw, just as there were five Clans. Was the extra claw a sixth Clan? Was StarClan promising to help them? Were *they* the sixth Clan? "What did the cat look like?"

"I don't know. It was too dark. I don't even know if it was a tom or a she-cat. The only thing I remember is the toes. I think that's all StarClan wanted me to see."

Alderheart sat down. "Do you know about the prophecy?"

"Which prophecy?" Willowshine looked puzzled.

"When we shared with StarClan at the Moonpool, Echosong told us all, 'The dark sky must not herald a storm.' We tried to tell you, but Duskfur—"

Willowshine interrupted him, her thoughts already on the prophecy. "'The dark sky must not herald a storm'? What does that mean?"

"We don't know." Alderheart shifted his weight onto his haunches. "Rowanstar thinks the dark sky must mean Sky-Clan. Harestar thinks something bad is coming, and he's ordered extra patrols. Leafstar says she's too busy building a new home to think about it." He frowned. "Bramblestar doesn't seem too bothered either."

Willowshine widened her eyes. "Mistystar reacted the same way to my vision! I told her what I'd seen, and she said she had too many real things to worry about without wasting her time on stuff she couldn't see."

Alderheart's pelt prickled. "Why don't leaders understand that StarClan is their best ally?" He grunted. "Patrols and borders," he muttered under his breath. "That's all leaders care about."

"We have more information now," Willowshine pointed out. "I only had my vision and you only had yours. But if we tell them about *both*, then they'll *have* to listen."

Alderheart blinked at her. She was right. Her vision had given them an important clue. Now at least they knew what would help them avoid the storm. If only they knew what the cat with the six toes meant. "Come on." He got to his paws. "We have to tell this to Bramblestar."

"But I need to get back." Willowshine glanced anxiously toward the lake. "I sneaked out."

"Your Clanmates will think you're gathering herbs," Alderheart reassured her. "That's what I was doing just now. That's what *all* medicine cats do at the start of leaf-fall." He didn't give her chance to argue and began to head toward the ThunderClan camp. It had been too long since he'd heard from RiverClan. He wanted a chance to talk to her. She needed to know that Duskfur had turned them away when they'd tried to share the prophecy. If RiverClan cut themselves off from StarClan as well as the other Clans, that could only lead to trouble. "We missed you at the Moonpool meeting," he mewed as he followed a rabbit track across the border into ThunderClan territory.

"I'm sorry I couldn't come. Mistystar ordered me and Mothwing to stay in camp." Willowshine hurried after him, her pelt ruffling uneasily.

"I tried to visit to tell you the prophecy. Jayfeather, Kestrelflight, and Puddleshine were with me, but Duskfur wouldn't let us cross the border."

"I know." Willowshine fell in beside him as he began to follow the stream that flowed down to the lake.

She *knew*? Alarm jabbed Alderheart's chest. Didn't she care?

She went on. "The patrol made their report to Mistystar loud enough for the whole camp to hear. Duskfur was furious that you tried to reach the camp. When Mothwing pointed out that medicine cats are allowed to cross borders, she wouldn't listen."

"Did Mistystar agree with her?" Alderheart glanced at her anxiously. He'd hoped that Duskfur's attitude wasn't shared by the whole of RiverClan.

Willowshine avoided his eye. "She said she was right to send you away."

Alderheart's heart sank. Why was RiverClan behaving like this? Mistystar hadn't seemed this hostile at the Gathering.

Now it sounded like she was following in the paw steps of Onestar, the late WindClan leader who'd acted so oddly before Darktail was driven off. "StarClan is unhappy about RiverClan cutting themselves off," he mewed softly. He didn't want to upset Willowshine, but he hoped she might pass on his words to Mistystar.

"Mistystar feels betrayed by the other Clans," Willowshine murmured, as though she feared being overheard. "She feels they should have stopped Darktail before he caused so much harm."

Alderheart glanced at her sympathetically. "RiverClan suffered. We all did. But how could the Clans have known Darktail was so evil? How could we imagine the unimaginable?"

Willowshine didn't answer. She was clearly torn between loyalty to her Clanmates and loyalty to StarClan. Instead she changed the subject. "How is SkyClan?"

Alderheart remembered that RiverClan had left the Gathering before SkyClan's fate had been decided. "They have their own territory now. Rowanstar gave them a piece of ShadowClan land."

Willowshine blinked at him in surprise. "Why?"

"Tigerheart suggested it," Alderheart told her. "He said it made sense to have a grateful ally on their border."

Willowshine was quiet for a moment. Then she mewed, "Should Rowanstar have let Tigerheart make such an important decision? After everything ShadowClan has been through, they need their leader to be strong."

"Perhaps having a strong deputy is as good as having a strong leader." Alderheart cut away from the stream and began to head for the rise, which led to the camp. He hadn't thought about Tigerheart's speech much; he'd been too worried about SkyClan's fate. But Willowshine was right. By speaking up, Tigerheart *had* made Rowanstar seem less powerful.

The sight of the thorn barrier distracted him from the thought. What would Bramblestar say about Willowshine's vision? *Please let him take it seriously this time.* Worry pricked at his paws as he padded into camp.

Bramblestar sat alone on Highledge. Dovewing was talking with Millie and Graystripe outside the elders' den. Blossomfall was encouraging her kits to chase a moss ball beside the nursery, knocking it softly away from them as they stumbled to catch it. They were still unsteady on their paws, blinking at the daylight.

Stemkit's white-and-orange fur was fluffed out as he scrambled ahead of his littermates and reached the moss ball first. "I got it!" he squeaked triumphantly.

Eaglekit hooked it away from him with a delighted mew.

Willowshine purred. "They look well."

"They are healthy and strong," Alderheart reported proudly. "In SkyClan, Tinycloud's had her kits too. Two she-kits and a tom."

Graystripe called across the clearing. "Willowshine! It's good to see you. How is RiverClan?"

"They're fine," she reported, not meeting the old tom's eye.

"Has Mistystar opened the border?" Dovewing asked.

"No." Willowshine's pelt ruffled. "I just came to discuss something with Alderheart."

Dovewing shrugged and headed toward the nursery. As she began playing with the kits, Alderheart led Willowshine up the tumble of rocks.

Bramblestar met them at the top. "Willowshine." He flicked his tail uneasily. "What are you doing here? Is everything okay in RiverClan?"

"RiverClan is fine." Willowshine dipped her head. "I came to share a vision I had with Alderheart."

Bramblestar's gaze sharpened. "Did StarClan send you their message about the dark sky?"

"It wasn't the same as the prophecy they shared with us," Alderheart told him. "It's a new message."

Willowshine met the ThunderClan leader's gaze. "I had a vision of a six-toed cat. StarClan told me that to fend off the storm, we will need an extra claw."

Bramblestar's gaze narrowed.

At last! Relief washed Alderheart's pelt. His father finally seemed interested in the prophecy.

"Do you know what it means?" Bramblestar looked from Willowshine to Alderheart.

"I was thinking maybe the claws could mean Clans," Alderheart said tentatively. "Five claws . . . five Clans."

Bramblestar looked into the distance and flicked his tail, agitated. "So it means *another* Clan? A *sixth* Clan?"

"It could mean StarClan," Alderheart told him.

Willowshine shook her head. "That's not what it felt like

in the vision," she mewed. "I think the cat I saw is a real cat. I think we have to find it."

Alderheart turned to her. "Are you sure it's that simple?"

Willowshine blinked at him. "Perhaps not . . . but we must start somewhere."

"Well, assuming it is a cat, do you know what the cat looks like?" Bramblestar asked.

"Only that it has six toes on its hind paw. I don't even know if it's a tom or a she-cat." Willowshine dipped her head. "I wish I could tell you more."

"It was good of you to come and share this much," Bramblestar meowed. "I'll certainly keep thinking."

Alderheart shifted his paws impatiently. "If it *is* a real cat . . . do we know any six-toed cats in the Clans?"

Willowshine shook her head, and Bramblestar tipped his head to one side thoughtfully. "None that I can think of," he meowed.

Alderheart sighed and nodded. "There's one way to find out," he mewed. "Can we travel to the other Clans?"

"Now?" Bramblestar blinked.

"Yes."

"You should have an escort." The ThunderClan leader glanced around the camp. Dovewing had left. Only Graystripe, Millie, Blossomfall, and her kits remained. "Can you wait until Brackenfur's patrol gets back? They won't be long."

Willowshine's tail twitched nervously. "I should get back to my camp. Mothwing will be worried."

Alderheart glanced at her. He wanted Willowshine to

share her vision with the other leaders. They wouldn't question it as much if they heard it from her directly. "If we leave straight away, we could visit ShadowClan and SkyClan before sunhigh—it won't take long." It would be a start. They could make the longer trip to WindClan another day.

Willowshine shifted her paws. "All right, but we'll have to hurry."

Alderheart nodded and stared straight at his father. "We're medicine cats. We don't need an escort."

Bramblestar dipped his head. "All right, but be careful."

As Alderheart turned to head down the rocks, he remembered Jayfeather. "Share the news with Jayfeather!" he called over his shoulder. "Tell him I'll talk to him when I get back." He knew Jayfeather would be angry that Alderheart had acted without him, but there wasn't time to guide a cantankerous blind cat through the woods.

Willowshine raced beside him as he headed out of camp. Together they burst into the woods and ran for the border. Alderheart slid into the lead, showing Willowshine the way as they crossed SkyClan territory and headed toward Leafstar's camp.

They arrived, panting, and burst through the fern tunnel.

Leafstar looked up from the mouse she was sharing with Macgyver and got to her paws, her eyes round with worry. "Has something happened?" she asked, eying their ruffled pelts.

"Willowshine had a vision." Alderheart nodded toward the RiverClan medicine cat as he struggled to catch his breath.

"I saw a six-toed cat," Willowshine puffed.

Leafstar blinked at her. "Where?"

"In my vision." Willowshine took a long gulp of air. "StarClan told me that we will need an extra claw to fend off the storm. They want us to find a six-toed cat."

"Do you know any?" Alderheart urged. "Have there ever been any six-toed cats in SkyClan?" Perhaps Hawkwing's patrol would bring back an old Clanmate with six toes.

Leafstar shook her head. "We've never had a six-toed cat."

Macgyver padded to join them, still chewing. "Have we counted the toes on Tinycloud's kits?"

"She'd have told us by now." Leafstar gazed at Alderheart. "Are there any six-toed cats in the other Clans?"

"Not that we know of."

"At least we know that there *is* a way to fend off the storm." The SkyClan leader looked relieved.

"If it really is a cat." Alderheart didn't want her to think their troubles were over. "And we can find the cat."

Leafstar turned back to her mouse. "I'm sure we'll figure it out," she mewed, settling down beside it.

Macgyver swished his tail. "StarClan is watching over us. They'll help you find the cat you're looking for."

As he turned away, Alderheart sighed and glanced at Willowshine.

She met his gaze. "Don't they care?" she whispered.

Alderheart headed out of the camp. "Perhaps SkyClan's ancestors never sent prophecies. Maybe *their* StarClan solved SkyClan's problems themselves instead of warning them."

He headed toward the ShadowClan border, his pelt ruffled. At least Rowanstar would understand that beside the lake, StarClan didn't have the power to save anyone. *They can only guide our paws.*

At the ShadowClan border, they met Juniperclaw and Ratscar. Alderheart had been surprised to see an elder patrolling but, as Juniperclaw had explained, with so few Clanmates left, every cat must help. And Ratscar had seemed happy with his duties. "I'm old," he had told them. "But I'm not dead yet."

Now they faced Rowanstar at the head of the Shadow-Clan clearing. Beside him, Puddleshine listened eagerly. Juniperclaw and Ratscar waited at the entrance. Scorchfur, Grassheart, and Stonewing watched from the edge of the camp as Whorlpaw and Flowerpaw shifted nervously nearby. Tawnypelt stood beside the wide, flat rock beside Rowanstar's den while Tigerheart hung back in the shadows. The dark tabby's eyes narrowed with interest as Willowshine told Rowanstar her vision.

"We will need an extra claw." The ShadowClan leader repeated her words thoughtfully.

"Do you know any cats with six toes?" Alderheart asked.

"Not in ShadowClan," Rowanstar answered.

"One of the rogues, perhaps?" Alderheart pressed.

Willowshine shuddered beside him.

Scorchfur growled from the edge of the clearing. "Why would a *rogue* help us fend off a storm?"

Willowshine flashed a look at the ragged-eared warrior.

"You once thought rogues would solve all your problems." There was bitterness in her mew.

Alderheart flicked his tail. "We need to look forward, not backward," he mewed quickly. "If we can find this cat, then everything will be okay."

"We should send out a search party," Grassheart meowed.

"Perhaps we should look in Twolegplace," Stonewing suggested. "Maybe there's a kittypet with six toes."

"A *kittypet*!" Juniperclaw snorted scornfully.

Scorchfur's ears flattened. "How can we send out a search party? We have barely enough cats to patrol our borders."

"The SkyClan border can't be left unguarded," Rowanstar agreed.

Alderheart prickled with frustration. "SkyClan is not your enemy. They are your allies. Wasn't that what Leafstar said when you gave her the land?" He looked at Tigerheart, hoping the ShadowClan deputy would speak up. He wanted support. If there really was a six-toed cat, it must be found.

But Tigerheart only watched as Rowanstar shifted his paws.

"Leafstar *did* promise us friendship," the ShadowClan leader conceded.

Scorchfur glared at him. "And you believed her!" he mocked.

"It was Tigerheart's idea," Rowanstar reminded him.

"'It was Tigerheart's idea.'" Scorchfur mimicked his leader as though teasing a kit. "When was the last time you had an idea of your own?"

Alderheart's belly tightened.

"I'd like to see you try to lead a Clan!" Rowanstar snapped. "Perhaps you could use the skills you learned from *Darktail*."

"At least he knew how to lead!"

Tawnypelt glared at Scorchfur. "You betrayed your Clan. Now you insult your leader? Show him some respect!"

"He's done nothing to earn it," Scorchfur spat back. "If he'd chased Darktail off in the first place, none of us would have followed those rogues. Instead he let them hunt on our land, while our apprentices grew arrogant and reckless. He couldn't manage to stop any of it."

"Whatever his mistakes, he still has the blessing of StarClan!" Tawnypelt hissed.

Grassheart and Stonewing exchanged glances. Whorlpaw and Flowerpaw stared at the ground uncomfortably. Alderheart felt his belly churning as the air seemed to sour around him.

Ratscar padded forward. "We must stay united," he rasped. "I know we have had our differences, but Alderheart is right. We must look forward, not back. There are so few of us left. If we are to remain a Clan, we must work together."

Grassheart whisked her tail. "Let's send out a search party and find this six-toed cat. Then we won't have to face any more storms."

"*ThunderClan* can send out search parties!" Juniperclaw called.

"Or WindClan," Stonewing chimed. "They've got nothing better to do."

Scorchfur glared challengingly at Rowanstar. "So?" he snarled. "What *should* we do?"

Alderheart saw hesitation in the ShadowClan leader's gaze. *He's not sure.* The thought shocked him. Bramblestar always knew what to do, even if it meant doing nothing. "I must do what's right for the Clan," Rowanstar meowed at last.

"Isn't it a bit late for that?" Scorchfur curled his lip.

Tawnypelt darted forward, facing the dark gray tom. "Rowanstar has always done what's best for this Clan!"

Scorchfur scanned the half-empty camp, contempt in his eyes. "So we have Rowanstar to thank for the state we're in?"

"Do you think you could have done any better?" Tawnypelt hissed. "You blame Rowanstar. But it was his Clanmates' disloyalty that killed them. If our apprentices grew arrogant, blame their mentors, not him. He cared about ShadowClan when none of you did. Rowanstar still wakes in the night, haunted by nightmares about the Clanmates he's lost."

Scorchfur flattened his ears. "He's lucky. He has nine lives to dream about lost Clanmates. They only had one."

"That's not fair!" Puddleshine blinked anxiously at Rowanstar. "You can't let him say that. StarClan gave you those lives because they believed in you."

Scorchfur's eyes narrowed to slits. "They believed in him once. Perhaps Rowanstar is the dark sky they're trying to warn us about."

Tawnypelt's green eyes glittered. "If anyone's the dark sky, it's *you*!" Her gaze flicked angrily around her Clanmates. "You let the rogues take over the Clan. You let them drive

Rowanstar away. Don't blame him for your treachery."

"And why do you think we chose a rogue over Rowanstar?" Scorchfur lashed his tail. "He was a weak leader then, and he's a weak leader now."

Tawnypelt's fur bristled. Spitting with fury, she lashed out at Scorchfur, slicing her claws across his muzzle.

Alderheart backed away, his pelt bushing. What was happening here? Clanmates shouldn't *fight*.

Scorchfur reared and slammed his paws onto Tawnypelt's shoulders. Hooking his claws in, he pulled her to the ground. She flipped over and, tucking up her hind legs, clawed viciously at his belly.

He struggled free and turned on her. Face to face, they snarled at each other. With a hiss, Scorchfur lashed out, raking Tawnypelt's eye with his claws.

Alderheart froze as she lurched away. ShadowClan gasped around him. What was Scorchfur doing? No warrior should *ever* attack another warrior's eyes! Tawnypelt shook her head, blinking. With a rush of relief, Alderheart saw that Scorchfur's claws had only sliced her cheek. Her eyes shone, unharmed. She'd been lucky.

She showed her teeth, hatred twisting her face, as she advanced on Scorchfur. "You're no better than a rogue."

"Stop!" Tigerheart moved at last. Fast as a fox, he crossed the clearing and pushed between the two warriors.

Rowanstar stared, his gaze stricken with shock. "We mustn't fight."

Alderheart backed away from the bristling cats. *It's not safe here. No one's in control.* He nudged Willowshine toward the camp entrance. Puddleshine's light blue eyes were round with shock. He gazed imploringly at Alderheart.

There nothing I can do. Guilt squeezed Alderheart's belly. He retreated through the entrance, beckoning Willowshine after him.

"Poor Puddleshine," Willowshine mewed as they hurried away from the camp. "Should we have stayed?"

"It's not our fight," he told her. *And I didn't want to put you in danger.* "I think ShadowClan needs to be alone to sort out their differences." Alderheart padded quickly over the needle-strewn earth. ShadowClan seemed more like a group of rogues than a Clan. Fear hollowed his belly. *What if they can't recover from all that has happened to them? What if they aren't strong enough to remain a Clan?*

CHAPTER 12

The gorge was smaller than Violetpaw had imagined. Its sandy walls glowed yellow in the evening sun, but its depths were swathed in purple shadow. The scent of water mingled with the fragrant tang of the scrubby bushes that clung to the sides of the narrow canyon.

Beside her, Hawkwing stood as still as a rock. Blossomheart, Rabbitleap, and Molewhisker flanked them, their pelts dusty from the journey.

Hawkwing's gaze was fixed on the ravine he'd called home for so long. "Listen."

Violetpaw pricked her ears, wondering what she was meant to be listening to.

"Can you hear it?" Hawkwing's words were hardly more than a breath.

"What?" Molewhisker blinked at him.

Blossomheart's eyes shone. "The stream."

Violetpaw leaned forward. Through the soft whisper of the wind, she could hear a stream echoing far below.

Hawkwing looked at her, his yellow eyes clouded. "That sound will always remind me of home."

For the first time, Violetpaw felt distance between them. He'd seen so much that she'd not shared. She hoped that, one day, the sound of the stream in their new home would touch him the same way.

He padded to the edge, his paws showering grit into the gorge. Violetpaw could see by the stiff way he held his tail that he was anxious. She could understand why. Although she didn't know every detail of the story, she knew that the rogues had driven SkyClan from their home many moons ago. Some cats, unable or unwilling to make the long journey in search of the other Clans, had stayed nearby. Hawkwing was hoping that some of them would have returned to the gorge.

Paw steps scuffed the ground behind them.

Violetpaw spun around. Two young cats raced toward them, ears flat, teeth showing. One was a black-and-white she-cat; the other a tan tom. She backed up against Hawkwing, her heart lurching.

The she-cat skidded to a halt in front of the patrol and glared at Molewhisker. "What are you doing here?"

"This is our land!" The tom stopped beside her and hissed.

Molewhisker glanced coolly at Hawkwing. He was clearly unruffled by the two young cats. They were hardly bigger than Violetpaw. They were certainly no match for warriors. "Are these your Clanmates?" the ThunderClan warrior asked Hawkwing.

Hawkwing shrugged. "I've never seen them before."

The black-and-white she-cat bristled. "I don't know who you are, but get off our territory!" Her amber eyes flashed with hostility.

Violetpaw admired her courage. "We're looking for our Clanmates."

The she-cat's gaze snapped to her. "Then you're looking in the wrong Clan," she snarled.

"Palepaw!" A meow sounded behind the she-cat. A black-and-white tom padded from the gorse and flicked his tail. "We should welcome our friends."

"They're not friends." The tan tom curled his lips. "They're probably rogues. We should drive them away."

"You're not driving anyone away, Gravelpaw." The black-and-white tom padded closer, his eyes glowing.

Violetpaw heard her father's breath quicken.

"Fidgetpaw!" Hawkwing sounded like he could hardly believe his eyes.

Fidgetpaw whisked his tail. "Hawkwing!" He broke into a run.

Palepaw frowned angrily. "Do you know these cats?"

Fidgetpaw pushed past her. "Of course I know them. They're SkyClan cats. Hawkwing's father was Sharpclaw."

"Sharpclaw?" Gravelpaw sounded surprised. "The old deputy?"

Fidgetpaw didn't reply. He was staring happily at Hawkwing. "You came. I dreamed you would. I've been waiting for days." He turned to Blossomheart and Rabbitleap. "It's great to see you all."

Hawkwing thrust his muzzle against Fidgetpaw's cheek, purring loudly. "You escaped!"

Fidgetpaw joined the purring as Blossomheart and Rabbitleap wound around him. "Of course I escaped. You didn't think Twolegs could hold me for long, did you?"

"I'm so sorry we couldn't save you." Emotion thickened Hawkwing's mew. Violetpaw heard guilt there. "There was nothing we could do."

Fidgetpaw blinked at him. "I know," he mewed solemnly. "It's okay."

Hawkwing's stiffness seemed to soften as though a weight had been lifted from him. He glanced at Violetpaw. "Twolegs caught Fidgetpaw and took him away," he explained. "I thought I'd never see him again. He was SkyClan's medicine-cat apprentice."

Paws scrabbled below them. Violetpaw turned, ears twitching, as a gray tabby she-cat and a pale brown tom climbed out of the gorge and gasped, their eyes landing on Hawkwing. Two young cats—one black, one brown—jumped up behind them.

"Is it really you?" asked the pale brown tom.

Palepaw blinked at them. "We thought these cats were intruders." She puffed out her chest. "But Fidgetpaw won't let us drive them off."

"He says they're SkyClan cats," Gravelpaw grunted.

"They are indeed," whispered the gray tabby she-cat, moving forward. "Blossomheart! Hawkwing!"

Hawkwing dipped his head to the she-cat. "Mintfur." His eyes shone in the dying sunlight. "It's good to see you."

Mintfur nodded, seeming to try to compose herself, as Blossomheart blinked happily at the pale brown tom. "You look well, Nettlesplash."

"So do you." Nettlesplash beckoned the two young cats forward with his tail. "These are our kits, Nectarpaw and Fringepaw." He nodded to Palepaw and Gravelpaw. "It looks like you've already met the rest of our litter."

Mintfur paced around Hawkwing's patrol. She stopped beside Molewhisker, her nose twitching. "And you are? Your scent is strange."

Molewhisker nodded politely. "I'm ThunderClan," he explained. "I came to show them the way."

"And who's this?" Nettlesplash blinked kindly at Violetpaw.

Violetpaw moved closer to Hawkwing, feeling suddenly shy. "I'm Violetpaw."

"She's my kit." Hawkwing licked her head. "I have another kit too, Twigpaw. She stayed beside the lake."

Mintfur lifted her tail. "Where's Pebble—"

Violetpaw interrupted her. "Pebbleshine died when Twigpaw and I were kits," she mewed quickly. She wanted to save Hawkwing from having to tell the story again.

"I'm sorry." Mintfur locked gazes with Hawkwing, compassion filling her round, blue eyes. "We have all lost so much. But to lose someone so precious must be hard."

Violetpaw's throat tightened with emotion as Hawkwing answered.

"It was. But in losing Pebbleshine, I found my kits and a new home."

"Have you traveled far?" Nettlesplash seemed eager to move the conversation on.

"We've walked for a quarter moon," Hawkwing told him.

"You must be tired," Nettlesplash meowed. "Come and rest in the gorge. The fresh-kill pile is full."

Violetpaw followed her father as the gorge cats led them down a steep trail that wound down the side of the narrow canyon. She shivered as they padded from evening sunlight into violet shadow. But as the trail reached the bottom, Nettlesplash headed along the stream and showed the way into a sheltered hollow beside it, where the stone still held the day's warmth. Spiky bushes jutted from the cliffs above it, shielding the space from the chilly evening air. A pile of prey lay at one end.

"This is where we sleep now," Mintfur told them.

Hawkwing looked up at holes in the sides of the gorge. "Don't you use the caves?" he asked in surprise.

"There are so few of us left." Mintfur watched her kits follow Rabbitleap, Blossomheart, and Molewhisker into the hollow.

Fidgetpaw padded in last. "It feels safer to stay together. We post a guard while we sleep," he mewed.

"Foxes come at night," Gravelpaw added.

Violetpaw tried to imagine how the gorge had been when it was home to a whole Clan. She imagined cats patrolling the top and slipping in and out of the caves and following the narrow paths around its sides. Where had Hawkwing slept when he was an apprentice? She pictured him practicing battle moves beside the stream. It would have been a fun place to grow up. She wished Twigpaw were here to see it.

Hawkwing was gazing around the stone walls; she wondered

if he was remembering. He blinked at Mintfur. "Why have you stayed?"

"Where else could we go?" she answered.

Fidgetpaw padded forward. "We wanted to rebuild the Clan, but surviving with so few warriors is hard."

Mintfur and Nettlesplash exchanged glances. "And it's difficult to trust new cats," Nettlesplash admitted. "After Darktail."

Violetpaw glanced at her father. *They're not rebuilding SkyClan here, are they? They're supposed to come back with us!* But Hawkwing wasn't looking at her as he padded around the hollow, mouth open as though breathing in old scents. "Darktail's dead," he mewed.

Mintfur's eyes flashed maliciously. "Good."

"And his rogues?" Nettlesplash narrowed his eyes.

"The Clans chased them off." Rabbitleap bent to smell the fresh-kill pile. A thrush lay on top.

Fidgetpaw hurried to his side. "Help yourself." He spread the prey out with his paw and stepped back to let the patrol choose from it.

Violetpaw glanced at Hawkwing. Her belly was hollow with hunger, but she didn't want to steal prey from this tiny Clan. It might have taken them all day to fill the pile.

Hawkwing nodded her forward. "Take what you like. We can help restock the pile tomorrow."

"There's plenty of prey around here." Fidgetpaw seemed to guess her reluctance. "It's flourishing with so few cats to hunt it."

The gorge cats hung back politely while their visitors took a piece of prey each, waiting for them to settle before choosing food for themselves.

Violetpaw sat beside Hawkwing and took a bite from a soft, juicy mouse. It was sweet, ripened by leaf-fall, and she relished the flavor on her tongue. Pleasure warmed her belly. They had made it to the gorge and found Clanmates. But would these cats return to the lake with them? She swallowed and licked her lips. "When are you going to ask them?" she murmured to Hawkwing as she took another mouthful.

"Ask us what?" Palepaw looked up from the robin she was eating, her ears twitching.

The other gorge cats paused and stared at Violetpaw. She froze, the mouse turning dry on her tongue, and wished she'd never spoken.

Hawkwing wrapped his tail around her. "We came to ask you to return to the lake with us. We've found the other Clans, and we have territory. The land is good. There is prey and shelter, and the other Clans say that Twolegs come in summer, but they don't disturb our camps."

The gorge cats looked at each other.

Gravelpaw blinked. "We can't leave the gorge," he mewed. "It's our home."

Mintfur looked thoughtful. "Our home is with SkyClan."

"We *are* SkyClan," Palepaw pointed out.

"We are," Nettlesplash agreed. "But our leader and deputy are not with us."

"Then they should come here," Palepaw mewed.

Fidgetpaw peered out of the small hollow, his gaze following the stream as it flowed along the gorge. "I think StarClan would want us to be with the other Clans," he meowed softly. "They led Leafstar and Hawkwing to the lake for a reason. I think we should go with them. The gorge will never be what it once was to us." He looked from Mintfur to Nettlesplash.

"It might be good to leave the bad memories behind us," Nettlesplash agreed.

Mintfur's pelt ruffled. She looked at Fidgetpaw. "What about Frecklewish?"

Fidgetpaw dropped his gaze.

"We can't abandon her!" Mintfur stared at him, her pelt twitching.

Hawkwing scrambled to his paws. "You know where she is?" He sounded amazed. "She's been missing for so long, I thought she was dead."

Fidgetpaw looked up, his eyes glittering in the half-light. "Twolegs took her," he meowed darkly. "They're holding her captive."

"Where?"

Violetpaw heard excitement in her father's mew.

Nettlesplash turned his vole over and took a bite. "Rest tonight, and in the morning we'll show you."

Violetpaw gazed out from the woods. Ahead, the forest opened onto stone where a huge Twoleg den rose into the sky. Violetpaw's neck ached from craning to see the top. "It must touch the clouds," she whispered breathlessly.

Blossomheart and Hawkwing flanked her. Rabbitleap, Nettlesplash, and Mintfur clustered beside them while Palepaw and Gravelpaw hung back in the shade of the trees with Fringepaw and Nectarpaw.

Fidgetpaw padded from the forest, his black-and-white fur glossy in the early morning light. Monsters slumbered on the stone at the far side of the nest. "It's full of Twolegs." His mew was tight with fear. "We've seen them come and go."

Violetpaw's pelt prickled anxiously. "It's like a camp."

"Full of nests," Blossomheart breathed.

"It's more like a beehive," Mintfur growled.

"Why do they want to live so high in the air?" Bellaleaf asked. "They can't fly."

Fidgetpaw shrugged. "Perhaps it's so they can see if danger's coming."

"Why do Twolegs need to look out for danger?" Blossomheart grunted. "They cause most of it."

Hawkwing padded to Fidgetpaw's side. "Is Frecklewish in there?"

Fidgetpaw looked up to a row of shiny squares near the top. "I've seen her through one of the clear walls up there." He nodded to the trees that grew beside the great hive. Their tops reached just a little higher than Frecklewish's prison. "From up there, I could see her moving around inside."

"You've climbed to the top?" Violetpaw gasped, her paws prickling with fear.

Fidgetpaw nodded. "One of the clear walls slides open sometimes, and she comes out onto the ledge." Outside

Frecklewish's nest, a wide slab of stone jutted out, edged by a low wall. "But it's too far to jump from the ledge to the tree."

Violetpaw felt dizzy at the thought. The trees tapered at the top, and the gap between the ledge and the treetop was wider than any cat could jump. "If only she were being held in a nest near the bottom." There, the longer branches reached close to the camp walls. "She could make the jump easily."

Gravelpaw edged forward. "Nettlesplash managed to sneak through the hive entrance once."

"It's like a rabbit warren in there. So many smells and so many Twolegs coming and going." Nettlesplash shuddered. "I didn't find Frecklewish's nest. I was lucky to find my way out."

Violetpaw scanned the Twoleg hive, her gaze sweeping the smooth walls from the great slab of stone sticking outside Frecklewish's nest to the ground. The trees weren't the answer. There had to be another way down. To one side she saw other ledges, smaller than Frecklewish's. They clung to the side of the huge nest, one under another, from the roof nearly to the ground. They were woven from what looked like thin, black branches. Her pelt prickled with excitement as she realized that each ledge was joined to the one below by a small stretch of steps. At the bottom, there was a long drop to the ground, but the lowest branches of a tree nearly touched the final ledge. If Frecklewish could reach *those* ledges, she'd be able to use them as an escape. Heart quickening, Violetpaw looked back at Frecklewish's nest. The stone slab was several tail-lengths from the closest woven ledge. Violetpaw's breath caught in her throat. Could Frecklewish make the jump? The drop to the ground would be deadly. But it might be Frecklewish's only chance for escape.

She nudged Hawkwing's shoulder with her nose. "I'm not sure," she whispered. "But I think I have an idea."

CHAPTER 13

❧

The blustery wind threatened rain. Twigpaw glanced anxiously at the swishing branches above the camp.

Finpaw nudged her. "Don't worry," he mewed. "You're safe with me. There's no way StarClan would let another branch drop on me."

They had the clearing to themselves. Leafstar was in her den. Tinycloud had taken her kits to the shelter of the nursery. Plumwillow, Harrybrook, and Sandynose were all hunting. Dewpaw was training with Macgyver in the forest, while Leafpool had taken Fallowfern to collect herbs.

Twigpaw had asked to stay in camp. "Finpaw needs company."

Sandynose had looked unconvinced, but Finpaw had begged and Leafstar had agreed. "Apprentices learn more together than alone," she had said. Sandynose had frowned but hadn't argued with the SkyClan leader.

Now Finpaw batted a moss ball toward her.

Twigpaw caught it distractedly. "I hope Violetpaw and Hawkwing are staying dry and warm." They'd been gone a quarter moon.

"They'll be fine." Finpaw hooked the moss ball from her.

She blinked at him. "What if they're not?"

"What if they're having a great time?" He flipped the ball into the air and swiped at it, missing. "Are you worried you'll have nothing to worry about?"

"No." She nudged him, pretending to be indignant. "Aren't I allowed to worry about my kin?"

"Not when there's nothing you can do to help them."

Twigpaw reached out and knocked the moss ball away from him. "Don't be such a smart-ears." A new scent touched her nose. She recognized it at once. "ShadowClan!"

"Where?" As Finpaw looked around, the fern entrance quivered and Juniperclaw strode into camp.

Fallowfern hurried after him. "You can't just walk into our camp!"

"Really?" Juniperclaw turned on her, pelt bristling. "But *you* can invade *our* territory?"

Fallowfern stared at him blankly.

Leafstar shot out of her den in the hollow cedar and slithered down the roots. She crossed the clearing and stood between Fallowfern and Juniperclaw. "She can't hear you," she told the ShadowClan warrior.

"Is that why she doesn't know that you don't just wander onto another Clan's land and steal their herbs?"

Fallowfern tipped her head. "Did I do something wrong?"

"No." Leafstar shooed her away gently with a nod of her head. "I'll take care of it."

Fallowfern moved away, her eyes glittering anxiously. "I'm sorry, Leafstar."

Juniperclaw lashed his tail. "Aren't you going to punish her?"

"Why?"

"She crossed our border!" Juniperclaw spluttered with outrage. "When I tell Rowanstar, he'll be furious."

"Then don't tell him." Leafstar sat down.

"Is this how SkyClan acts like our ally?" Juniperclaw growled. "We gave you *some* of our land, not *all* of it."

"She probably didn't smell your scent line," Leafstar meowed.

"She's deaf, not stupid!" Juniperclaw's ears twitched angrily.

"ShadowClan hasn't exactly been marking their borders regularly!" Leafstar snapped back.

Juniperclaw glared at her.

Leafstar took a breath. "I'm sorry it happened," she apologized. "We're still getting used to our new home."

As she spoke, Leafpool padded quickly into camp, a bundle of herbs in her jaws. She dropped them and hurried to Leafstar's side. "Is Fallowfern okay? I saw her following Juniperclaw. She looked worried." She glanced at the ShadowClan tom. "Why's he *here*?"

"I caught that fleabag stealing our herbs!" Juniperclaw snarled.

Leafpool looked distraught. "That's my fault. I'm not used to the new borders. I probably sent her to the wrong herb patch."

Juniperclaw rolled his eyes. "What sort of Clan *is* this? You have a borrowed medicine cat who knows even less about your territory than you do." He looked around the camp. "Where is every cat?"

"Busy." Leafstar straightened defensively. Twigpaw guessed that she didn't want to admit that the Clan was so small right now that even one hunting patrol left the camp empty.

"When they stop being busy"—the black tom curled his lip—"tell them to pay more attention to their borders. We will shred the next SkyClan cat we find on our territory." He stormed off.

"Sorry." Leafpool shook her head and turned to Leafstar. "I should have been more careful."

"It's okay," Leafstar assured her. "The borders probably weren't properly marked. ShadowClan is just as short on warriors as we are."

"They'd never admit it," Leafpool grunted.

"Nor would we," Leafstar pointed out. "But we don't try to make up for it by throwing our weight around like a troop of badgers."

Twigpaw poked the moss ball nervously. Border tension was never a good sign. Was ShadowClan beginning to regret giving some of their land to SkyClan? Would they ask for it back?

As Leafpool walked toward Fallowfern, her eyes filled with remorse, Leafstar headed back to her den.

The SkyClan leader glanced at Twigpaw and Finpaw as she passed them. "Why don't you two make yourselves useful?" she mewed crossly.

"How?" Twigpaw blinked at her.

"Clear out the warriors' den." Leafstar lashed her tail.

Twigpaw dipped her head. "Okay."

As Leafstar padded to her den, Finpaw screwed up his nose. "Why should *we* clean out dens?" he muttered. "We're here because of my tail, not because we're in trouble."

"Some cat's got to clean them," Twigpaw pointed out.

"Let the warriors clear up their own mess." Finpaw jerked his muzzle toward the camp entrance. "We should have fun. Let's go find another frog for Dewpaw's nest."

Twigpaw's whiskers twitched with amusement as she remembered how Dewpaw had shot out of his nest when the frog had wriggled beneath his bedding. She glanced at Finpaw out of the corner of her eye. His mischievousness was infectious. "Let's find a *hedgehog*!"

"How would we get a hedgehog back to camp?"

"We could lay a trail of worms for it to follow."

Finpaw's eyes brightened. "Great idea!" He headed for the entrance.

"I was joking!" Twigpaw hurried after him.

"I know." He paused at the entrance while Leafpool and Fallowfern disappeared into the medicine den. "But we can clean out dens later, while everyone else is showing off their catch or reminiscing about the gorge." Winking at her, he scampered out of camp.

Twigpaw followed. "I guess we could hunt," she suggested. They could share their catch with their Clanmates. And it would be great to hunt without Sandynose for a change. He was always criticizing where she put her paws or how she killed her catch. "I know a great place for mice."

Without waiting for an answer, she headed to where one of

ShadowClan's ditches ran onto SkyClan land. Wind whirled through the canopy and whipped through her pelt. She smelled the musty flavors of leaf-fall, her heart pricking as she remembered ThunderClan's forest. Leaves would be fluttering down like snow there, lining the paths and choking the ferns. Here the pines stood green and straight, heedless of the changing season.

"Mouse dung!" Finpaw cursed behind her. She glanced back and saw him stagger as he followed her over an uneven stretch of ground. His stubby tail flicked back and forth wildly as he tried to steady himself.

Twigpaw slowed down and let him catch up to her. "You'll get used to your tail eventually."

He glanced at her. "But I'll never be a normal cat again."

"Who wants to be normal?" she mewed lightly.

As the trees thinned, she saw the ditch. She could smell mouse already. She stopped at the edge and peered in. Weeds sprouted from the sides, and beneath their shriveling leaves she saw movement. "Quick! Get down." She dropped into a crouch.

Finpaw squatted beside her. "Prey?"

"It's a mouse." Twigpaw could hear it pattering over the pine needles at the bottom of the ditch. She flicked his haunches with her tail-tip. "You can have the first catch."

Finpaw edged forward and peeked into the ditch. His hindquarters quivered with excitement. He bunched his paws tightly beneath him and held his breath. Twigpaw could sense he was about to pounce but, as his stubby tail swept the forest floor, he wobbled. His hind paw shot out to stop himself toppling. Pine needles sprayed the ditch. The mouse darted away.

Finpaw lunged after it, slapping his front paws down hard. But the mouse skittered free as he staggered and thumped clumsily against the side of the ditch.

Twigpaw saw his hackles lift. He was angry with himself.

"I'm never going to be able to hunt!" He turned on her, eyes flashing. "I'm going to be the worst warrior ever."

Twigpaw's heart twisted. *Poor Finpaw!* But she hid her pity. "You will if you think like that," she mewed sharply. "You can be as good or as bad as you want to be."

"How can I ever be any good when my tail throws me off balance all the time?"

"You'll just have to train harder," Twigpaw told him. "Feeling sorry for yourself won't make your tail grow back."

Finpaw stared at her, emotion welling in his eyes.

"You can do it," she urged. "You can be the best warrior in SkyClan if you practice."

He blinked. "Do you really think so?"

"Of course I do! You're clever and determined and so full of energy. Why wouldn't you be a brilliant warrior?"

Finpaw's fur smoothed and he lifted his chin. "I can do anything I want."

"Yes!" Twigpaw purred, pleased to see him looking happier.

"Twigpaw!" Leafpool's mew rang through the forest. "Finpaw!"

Twigpaw's heart fell. They'd been discovered. She glanced

guiltily at Finpaw, then turned to face Leafpool.

The ThunderClan medicine cat was hurrying toward them, swerving between the trees. "What are you two doing out here?" Her voice was hushed, as though she was worried about being overheard. "Get back to camp. Sandynose will be back soon and wondering where Finpaw is. You know how annoyed he was the last time you sneaked out."

"Why does he care?" Twigpaw bristled with annoyance. "You'd think he'd *want* Finpaw to be training instead of hanging around camp all the time."

"He's worried about him," Leafpool told her.

Finpaw hopped out of the ditch. "I wish he'd find something else to worry about."

"Until he does, you'd better do as you're told." Leafpool whisked her tail. "Didn't Leafstar ask you to clean out the warriors' den?"

Twigpaw's tail drooped. "But I've been doing apprentice duties for *moons*!"

"I'll do it." Finpaw padded to her side. "You've spent enough time in camp with me. You should have some fun."

Twigpaw *had* been looking forward to a chance to hunt without Sandynose. "But what about you?"

"I can have fun later."

Leafpool nosed Finpaw toward the camp. "Once the warriors' den is clean," she mewed briskly. "The sooner you get the forest smell off your fur, the better. That's how Sandynose caught you last time."

Finpaw glanced back at Twigpaw as Leafpool hurried him away.

She watched him go sadly. Hunting would have been more fun with Finpaw. She shook out her fur. There was no point being miserable. One day, she and Finpaw would both be warriors and they could hunt together whenever they liked. Even Sandynose wouldn't be able to stop them then.

Why was Sandynose such an old badger? He didn't like anything she did. He'd probably frown if she brought him a mouse.

Small paws skittered over the forest floor. Excitement sparked beneath Twigpaw's pelt as a squirrel jumped the ditch and shot toward the ThunderClan border.

Twigpaw hared after it. She skimmed the forest floor, zigzagging between the pines. The squirrel was fast, but so was Twigpaw. And the wind was on her side. Her scent streamed out behind her, and the swishing treetops disguised the sound of her paw steps. As the squirrel neared the ThunderClan border, she ran harder. She was closing on it. As it raced across the border, she leaped. Stretching out her front paws, she sailed across the scent line.

Silver fur flashed in front of her face. With a yelp, she crashed into the muscly flank of another cat. She staggered backward and regained her balance. Catching her breath, she blinked at the cat she'd collided with. "Ivypool!"

Her mentor shook out her fur and glanced glumly at the squirrel as it leaped for the trunk of an oak and swarmed up into the branches.

"I'm sorry," Twigpaw panted. "I chased it across half of SkyClan's territory. I thought a few more tail-lengths wouldn't matter." She glanced apologetically at the border behind her.

Ivypool eyed her warily. For a moment, Twigpaw wondered if she recognized her.

"It's me," she mewed. "Twigpaw."

Ivypool flicked her tail. "I *know*," she snapped.

Wasn't Ivypool pleased to see her? Twigpaw wanted to tell the silver-and-white warrior how much she missed her, but Ivypool was acting strangely. "Is everything okay?"

Ivypool scowled. "Yes. If *okay* means that the apprentice I spent moons training decides that she doesn't want to become a ThunderClan warrior and leaves to join another Clan."

Guilt clawed Twigpaw's belly. "I had to," she mewed. "I needed to be with Violetpaw and Hawkwing."

Ivypool sighed heavily. "I suppose," she conceded. "But I miss you. And it feels strange to train a cat who leaves to fight for another Clan."

Twigpaw dipped her head. "I'll always be grateful for what you taught me."

Ivypool huffed. "Alderheart said you haven't gotten your warrior name yet."

"Leafstar wants me to do some SkyClan training."

"Isn't ThunderClan training good enough?" Ivypool sniffed.

"Of course." Twigpaw's pelt prickled self-consciously. "But SkyClan cats use different skills."

"There's only so many ways to catch a mouse."

Twigpaw swallowed back a purr. "You sound like Gray-stripe."

Ivypool caught her eye, her gaze warming. "I guess I'm

getting a little set in my ways."

"No, you're not," Twigpaw reassured her. "How's Fernsong?"

"Fernsong's great." Ivypool purred. "He wants kits. He's even offered to move into the nursery and raise them."

"A tom in the nursery?" Twigpaw blinked at her. It wasn't something she'd ever considered before. "I guess that could work. Fernsong would make a great father."

"Yes." Ivypool's eyes shone.

The affection in Ivypool's gaze jolted a memory from the back of Twigpaw's mind. "How's Dovewing?" she asked warily.

"Why?" Ivypool narrowed her eyes suspiciously.

Twigpaw's belly tightened. Did Ivypool know about her sister and Tigerheart's secret meetings?

"What are you hiding?" Ivypool padded closer.

"Nothing." Twigpaw stared at her paws.

Ivypool's stare burned her pelt. "I know you well enough to see when something's bothering you."

Twigpaw didn't want to tell Ivypool what she knew. But she couldn't lie to her former mentor. "I saw her," she murmured softly.

"Where?" Ivypool flexed her claws.

"Near the ShadowClan border." Twigpaw avoided Ivypool's gaze, feeling as guilty as if *she'd* been meeting the ShadowClan deputy in secret. "She was with Tigerheart."

Ivypool didn't respond.

Twigpaw looked at her and saw worry spark in her gaze.

"I knew it!" The white-and-silver warrior suddenly lashed

her tail. "I knew she'd been up to something. Did you hear what they were saying?"

"I couldn't really tell what they were talking about. Tiger-heart was worried about ShadowClan," Twigpaw mumbled. She couldn't tell Ivypool that the two warriors were in love. "Dovewing seemed upset."

A growl rumbled in Ivypool's throat. "*Upset?* Why does she care what happens in ShadowClan? Her loyalty should be to us."

Twigpaw squirmed beneath her pelt. "I'm sure it is."

Ivypool glared at her. "Then why is she meeting Tigerheart in secret?"

"I don't know." Twigpaw backed away. She was shocked by the fury in Ivypool's mew. *Does she think my loyalty should still be with ThunderClan?* She searched the warrior's gaze.

"I'm sorry." Ivypool fluffed out her fur. "It's not your fault. I shouldn't be angry with you."

"I'm sorry I left ThunderClan," Twigpaw blurted.

Ivypool blinked at her. "I know it was a hard decision to make."

"Are you worried Dovewing might switch Clans too?"

Ivypool looked away. "She'd never do that. She's fought too long and risked too much for ThunderClan."

A meow sounded between the oaks. "Ivypool!"

"That's Thornclaw," Ivypool told her.

"I know." Twigpaw recognized the ThunderClan tom's mew with a pang.

"I'd better go." Ivypool dipped her head. "You should head

back to your own territory."

Twigpaw followed Ivypool's gaze toward the SkyClan border. Part of her wished she were returning to the ThunderClan camp. But then she'd miss Finpaw. With a sigh, she turned and crossed back over the scent line. "Take care!" she called to Ivypool.

"You too." Ivypool headed away.

As the undergrowth swallowed her, Twigpaw's heart felt heavy. She missed her mentor. She missed ThunderClan. And she wished she hadn't been the one to share the news about Dovewing. She felt a sudden spark of sympathy for Dovewing. It must be hard having feelings for a cat in another Clan. What if someone tried to stop her from seeing Finpaw? She tried to imagine how she'd feel if she were still in Thunder-Clan and could only meet with him in secret. She shuddered. *I wouldn't like it. I wouldn't like it one bit!*

CHAPTER 14

Clouds filled in the sky, as gray as doves. Alderheart fluffed out his fur against the damp chill. The air tasted of rain. The fine leaf-fall days were giving way to darker weather.

He glanced at the forest closing behind him, wondering how far he'd traveled. ShadowClan scents still emanated from the pines beside him. Surely he must be nearing RiverClan by now? He'd been walking since the sun had risen above the camp, skirting SkyClan territory, and then ShadowClan territory, hoping no cat would spot him as he headed toward the stretch of land that ran down to the lake between Shadow-Clan and RiverClan. There, Twolegs inhabited dens during greenleaf. He might find what he was looking for.

He didn't want the help of any cat. This was a quest he wanted to make alone. Why involve others in a journey that would probably be a waste of time?

As the forest thinned and the land opened into rolling meadows, he narrowed his eyes. The Twoleg dens dotted the hillside where it dipped toward the lake. Would Twolegs still be there now that greenleaf had cooled into leaf-fall? He didn't *want* to find Twolegs, but if there were no six-toed cats among the Clans, perhaps he'd find one here among their kittypets.

It's a dumb hope.

He ignored the doubt that was drowning his thoughts. He had to try. RiverClan had cut themselves off entirely. ShadowClan seemed as divided as they'd been when the rogues moved onto their territory, and SkyClan had so few cats that they hardly seemed a Clan at all. Alderheart couldn't shift the sense of dread that pressed in his belly during the lengthening nights. The Clans seemed to be falling apart; not even their history seemed able to bring them together. *This prophecy must be the answer.*

He could only hope that they were interpreting StarClan's words correctly. That they would find the six-toed cat, and that the cat would help lift the darkness that seemed to hang heavier than the storm clouds threatening the forest. He'd traveled to WindClan the day before to ask Harestar if he knew of a six-toed cat. But Harestar had only stared at him uneasily, and Alderheart had left the camp wondering if he'd simply made the WindClan leader more anxious.

He headed downslope, his mouth open as he tasted the air for kittypet scent.

A high-pitched bark made him freeze. His pelt bushed as he glanced over his shoulder and spotted a white-and-brown dog yapping at the top of the hill. It was held by a Twoleg kit, which pulled on the vine attached to the dog's neck.

Alderheart hesitated. The dog was glaring at him. Its eyes glittered wildly as it barked. With a yelp, it showed its teeth and tugged at the vine, paws scrabbling against the ground.

The Twoleg kit yowled angrily as the dog barked harder. Suddenly, with a snarl, the dog jerked the vine free of the Twoleg's paw.

The dog streaked toward him, and fear seared like fire beneath Alderheart's pelt. Alderheart scanned the grassy slope. There was nowhere to hide. He ran, pelting over the grass, terror pounding in his ears. He headed for the Twoleg nests, then veered, his thoughts spinning. What shelter could Twolegs give him? He raced across the slope. The sound of the barking was growing louder. He glimpsed the brown-and-white fur of the dog at the corner of his gaze. It was closing fast. He swerved again, running blindly now, with a vague hope of reaching the lake's edge, as though somehow the water could protect him.

Tree. The thought sparked a moment before he spied the young rowan. It sprouted at the edge of the slope. *Dogs can't climb!* He raced for it, his heart lurching as he saw that he'd have to cross the dog's path to reach it. Pushing harder against the ground, he ran faster. Wind streamed through his fur. Air burned his lungs. He felt the hot breath of the dog on his flank as he flashed in front of it and leaped for the tree. He hooked his claws into the bark and hauled himself up, his hind legs scrabbling in desperate panic as the dog yelped, a whisker beneath him. He pulled his tail clear of the snapping jaws and scrambled onto the lowest branch.

He stared down, his flanks heaving.

The dog jumped and twisted beneath him, its ears flapping, its eyes rolling with rage.

Alderheart flattened his ears against its yapping and tried to catch his breath. He was trembling so hard he thought he might lose his balance. He dug his claws deep into the bark and squashed himself flat.

The Twoleg kit was racing toward the tree, wailing at the dog. As it neared, it lunged for the vine, which still trailed from the dog's neck. It jerked the dog backward and, growling with effort, dragged it away.

Alderheart watched them go, his mouth dry with fear. Perhaps he should have asked for an escort after all. He stayed in the tree until the kit and its dog had disappeared from view. Then he waited a while longer until he could no longer hear the dog yapping. Unpeeling himself from the branch, he scanned the hillside.

Something was moving near the top. He strained to make out a shape, but the wind was streaming through the long grass and it was hard to see anything clearly against the rippling pasture. He shrugged. It was probably a RiverClan warrior, or ShadowClan. Their territories lay on either side. Or perhaps it was one of the kittypets he'd come here to find. For now, he climbed cautiously down the tree and looked toward the Twoleg nests. He would start there.

A dirt Thunderpath trailed from the cluster of Twoleg dens. It smelled stale, its stench softened by the wind. Alderheart followed it, keeping to the side, his ears pricked for the low roar of a Twoleg monster. Wooden Twoleg dens rose on either side, and he glanced at them nervously. There was no sign of life. Perhaps the Twolegs had gone back to their leaf-bare camp? He ducked under a fence around the edge of a low den, wrinkling his nose as he scented rancid food. Perhaps there were Twolegs here after all. . . .

A hiss made him freeze. A black tom was glaring at him from beside a tall shrub. A tabby she-cat stalked out from behind the foliage. They faced him, their pelts prickling with hostility.

Kittypets!

"I'm not here to steal anything," Alderheart called out.

The black tom narrowed his eyes. "What did you come for?"

Alderheart hesitated. There was something familiar about the tom. And he seemed to recognize the scent of the tabby she-cat. He searched his memory, wondering if he could have seen these cats before.

The tabby tipped her head, her eyes hard. "Well?" she snarled.

"I'm looking for someone." Alderheart's pelt ruffled nervously.

"Are you a rogue?" The tom padded closer. "Did Darktail send you?" Was that fear glittering in his gaze?

Suddenly, Alderheart remembered them. They'd been held captive by Darktail, hadn't they? He'd seen them fighting in the battle with the rogues. He remembered the she-cat's name. "Zelda!"

She backed away, looking scared. "How do you know me?"

"I'm Alderheart," he told her. "I'm ThunderClan's medicine cat. I saw you in the battle with the rogues."

The tom stretched his muzzle forward and tasted the air. "You helped fight the rogues?" he asked.

"I didn't exactly fight," Alderheart told him. For the first time in moons, he felt self-conscious about his role as a medicine cat. Would these cats understand that fighting wasn't always the bravest thing a cat could do?

The tom padded forward and sniffed him. "I'm Loki." He stood back, clearly satisfied that Alderheart wasn't a threat. "Who are you looking for? There aren't any Clan cats here."

"I know." Alderheart's pelt smoothed. "The cat I'm looking for doesn't have to be a Clan cat. It just needs to have six toes."

Zelda's eyes widened. "Six toes?"

"Cats don't have six toes," Loki grunted.

"Sometimes they have four." Loki glanced at the fence behind Alderheart. "Like Jasper."

Alderheart looked around, his heart lurching as he saw a stocky kittypet crouching on top of the fence. The russet tom was glaring at him.

"Jasper lost a toe after it got infected," Zelda explained.

"That must have hurt," Alderheart mewed to the russet tom kindly.

"Why do you care?" Jasper curled his lip.

"I'm a medicine cat," he explained. "It's my duty to care."

Jasper hissed. "I don't need the sympathy of a mangy old stray."

"He's a Clan cat, Jasper." Zelda padded to Alderheart's side.

"I've heard enough about Clan cats to know that they're

a bunch of mangy old strays," Jasper hissed. "Didn't you say they held you prisoner?"

"That was the rogues," Loki told him. "Rogues are different."

"Wild cats are all the same." Jasper watched Alderheart coldly.

Zelda blinked apologetically at Alderheart. "Jasper's okay, really," she mewed.

"It's all right." Alderheart tried to pretend he wasn't unnerved by Jasper's open hostility. "We have bad-tempered cats in the Clans too."

Jasper slid off the fence and stalked away, his tail high.

Relieved, Alderheart blinked hopefully at Zelda. "Do you know of any six-toed cats?"

Zelda shook her head. "Not around here."

"I've never heard of any," Loki agreed.

"Sorry we can't help." Zelda whisked her tail. "Why are you looking for one?"

Would kittypets understand the importance of a StarClan prophecy? Probably not. Alderheart dipped his head. "It doesn't matter," he mewed. "I should go home. Thanks for your help."

"I wish we could have helped more," Loki meowed.

"Are you hungry?" Zelda asked. "There's food outside my Twoleg's nest. It's really tasty."

Alderheart tried not to let his shudder show. He'd heard about kittypet food. Graystripe had told him that it tasted like dried leaf mold. "No, thanks," he meowed politely. "I need to go home."

"Okay." Zelda headed across the grass. "Take care."

Loki followed her. "Bye, Alderheart. I hope you find what you're looking for."

"Thanks." Alderheart headed for the fence and squeezed under it. Disappointment weighed in his paws. He knew there had only been a slim chance that he'd find the answer to StarClan's prophecy here, but hope had kept his spirits high. Where else could he look for a six-toed kittypet? Perhaps he needed to head farther out of Clan territory. But not today. His Clanmates would worry if he didn't return soon. He headed along the dirt Thunderpath that led out of the Twoleg camp.

Flattening his ears against the cold, he cut across the grass, leaving the Twoleg camp behind. The wind whistled past his ears, and he narrowed his eyes against it so that he could barely hear or see.

Suddenly, paws slammed into his side. A flurry of russet fur caught his eye as he staggered sideways. The smell of kittypet washed over him. Instinctively, he lashed out, hooking thick folds of pelt, but his attacker was bigger and tugged easily free before swiping Alderheart's cheek with a hefty blow. Pain scorched through Alderheart's head as he felt claws rake his flesh. With a yowl he hit out blindly, gasping as another powerful blow knocked him off-balance. He fell and felt the weight of the other cat pin him to the ground. Thrashing his hind legs, he tried to wriggle free, but the kittypet held him fast. *Jasper!* He recognized the pelt and the scent now. Rage swelled in his chest as he tried to fight the tom off.

"So you have bad-tempered cats in your Clan, do you?"

Jasper sneered, looming over Alderheart, pressing him into the earth. "Are they as bad-tempered as this?" Jasper lifted a wide paw and began to swing it toward Alderheart's muzzle.

Alderheart braced himself for pain, furious at being so helpless.

But the blow didn't land, and suddenly, the weight lifted from his chest. Alderheart scrambled to his paws, confused. Had Jasper just been trying to scare him? Then he heard a yowl and saw a flash of Sparkpelt's orange fur. Jasper staggered as Sparkpelt lunged at his forepaws and knocked them from under him. As he collapsed onto his chin, she reared and thumped his flank with her paws. He rolled onto his side, his hind legs churning frantically. Sparkpelt hopped clear of the kittypet's flailing claws and grabbed Jasper's throat from behind. She jerked his head backward and hissed in his ear. "If my brother tells you we have bad-tempered cats in our Clan, you'd better believe it." She sliced her claws along his throat, not hard enough to draw blood, but tugging out fur. Then she let him go.

Jasper leaped to his paws and faced Sparkpelt and Alderheart, his eyes flashing with shock. As he backed away, Alderheart felt relief flood him, and yet his pelt prickled with embarrassment. Medicine cat or not, he should have been able to defend himself from a *kittypet*.

Sparkpelt hissed at Jasper, and the russet tom turned and fled. "So brave!" she yowled after him. Purring with amusement, she turned to Alderheart. "Are you okay?"

He ran a paw over his cheek. It was wet with blood and it

stung, but the cuts didn't feel deep. "I'll be fine." He met her eye, feeling hot with shame. "Thanks."

She shrugged. "It was nothing."

Nothing? She'd just fought off a tom nearly twice her size. Alderheart hadn't even been able to defend himself. Was she trying to rub it in?

Alderheart headed upslope.

Sparkpelt hurried after him. "Where are you going now?"

"Home," he mewed curtly. "Have you been following me?"

"Of course I've been following you." Sparkpelt fell in beside him. "You slunk out of camp like you were up to something. I wanted to know what. And it's a good thing I did. That cat would have shredded you."

"No, he wouldn't," Alderheart snapped. "I was just planning my next move."

Sparkpelt didn't respond. Instead she changed the subject. "Why did you come here?"

"Medicine-cat stuff," he answered. "You wouldn't understand."

"Try me."

Alderheart kept walking. He felt mean. She'd just saved him and he was acting ungrateful, but he couldn't shake the embarrassment from his pelt. Was she going to tell their Clanmates that she'd had to rescue him like a kit?

Sparkpelt blocked his path. "What's wrong?" She gazed into his eyes anxiously. "Are you annoyed with me?"

Thoughts flashed like shooting stars through Alderheart's mind. Where should he start? She had wanted SkyClan to go back to the gorge after he'd spent moons finding them. She'd been so busy flirting with Larksong like a feather-headed apprentice that she hadn't even noticed that Alderheart had hardly spoken to her in a moon. And now she had totally humiliated him and didn't even realize it. He glared at her. "What's wrong with *you*?" he snapped. "We were always close. Now I feel like I hardly know you!"

"We still are close, aren't we?" Hurt flashed across Sparkpelt's intense green gaze. "I know I've been kind of distracted lately with Larksong."

"*Kind of?*"

"Is that what's bothering you?" Sparkpelt blinked at him.

"Not exactly." Alderheart didn't want to sound dumb. "But you haven't noticed anything! You didn't care how I felt about SkyClan. Or that I've been worried about the prophecy or that it might be embarrassing to need saving from a kittypet! You're always so sure of yourself—you act like everything you do is okay, and sometimes it's *not* okay!"

Sparkpelt's fur ruffled along her spine. "I know you wanted SkyClan to stay. But that didn't mean I had to agree. I can have my own opinion. And of course I care that you're worried." She began to pace back and forth. "But you're right. I guess I've been too caught up with Larksong to take the time to talk to you about stuff that's important. And I'm sorry I saved you from that fat kittypet. . . ." She paused. "I'm not *sorry* exactly. I wasn't going to let you get your fur ripped off. But I trained as a warrior and you trained as a medicine cat. If I was bleeding to death right now, you'd save me, wouldn't you?

Because that's what you do. *You* save cats. *I* hunt and fight."
She stopped and gazed at him.

Guilt jabbed Alderheart's belly. "I'm sorry." He stared at the
ground. "I know I'm being oversensitive. And you are allowed
to have your own opinions." He glanced at her quickly. "Even
if they're wrong."

She purred. "I'm glad you're sensitive. It makes you a great
brother." She nudged his shoulder with her nose. "Let's go
back to camp and take the biggest piece of prey from the pile,
and if anyone complains, I'll just tell them that you traveled
all the way here and fought off the fiercest cat in the forest."

Alderheart began to climb the slope. "Okay, but let's not
take the biggest piece. Just the second biggest piece."

"Okay." Sparkpelt fell in beside him. "Why did you come
all the way here? And don't tell me it's *medicine-cat stuff* again."

"I was hoping one of those kittypets might be the six-toed
cat," Alderheart told her.

"The one who's going to save the Clans from the storm?"
He nodded.

"But no luck?" she asked.

"No." Alderheart's tail drooped.

"Don't worry," Sparkpelt mewed softly. "You'll work it out.
After all, you did find SkyClan."

"*Twigpaw* found SkyClan," he corrected her.

"Only because you told her where to look." Sparkpelt lifted
her tail. "And perhaps this prophecy isn't as bad as you think.
Maybe StarClan is just being cautious because so much bad
stuff has happened already."

They reached the top of the slope and turned toward the forest. *Perhaps this prophecy isn't as bad as you think.* Alderheart tried to imagine that Sparkpelt was right, but anxiety still tugged in his belly. "No," he murmured. "I can *feel* it's important. StarClan wants us to figure it out. RiverClan has turned its back on us. ShadowClan is close to falling apart. I don't know how a six-toed cat can fix everything, but even if it only leads us to the next clue, it's worth trying for."

As they headed into the trees, Sparkpelt padded closer, letting her fur brush his. "Tell me if you need help," she mewed. "If you need to make another journey like this, I can come with you."

He blinked at her gratefully, pleased that the anger that had been sitting like a stone in his belly for so long had dissolved. Affection swelled in his chest. The forest muffled the wind, but above the trees the sky was growing darker. "Tell me about Larksong. Do you really like him?"

Sparkpelt shrugged. "Yeah. A lot. But . . . I don't know. I want to enjoy being a warrior right now. I don't want to get serious. But I like being with Larksong, and I think he likes being with me." She glanced nervously at Alderheart. "Do you think he likes being with me?"

"Why wouldn't he?" Alderheart mewed. "You're funny and smart and a great warrior."

She nudged him. "Thanks, Alderheart."

As Alderheart purred, an ominous growl sounded from the bracken beside them. The stench of dog washed his muzzle. Panic shrilled through him as the brown-and-white dog lunged from the undergrowth. Alderheart recognized it at once. Its vine trailed on the ground beside it. Its growl exploded into ugly barking.

Sparkpelt knocked Alderheart backward and swiped a paw at the dog's muzzle. Fast as a fox, the dog thrust its nose low and snapped its jaws around Sparkpelt's hind leg. With a tug, it yanked her onto her back and dragged her toward the bracken.

Alderheart's chest seemed to burst with terror. Without thinking, he flung himself at the dog. Flailing with every paw, he clung to its head and tore at it wildly.

The dog yelped in pain, thrashing its head back and forth. Alderheart clung harder. Jaws snapped beneath him. Hot breath billowed around him. Blind with terror, he hooked his hind claws into the folds of fur around the dog's neck and began churning.

Whimpering, the dog thumped Alderheart against a tree, and Alderheart let go. Winded and trembling, he scrambled to his paws, ready to fight for his life. But the dog turned and, with a howl, pounded away through the bracken and disappeared between the trees.

Blood roared in Alderheart's ears. "Sparkpelt?" He saw her orange pelt beneath the bracken fronds. "Sparkpelt!" Throat tight with fear, he darted to her side.

She rolled over and stared at him, her green eyes wide. "That was the bravest thing I've ever seen."

Weak with relief, Alderheart scanned her flank. Blood was welling around her hind leg.

She heaved herself to her paws and gingerly touched her injured hind leg to the ground. "Nothing broken," she breathed.

"That bite will need treating," Alderheart mewed anxiously.

Sparkpelt shooed him forward with a flick of her tail. "It's bad enough you had to chase the dog off. *I'm* supposed to be the warrior. Don't rub nettles into the wound."

He glanced at her teasingly. "I was going to use oak leaf. It's better for infections."

"Smart-ears." Purring, Sparkpelt limped toward the ThunderClan border.

Alderheart hurried after her. Pride washed his pelt. As he lifted his muzzle happily, the skies opened and rain began to pound the canopy.

CHAPTER 15

❧

"You don't need to climb up with us, Violetpaw." Hawkwing craned his neck and looked into the branches of the oak. He narrowed his eyes against the rain, which dripped through the branches.

Violetpaw puffed out her chest, hoping to look braver than she felt. "I want to." It was her plan. She was asking Frecklewish to take a big risk. She had to be there to help.

The rain had started before dawn. It had lashed the gorge so fiercely that the stream had risen by the time the sun climbed above the trees. As water began to wash over the banks, the cats left their camp in the small hollow and moved to higher ground. Before long, they watched their nests get carried away by the flood.

"There's nothing left for us here." Fidgetpaw had been the first to say the words. "Let's fetch Frecklewish and leave."

Nettlesplash had argued. How could Frecklewish escape in weather like this? But Mintfur had pointed out that, with their camp washed away, they had no home left. And who knew when the rain would stop. Finally Nettlesplash had agreed. It was time to head for SkyClan's new home.

Now, below the oak, Violetpaw shook out her sodden pelt, hoping Hawkwing would think her fur was spiked because of the rain. She didn't want him to see her fear. What if Frecklewish didn't make the jump to the woven ledge? What if she fell?

She peered at the towering Twoleg hive. Rainwater streamed down its smooth walls and ran in rivers across the stone that surrounded it.

Nettlesplash circled the thick trunk of the oak. "It's an easy climb to the top," he meowed.

Rabbitleap and Blossomheart looked up, clearly unconvinced. "I'm glad I'm keeping my paws on the ground," Rabbitleap growled.

Gravelpaw lifted his forepaws and pressed them against the gnarled bark. "Can I come?"

"You're staying down here," Mintfur told the young tom. Her gaze swept over Palepaw, Fringepaw, and Nectarpaw. "All four of you."

"But *Violetpaw* is going," Palepaw objected.

"It was her plan." Hawkwing inspected the trunk.

Violetpaw looked down self-consciously. Gravelpaw and the other apprentices would be her denmates soon. She didn't want to annoy them. "I guess I could stay down here with you," she murmured.

"No!" Nectarpaw splashed over the wet earth and stopped in front of her. "You've got to go. We don't mind staying here."

"Speak for yourself," Gravelpaw huffed.

"Just be careful," Nectarpaw mewed. "And ignore

Gravelpaw. He thinks he's already a warrior."

Violetpaw looked at the tan tom. "I promise to tell you everything when I get down," she offered.

"*If* you get down," Gravelpaw sniffed.

Palepaw nudged her brother. "She won't get stuck up there like you did last half-moon."

"I wasn't stuck." Gravelpaw flicked his tail crossly. "I was hunting owls."

"Then why did Mintfur have to climb up and fetch you?"

Nettlesplash circled the tree again, frowning. "Stop bickering. This is serious." He reached his front paws up the trunk and then, gracefully, bounded up to the first branch.

"Good luck." Rabbitleap brushed his tail along Violetpaw's spine. "Dig your claws in deep."

"I'll look after her," Hawkwing promised, and scrambled after Nettlesplash.

Violetpaw's heart quickened. Breathing fast, she watched Mintfur and Fidgetpaw follow him. Hooking her claws into the soaked bark, she hauled herself up.

Splinters of bark peeled away as she climbed and showered onto the cats below as she followed the warriors higher into the tree. Nettlesplash seemed to know the route; he moved swiftly from branch to branch, tracing a path that took them past ledge after ledge of the Twoleg camp. The tree had already lost half its leaves, and the other half were brown. They fluttered around Violetpaw's face as she wove around the trunk, following Hawkwing and the others higher into the branches.

Rain drenched her pelt and streamed from her whiskers.

She didn't dare look down, scared of losing her balance. She glanced instead at the wide slab outside Frecklewish's Twoleg nest. The stone shone with rainwater. The top of the encircling wall was slick. Violetpaw glanced at the woven ledges nearby and saw that the narrow fences that edged them were dripping with rain. How would Frecklewish grip them?

Worry wormed beneath Violetpaw's pelt. *She may not want to risk it.*

In front of her, Hawkwing stopped, and Violetpaw realized that the patrol was level with the stone slab. Nettlesplash had led them onto a thick branch. Smaller branches jutted from it, and Mintfur and Fidgetpaw had fanned out so that they had a good view of Frecklewish's nest. Hawkwing edged forward onto the branch beside Fidgetpaw. He made room for Violetpaw and beckoned her forward. Gingerly, she padded over the wet bark and crouched behind him.

Warm light spilled through the clear wall of Frecklewish's Twoleg nest and reflected in the puddles outside on the ledge.

"Can you see her?" Fidgetpaw hissed to Nettlesplash.

Nettlesplash was peering through the clear wall. "Not yet," he meowed. "We'll just have to wait."

Rain seeped through Violetpaw's pelt, reaching her skin. She tried not to shiver and dug her claws deep into the bark. Cold to the bone, she waited beside Hawkwing. Time seemed to pass slowly, and with the sun hidden, she had no idea how long they waited.

At last, Nettlesplash straightened. "I see her!"

Through the rain streaming down the clear wall, Violetpaw could see a mottled tabby moving in the warm light.

Nettlesplash yowled. Frecklewish's face turned sharply toward him. Her eyes widened and she hurried closer. Violetpaw saw her talking. A Twoleg hurried to her side. Eagerly, Frecklewish escorted the Twoleg toward the clear wall.

Violetpaw could hear the medicine cat's muffled mewing now. Her heart seemed to stop as the Twoleg slid the wall open and Frecklewish hurried onto the stone slab.

Nettlesplash ducked close to the branch as the Twoleg glanced outside, then closed the glass wall and disappeared inside the nest, leaving Frecklewish outside.

Frecklewish hopped onto the slab's wall and called out excitedly. "What are you doing here? Is everything okay?"

"We're fine," Mintfur mewed.

"How are you?" Fidgetpaw asked anxiously.

"I'm fine," Frecklewish called across the gap. "The Twolegs treat me well, but I want to get out of here."

"That's why we've come," Nettlesplash told her.

"Have you thought of a way for me to escape?" Frecklewish looked down. Violetpaw followed her gaze, her head spinning as she took in the huge drop to the stone below. "I escaped through the nest entrance a few days ago, but I got lost before I made it all the way outside, and another Twoleg picked me up and brought me back."

Violetpaw shuddered at the thought of being picked up by a Twoleg. She blinked sympathetically at Frecklewish.

Frecklewish seemed to notice her. Her eyes widened as her gaze flicked from Violetpaw to Hawkwing. "Hawkwing. You're back!"

"We've come to take you to the lake," Hawkwing called.

"We have a new home there among the other Clans."

Frecklewish's eyes brightened. Happiness seemed to flood her gaze, then faded as she glanced down once more. "But how do I get out of here?"

"We have a plan." Hawkwing nodded to Violetpaw.

Frecklewish blinked hopefully at Violetpaw.

Dread gripped Violetpaw's belly. *My plan is so dumb!* She looked at the gap between the stone slab and the woven ledge, trembling as she realized how far it was from this angle. How had she ever imagined Frecklewish could make that jump? A thought flashed in her mind. There was another clear wall beside the woven ledge. Could Frecklewish get to it from inside?

Hesitantly, Violetpaw nodded to the woven ledge. "If you can get to that ledge, there's a way down."

Frecklewish followed her gaze, her wet pelt spiking.

"Can you get to it from inside the nest?" Violetpaw blinked at her hopefully.

Frecklewish shook her head. "No."

"Can you jump to it?"

Frecklewish narrowed her eyes. "I'm not sure. I've thought about it before, but it didn't seem to lead anywhere."

"It does," Violetpaw told her eagerly. "There are steps down to the next ledge. They go right to the bottom."

Frecklewish's eyes flashed with excitement. "All the way?"

"You'll be able to climb down far enough to jump into the tree," Violetpaw called through the rain. She wondered if she was doing the right thing. What if Frecklewish fell?

Nettlesplash edged closer to the end of his branch. "It's a long jump," he called, jerking his muzzle toward the gap between Frecklewish's stone slab and the woven ledge. "We'll understand if you don't want to try."

"But the lake!" Frecklewish stared at Hawkwing. "No. I can't let you leave without me."

Violetpaw stared at her through the pouring rain. Was she really going to try? *Why did I mention my plan?*

Frecklewish faced the woven ledge, her gaze fixed on the narrow struts that fenced it. The top shimmered with raindrops. She drew her hind legs in close, her forepaws curling over the edge of the stone. Her tail waved slowly back and forth as she balanced herself. She lifted her haunches. Violetpaw could see her bunching her muscles, ready to leap.

Suddenly, the clear wall opened behind her. A Twoleg stepped out into the rain, its eyes wide as it stared at Frecklewish.

Frecklewish leaped.

The Twoleg lunged toward her with a howl. As its hands slapped the wall, Frecklewish's hind paws slipped clumsily.

She's going to fall! Violetpaw's heart seemed to jump into her throat as Frecklewish sailed through the air, forepaws stretching.

Violetpaw darted forward, but Hawkwing steadied her with a paw. "Don't move!" Half-blind with terror, she looked down. The ground seemed to swim far below them. *Don't let her die!*

A clang jarred her from her stupor as Frecklewish hit the

thin fence of the woven ledge hard. Her forepaws curled over the narrow strut at the top. Her hind paws scrabbled against the slippery bars below. Pelt bristling with terror, she fought to get a grip. Then, with a long, low, grunt, she hauled herself over the top and slithered to safety.

Violetpaw melted against Hawkwing as relief washed through every muscle. "She made it." Her mew was no more than a breath.

"Quick!" Nettlesplash hurried toward the trunk and began scrambling down the tree. Fidgetpaw raced after him.

Frecklewish was already leaping down the first flight of steps, making the ledge rattle. The Twoleg stared after her for a moment, then turned and raced back into its nest.

"It's chasing her!" Mintfur stared after the Twoleg as it disappeared inside. She rushed after Nettlesplash.

Violetpaw followed, Hawkwing at her heels. Half jumping, half sliding, she climbed after the SkyClan warriors. She could hear Frecklewish keeping pace with them. The woven ledge rang with her paw steps. Near the bottom of the tree, Nettlesplash bounded nimbly along a long low branch. At the end, he leaned out as Frecklewish landed on the bottom ledge, a tail-length from the branch. She leaped over the enclosing fence, hardly touching it as she launched herself toward the tree.

Nettlesplash reached out a paw and hooked Frecklewish's pelt, then hauled her the final muzzle-length into the safety of the oak.

Behind her, the Twoleg climbed through a clear wall onto

the woven ledge and yelped.

Violetpaw stood frozen with shock beside the trunk.

Mintfur nudged her. "Let's get out of here." She bundled Violetpaw onto the branch below.

Violetpaw could see Gravelpaw, Palepaw, Fringepaw, and Nectarpaw staring up, their eyes wide. Rabbitleap and Blossomheart watched, pelts on end. She swung herself around the lowest branch and clung to the trunk. The bark scraped her belly as she dropped like a stone onto the ground. "We've got her!" she told the trembling apprentices. They surged past her as Fidgetpaw and Frecklewish scrambled down the trunk.

Violetpaw hung back as the SkyClan cats wound around each other, purring louder than the rain. Hawkwing rubbed his cheek along Frecklewish's. "It's good to see you."

Clattering sounded from the Twoleg hive. Huge paw steps pounded the stone. "Let's go!" Violetpaw yowled as she spied the Twoleg running toward the tree.

She pelted away, Gravelpaw darting in front of her. Mintfur and Palepaw raced at her side. She glanced back to see Hawkwing, Nettlesplash, and Frecklewish running after her with Rabbitleap and Blossomheart.

Behind them, the Twoleg slowed to a halt, its small eyes staring in surprise.

We did it! Joy surged beneath Violetpaw's pelt. They had rescued Frecklewish and found the last of SkyClan. In a few days, they'd be home.

CHAPTER 16

Twigpaw squeezed into the warriors' den and shook the rain from her pelt. She'd lost track of how long it had been raining. Days had passed since the dark clouds had rolled over the forest, and now every den was dripping and every nest was damp. Leafpool fretted over her herb store, worried that her carefully gathered leaves might begin to rot. Hunting patrols brought back soaked prey. Twigpaw wondered how Hawkwing and Violetpaw were managing to stay dry. Surely they'd be back soon? They'd been gone nearly a half-moon.

Macgyver's mew snatched her from her thoughts. "Have you brought a poultice for my paws?" The black-and-white tom blinked from his nest.

"Leafpool will bring some later," Twigpaw told him. "Sandynose sent me to groom you."

Macgyver had lost his grip on a tree trunk the day before and slithered down the wet bark, slicing his pads. He'd landed heavily and sprained his shoulder and now lay in his nest, too stiff to move.

Twigpaw's nose wrinkled at the smell of him. The dampness had turned his pelt sour, and she didn't relish the thought of working her tongue through his fur in search of fleas and ticks. He was a Clanmate in need and she didn't begrudge him. But she felt irritated with Sandynose for giving her the task.

Was he punishing her for something? She'd been trying hard to listen to him during training and follow his instructions carefully, no matter how rabbit-brained they seemed. She hoped that if she worked hard, her SkyClan apprenticeship would end soon.

Macgyver shifted in his nest with a grunt. "I've managed to groom my belly and my paws, but I can't reach my back." He turned it toward her. "Sorry about the smell."

Twigpaw padded to his nest. "The whole camp stinks," she mewed sympathetically. "The dens and nests are so damp, they're half rotten. It must be terrible being stuck inside."

"I'd rather have fresh rain in my fur," Macgyver agreed. "At least I wouldn't smell like a badger."

Twigpaw purred as she buried her muzzle in his thick fur and began to root for fleas. She found one and cracked it between her teeth before lapping the area clean.

Macgyver relaxed beneath her tongue. "Feels good," he meowed gratefully. "That flea has been nibbling me all night."

Twigpaw worked her way down his spine, nipping out fleas and washing his pelt thoroughly. At the base of his tail, she found a tick. It was fat with blood. She washed around it and leaned back on her haunches. "That tick will need mouse bile," she told him. "If I pull it, I can't promise to get it out cleanly. And you don't want an infection."

Macgyver lifted an injured paw. "I'd go to Leafpool's den if it didn't hurt so much to walk."

"I'll fetch some." Twigpaw got to her paws. She wondered if Finpaw was back from training. Bellaleaf, who had taken over as his mentor in Blossomheart's absence, had taken him out early. She was glad he was training again, but she missed seeing him around camp so much. She poked her head out of the den. Sandynose, Dewpaw, and Sagenose had returned from hunting. Reedpaw was helping Leafpool pile mud and moss against the walls of the medicine den to keep the rain out. While Sandynose crossed the swollen stream to talk with Leafstar, Dewpaw helped Sagenose push the prey they'd caught closer to the fern wall of the camp. Twigpaw guessed they were hoping to shelter it from the rain. But the ferns were shriveling now, and the rain was still falling. She doubted there was anywhere in camp where fresh-kill could stay dry.

"Twigpaw!"

As she headed toward Leafpool's den, Sandynose called her.

She turned, pricking her ears. The tabby tom was heading toward her, his gaze serious. Twigpaw swallowed back a sigh. What was he going to find fault with now?

She stopped and waited. "Was prey running well?" she asked as he reached her.

"As well as can be expected in this weather." Rain streamed from his whiskers but he didn't seem to notice. He blinked at her sternly. "I want to speak with you about Finpaw while he's out of camp."

Twigpaw frowned. What did he want to say to her that he couldn't say in front of Finpaw?

"I don't think you should be around him so much."

She stared. "We share a den!" How was she supposed to avoid her denmates?

"I know," Sandynose went on. "But that doesn't mean you have to go exploring with him or hunting with him every chance you get."

"You make it sound like I'm stalking him." Twigpaw's pelt bristled. "He *wants* to hunt with me."

Sandynose grunted. "Try to discourage him."

"Why?" Twigpaw could hardly believe her ears. Finpaw was a Clanmate. What was wrong with being with him?

Sandynose looked at her steadily. "He's trying to recover his confidence after his accident. Training is harder for him with half a tail. And he's got a lot of catching up to do. Seeing you doing everything so easily must be hard for him."

Twigpaw felt hot. Was that true? "But I've been helping him." Together, they had found new ways for him to stalk and pounce that took advantage of his short tail. "Yesterday we worked out a new hunting crouch."

"He's young and he's clearly fond of you." Sandynose didn't seem to be listening. "I don't want him taking risks to impress you."

"I'd never let him take a risk!" Twigpaw was angry. Why was Sandynose being so unfair?

"You're distracting him from his training." Sandynose's tail twitched impatiently. "Just stay away from him. It's for the good of *SkyClan*."

He walked away before Twigpaw could reply.

She stared after her mentor, her heart pounding with rage. How dare he tell her to stay away from her Clanmate? *For the good of SkyClan?* What did that mean? *I'm SkyClan too!* He talked as though she wasn't one of them.

Paw steps sounded at the entrance tunnel. Twigpaw glanced toward it. Hope flashed in her belly. Was it Hawkwing's patrol?

Her ears twitched with surprise as she saw Ivypool lead Lionblaze, Fernsong, and Thornclaw into the clearing.

The ThunderClan warriors stopped beside the stream as Leafstar padded toward them. Sandynose came closer and stared as Dewpaw and Sagenose watched uneasily from beside the fresh-kill pile.

Ivypool dipped her head low. "We waited at the border for a patrol," she meowed apologetically. "But no cat came."

Leafstar glanced at the falling rain. "No cat wants to be out on a day like this. And, until Hawkwing returns with our Clanmates, our patrols are a little thin."

As she spoke, Quailkit and Pigeonkit tumbled out of the nursery.

"Invaders!" Quailkit squeaked in alarm.

Sunnykit scrambled out, puffing her ginger kit-fluff against the weather.

Quailkit shook rain from his crow-black ears. "Are they rogues?"

"No, dear." Tinycloud followed her kits out. "They're ThunderClan warriors."

"I thought ThunderClan warriors were like foxes," Sunny-kit mewed.

"That's ShadowClan," Pigeonkit announced knowledgeably.

Tinycloud swept her tail around them and scooped them close, shielding them from the rain. "Be quiet, my dears, and listen."

Beside the medicine den, Reedpaw sat back on her haunches and poked Leafpool. "Your Clanmates are here."

Leafpool, absorbed in her work, looked up. "Thornclaw!" Her gaze warmed when she saw the golden-brown tom. She shook mud and moss from her paws and crossed the camp to greet him. "How's Blossomfall?"

"She's well." Thornclaw nodded graciously.

"And the kits?" Leafpool's eyes sparkled.

"Eaglekit and Shellkit are determined to climb the rock tumble and explore Bramblestar's cave," Thornclaw told her. "Stemkit and Plumkit prefer to hang around the medicine den."

Leafpool purred. "I expect Jayfeather isn't too pleased."

"No." Thornclaw's whiskers twitched. "But Alderheart says he enjoys having something to complain about."

A twinge of homesickness jabbed Twigpaw's heart. Jayfeather used to complain about *her*.

Ivypool looked at Thornclaw, her eyes dark. "We came to discuss a serious matter."

Thornclaw lowered his head as she went on.

"We're searching for Dovewing." Ivypool's mew was taut with worry.

Leafstar tipped her head to one side. "Is she missing?"

"She left camp two days ago and hasn't been seen since."

Twigpaw stiffened. *She's gone?*

"Did she say where she was going?" Leafstar asked.

Lionblaze's pelt rippled along his spine. "She left without a word to anyone."

Leafpool leaned closer. "Have you searched the forest?"

"We've searched ThunderClan's part of the forest," Ivypool told her. "We've also traveled to ShadowClan's camp to ask if they've seen her."

"Have they?" Leafstar asked.

"Rowanstar says they haven't." Ivypool's ears twitched uneasily.

Leafstar turned to Sandynose. "Has there been any sign of her on SkyClan territory?"

"No cat's reported any strange scents to me," he reported.

"No cat?" Ivypool looked at Twigpaw.

Twigpaw shifted her paws guiltily. Should she have reported seeing Tigerheart and Dovewing? Ivypool stared at her wordlessly until Leafstar followed her gaze. Sandynose narrowed his eyes.

"Twigpaw? Do you know something?" Leafstar asked.

Twigpaw's pelt prickled uncomfortably. "I saw Dovewing talking to Tigerheart near the ThunderClan border a quarter moon ago." She glanced at Ivypool quizzically. Why had her former mentor put her in this position? "But it didn't seem to be anything to do with SkyClan."

"Were they on our territory?" Leafstar asked.

"Yes, but they were talking about ShadowClan," Twigpaw mewed quickly.

Leafstar's ears pricked. "What were they saying?"

Twigpaw's thoughts seemed to tangle into knots. What should she say? Should she betray Tigerheart's fears for ShadowClan? Or his love for Dovewing? Words shriveled on her tongue. She felt she was being disloyal to everyone. "Tigerheart was worried about his Clan, that's all," she mewed at last.

Leafstar narrowed her eyes.

Sandynose padded toward Twigpaw. "Why didn't you report this at the time?"

"It didn't seem important."

"They were on *our* territory," Sandynose growled.

"But it was ShadowClan's land half a moon ago. I just figured borders weren't as fixed as they used to be."

Sandynose's gaze glittered with anger. "Since when were a Clan's borders *not fixed*?"

Twigpaw looked at the ground. "There have just been so many changes lately," she mumbled.

"Yes," Sandynose meowed icily. "Perhaps, for some cats, change isn't always good."

What did he mean by that? She looked at him, alarmed. His unwavering gaze pierced hers. Did he think she should have stayed with ThunderClan?

Leafstar whisked her tail. "Did you ask Tigerheart about Dovewing?" she asked Ivypool.

"I questioned him." Ivypool lifted her chin. "But he said he hasn't seen her."

"And you believe him?" Leafstar asked.

"Would you?" Ivypool retorted.

Leafstar shrugged. "All I know about Tigerheart is that it was his idea to give us this territory. Feel free to search our land." She dipped her head to Ivypool. "But you must be back across your border by sunset."

"Thank you." Ivypool stared for a moment at the SkyClan leader, then turned away. Lionblaze, Thornclaw, and Fernsong followed her to the camp entrance.

Twigpaw watched them leave, her belly tight. She wanted to run after Ivypool and ask her why she'd forced her to confess to seeing Dovewing. Did she want to make her life difficult in SkyClan? Was she still angry at her for leaving ThunderClan? *Was I disloyal?*

Sandynose growled beside her. "I see I was right to tell you to stay away from Finpaw."

Twigpaw flinched as he stalked away. Now he had reason to distrust her. She wished that Hawkwing and Violetpaw were with her. At least she'd have the support of kin. She knew that Tinycloud was Pebbleshine's mother, but she was busy with her new kits now. Her pelt tingled uneasily. Hawkwing and Violetpaw had been spending so much time together on their journey—now they would share all kinds of private jokes and stories that Twigpaw wouldn't understand. What if she felt even more isolated with them here?

Stop feeling sorry for yourself. She shook out her pelt. She was behaving like a kit. *You made a decision. Now live with it. You were born a SkyClan cat. This is the Clan you're supposed to be with.*

And yet a small voice sounded at the back of her mind. She'd been happy in ThunderClan. She knew their stories. She'd hunted at their side. It had felt easy to be around them. Here she had to work to feel like she belonged.

Twigpaw watched as Sandynose talked in hushed mews with Leafstar. Tinycloud shooed her kits back into the nursery. Dewpaw and Sagenose busily laid bracken fronds over the fresh-kill pile.

Macgyver would be waiting for his mouse bile. She headed for Leafpool's den. How strange that Dovewing had gone missing. Something told her that the ThunderClan warrior had been planning to leave. Twigpaw had heard it in the way she'd talked with Tigerheart. Dovewing had seemed at ease with the ShadowClan warrior. As though she were at home just being with him. And, for a moment, Twigpaw envied her.

CHAPTER 17

Alderheart unrolled a bundle of catmint.

Jayfeather's nose twitched. "It's starting to rot."

Alderheart examined the leaves. They were dark at the edges where they had begun to wilt. "Perhaps the rain will stop today."

"You said that yesterday." Jayfeather pulled a roll of comfrey from the herb store. Its pungent smell filled the medicine den.

Alderheart frowned. "Dried herbs shouldn't smell that strong."

"They're not dry," Jayfeather grunted. "Nothing in the whole forest is dry anymore."

Briarlight shifted in her nest. "Surely the rain must stop soon?"

"I hope so." Alderheart padded anxiously to the den entrance. Outside, the rain pounded the camp. A large puddle had swallowed the clearing, and ThunderClan had begun piling mud and sticks outside their dens, hoping to keep the water from seeping inside if the puddle grew larger.

His Clanmates hid in their dens. Only Graystripe was

outside, wading through the puddle to sniff at the drenched fresh-kill pile. His thick fur was plastered to his body. He glanced at Alderheart and lifted his tail halfheartedly. "Nice weather—if you're a duck."

"I guess." Alderheart blinked at him anxiously as the old tom lifted a dripping mouse from the pile and trudged back to the elders' den.

Bramblestar and Squirrelflight were out, hunting with Brightheart, Sparkpelt, and Berrynose. Prey was hard to sniff out in this weather, and he wondered how much they'd bring back.

He saw the thorn barrier quiver as Ivypool led Thornclaw, Lionblaze, and Fernsong into camp. Alderheart ducked from the medicine den and splashed through the puddle to greet them. "Did you find any sign of Dovewing?"

Ivypool blinked at him, rain streaming around her face. "Nothing," she meowed heavily. "Rowanstar and Leafstar say that no one has seen or smelled her."

"Her scent would be hard to pick up in weather like this." Alderheart looked up at the sky. *The dark sky must not herald a storm.* Was this the beginning of the storm StarClan had warned them about? Was Dovewing's disappearance something to do with it?

Lionblaze interrupted his thoughts. "Twigpaw told us she saw Dovewing talking with Tigerheart on SkyClan land."

"When?" Worry pricked Alderheart's belly. Was Tigerheart the reason Dovewing had left?

"A quarter moon ago," Ivypool mewed.

Thornclaw and Lionblaze exchanged glances.

Ivypool frowned. "We have to find her before she does anything stupid."

No one responded. Instead, Thornclaw turned his muzzle toward the nursery. "I'm going to see if Blossomfall and the kits are warm enough." The warrior headed toward the thick bramble bush and disappeared inside. Lionblaze padded to the warriors' den.

Ivypool looked anxiously at Fernsong. "Do they think she's a traitor?"

Fernsong touched his muzzle to Ivypool's cheek. "Dovewing could never be a traitor. Lionblaze knows that more than anyone. She helped him fight the Dark Forest, remember?"

Ivypool's eyes clouded. "I just hope she's safe."

As she spoke, pebbles clattered down from the top of the cliff and showered Highledge.

Alderheart looked up nervously. Rainwater was streaming down the rock face. Ferns and brambles sagged over the top, oozing muddy water from their roots. The earth groaned.

Ivypool's fur bristled. "Perhaps we should evacuate the camp." She glanced at the fallen beech where the elders' den nestled beneath dead branches. "Weather like this washed that tree from the top of the cliff. It killed Longtail and crippled Briarlight."

Alderheart looked toward the medicine den. It seemed safe, tucked into a hollow in the cliff face. But its roof opened to the sky. Could rocks fall inside? "I'll go and ask Jayfeather if we should move Briarlight to the warriors' den until the weather clears."

As he spoke, the cliff top groaned again. His heart lurched as a chunk of rock shifted at the top. With a creak, it broke away from the cliff face and dropped like a diving hawk, pulling soil and plants after it. Alderheart leaped for the edge of camp as it smashed onto Highledge, earth and stones cascading around it.

Dazed, he looked at Ivypool and Fernsong. They'd dived clear and were crouching against the walls of the elders' den.

Ivypool's eyes were wide with panic. She lifted her muzzle as cats scrambled into the clearing. "Clear the camp!"

Lionblaze shot from the warriors' den, Brackenfur at his heels. He looked at the cliff, where earth hung and bushes dangled over the edge. Cracks snaked through the rock below the rim. The crack of splitting stone rang across the camp. Lionblaze's amber gaze hardened. "Brackenfur." He jerked his muzzle toward his denmate. "Make sure the warriors' den and the elders' den are cleared. Get everyone to the lakeshore."

Brackenfur nodded. "Cinderheart! Bumblestripe!" He called to his Clanmates, who stumbled, wide-eyed, into the flooded clearing, and repeated Lionblaze's order.

They nodded curtly. Cinderheart disappeared inside the den while Bumblestripe stood outside and nosed warriors toward the thorn entrance tunnel.

Brackenfur called to Poppyfrost. "Get Graystripe and Millie out of camp," he ordered. As Poppyfrost raced toward the fallen beech, he ran to the entrance. "Head for the lakeshore," he yowled as Whitewing, Lilyheart, and Stormcloud streamed past him.

Ivypool and Fernsong waited at the nursery entrance. Thornclaw was already scrambling out, Eaglekit swinging from his jaws. Daisy followed him, running for the camp entrance as Blossomfall passed Shellkit and Stemkit through the opening in the brambles. Fernsong and Ivypool grabbed the kits by the scruff and raced away. As Blossomfall snatched up Plumkit and followed, an ominous crack sounded from the cliff top.

Alderheart stared, frozen with terror, as a lump of stone peeled away and fell toward the clearing. Lionblaze raced at him, shouldering him backward until he was pinned against the thorn barrier. Behind him, rubble and earth exploded as the stone hit Highledge and rolled into the clearing. It sent a wave of muddy water sweeping across the camp, drenching the fleeing cats.

Icy cold pierced Alderheart's pelt, shocking him from his panicked stupor. "Jayfeather!" He raced for the medicine den. "Briarlight!"

Lionblaze hared after him as he scrabbled over the mound of rubble at the heart of the camp. The golden tom called to his Clanmates. "Cloudtail! Birchfall! Snowbush! Come, help us!"

Alderheart burst through the lichen that draped the entrance to the medicine den. Jayfeather was shielding Briarlight, stretched over her as mud and stones showered down from the cliff top.

The earth above the den seemed to roar as more stone and mud cascaded into the camp.

Lionblaze shoved Jayfeather out of the way and grabbed Briarlight by her scruff. He dragged her from her nest. Birchfall ducked under her hindquarters and lifted her onto his shoulders. Between them, the two warriors carried her out of the den.

"My herbs!" Jayfeather screeched.

"Leave them!" Cloudtail yowled.

"They're half-rotten anyway." Alderheart tried to nudge Jayfeather toward the den entrance. But the blind medicine cat dug his claws into the ground. "We've been gathering them for a moon. They have to see us through leaf-bare." He glared at Alderheart and Cloudtail.

Snowbush darted to the crack in the cliff where the herbs were stored and began dragging them out, bundle after bundle. Cloudtail snatched up as many as he could hold in his jaws. Jayfeather grabbed a mouthful. Alderheart pawed the wads of catmint together and gripped them between his teeth. He turned to follow Cloudtail and Jayfeather out of the den.

Snowbush was still hauling out herbs.

"Leave them!" Alderheart tried to make himself heard through the leaves blocking his mouth.

Snowbush paused and blinked at him.

Alderheart beckoned the white warrior away with a panicked flick of his tail. Earth and stones were falling more heavily into the den. In a moment, they might be submerged in mud. Snowbush grabbed a fat bundle of thyme and mallow and headed for the entrance.

Alderheart slid ahead of him and raced across the camp.

Poppyfrost and Cherryfall were herding Millie and Graystripe through the thorn tunnel. Lionblaze waited there, herbs dangling from his jaws, his gaze scanning the clearing. Alderheart and Snowbush were the last cats left. Lionblaze beckoned them, his eyes glittering urgently. Alderheart saw him glance at the cliff top, terror swamping his gaze. He slowed and turned, looking up.

A massive piece of stone was breaking away from the cliff face. It seemed to slip like ice and drop toward the clearing. Soil, bushes, and stones showered around it. Time seemed to slow as Alderheart watched. Then he felt Snowbush's muzzle shove him from behind. Lionblaze hooked Alderheart's scruff with an outstretched paw and dragged him forward as the stone hit the clearing, splitting the air with a roar as it shattered into countless pieces.

The rush of air knocked Alderheart into Lionblaze. He dropped his herbs as he landed and waited for the blast of stone against his pelt. Earth showered around him. A wave of muddy water engulfed him. Then the camp fell silent except for the steady pounding of the rain.

Alderheart lifted his head.

Lionblaze groaned beside him and heaved himself to his paws. "Are you hurt?"

Alderheart moved, surprised to feel no pain. He pushed himself up shakily. "Snowbush." His mew was thick with mud. He spat it out and glanced back.

A white scrap of fur lay beside the heap of mud and rubble. Lionblaze raced toward it. "Snowbush!"

Alderheart scrambled to Lionblaze's side. "Is he breathing?" He pushed past the golden tom and pressed his ear to Snowbush's mouth. There was no sound. "Quick!" Alderheart jerked his nose to the rubble, which buried Snowbush's hindquarters. "Pull him clear."

Lionblaze thrust his muzzle beneath Snowbush's lolling head and grabbed his scruff. With a grunt, he heaved him clear of the debris and laid him at the edge of the clearing.

Alderheart rolled the white warrior onto his back and thumped his paws against his chest. Pressing them against his ribs, he pushed down and released, then pushed down again. *I have to get him breathing again.* "Fetch help," he told Lionblaze.

Lionblaze stared blankly.

"Hurry!" Alderheart growled.

Lionblaze turned and raced from the camp.

Alderheart pushed harder against Snowbush's chest. Feeling his way down, he pushed his paws beneath Snowbush's ribs and pushed again, grunting with the effort.

Snowbush jerked and spewed up muddy water.

Hope flashed in Alderheart's belly. He ran his paws over the tom's mud-smeared pelt, feeling for broken bones. He stiffened as he ran his pads down his hind leg. A bump betrayed a jagged crack in the bone.

Snowbush opened his eyes blearily, blinking against the rain that soaked his face.

"You're safe," Alderheart told him. "But your hind leg is broken. Lionblaze has gone to fetch help."

As he spoke, Lionblaze raced back through the entrance.

Molewhisker, Birchfall, and Larksong followed, Lilyheart behind them. Her eyes sparked with anguish when she saw Snowbush. She slid past her Clanmates and crouched beside her mate. He seemed small, his fur slicked by rain and mud, his eyes glittering with pain.

"He's okay," Alderheart told her. He wished Jayfeather were here. "His leg is broken, but that's all." He knew he wasn't telling her the whole truth: that for a moment Snowbush had stopped breathing, and that there might be worse damage beneath his pelt than a broken bone.

"Let's get him away from here." Lilyheart looked fearfully at the cliff top.

"Be gentle," Alderheart cautioned as Lionblaze and Birchfall crouched on either side of their injured Clanmate.

"I can walk." Snowbush rolled over and heaved himself to his paws, letting out a low groan. Lionblaze and Birchfall pressed against either side of him, lifting him as he limped weakly toward the camp entrance, holding his broken leg clear of the ground. Molewhisker and Lilyheart followed, keeping close.

Larksong glanced around the camp, his eyes wide with disbelief. Alderheart followed his gaze numbly. Highledge was hidden beneath a pile of dirt and stone. Rubble covered the clearing and reached to the edges of the camp. Mud and twigs plastered every den. Plants and bushes, dragged down by the mudslide, stuck out like wounded limbs from the debris. Stones blocked the entrance to the medicine den.

Alderheart looked at the storm-black clouds and let the

rain wash the mud from his face. "Will it ever stop?" he murmured.

Larksong looked at him hopefully. "Maybe this was the storm StarClan promised. Maybe it's over now."

"Perhaps," Alderheart breathed. *Or perhaps it's only just begun.*

CHAPTER 18

Violetpaw squinted as sunshine sliced through the evening air, its weak rays warming her damp pelt. Lifting her face, she closed her eyes and relished the brightness. The clouds were clearing at last.

In the days since rescuing Frecklewish, they had trudged through the relentless rain. And yet, despite the dismal weather, Violetpaw's heart had been light. Fidgetpaw and Frecklewish had shared stories, Mintfur and Nettlesplash joining in. Fringepaw and Nectarpaw had gradually lost their shyness, and they felt like denmates already. Their spirits had lifted with every paw step. Their excitement at seeing the land beyond the gorge was infectious. Even Gravelpaw and Palepaw were complaining less. Violetpaw couldn't wait to show them around SkyClan's new territory.

Molewhisker seemed almost more like a Clanmate than Sparrowpelt or Harrybrook. He shared his prey, and he was as protective of the apprentices as any of SkyClan's warriors. When Nectarpaw had wandered too close to a Twoleg patrol, he had rushed to shoo her away.

Rabbitleap had stayed close to Violetpaw, training her as

they traveled without ever being bossy. He'd hunted beside her, gently offering advice on stalking techniques and scent trails. Blossomheart and Hawkwing had stuck close to Cherrytail and Cloudmist. They were delighted that their kin had decided to leave Barley's farm and travel to SkyClan's new territory.

Violetpaw remembered how nervous Hawkwing had been as they'd approached Barley's farm just a quarter of a moon earlier. He hadn't said anything, but she'd been able to read anxiety in the stiffness of his tail and the way his ears twitched. What if his mother and sister had chosen to stay with Barley? He would have had to make his new home beside the lake without them.

They had arrived at Barley's farm the morning after Frecklewish's rescue, having traveled through a rainy night. The shelter and warmth of the barn had felt like a blessing from StarClan, and Barley had organized the hungry party into hunting patrols while Hawkwing faced Cloudmist and Cherrytail.

He hadn't needed to speak. They had met his hopeful gaze with round, anxious eyes. Violetpaw could see from the quiver along his spine that he thought for a moment that they were going to tell him they wanted to stay on the farm. But Cherrytail had stepped forward and touched muzzles with her son.

"We're coming with you."

Her words seemed to lift a weight from Hawkwing's shoulders. Purring, he wove around them, promising that they had made the right decision and would never regret moving to SkyClan's new territory.

Now, days later, as they trekked along another sweeping hillside, the lake glittered on the horizon.

"Look!" Violetpaw saw the water first, sparkling in the dying rays of evening sun.

Nectarpaw bounced excitedly beside her. "Is that it?"

"What?" Gravelpaw pushed between them, craning his neck.

"The lake! Over there." Violetpaw nodded with her muzzle. It looked wide even from here, stretching between hillside and forest. She felt the tug of home and wondered how Twigpaw was doing. It must have felt strange to be left alone in SkyClan. Violetpaw wondered again why Twigpaw had stayed behind. Perhaps she was hoping to show Leafstar that she was a loyal Clanmate. Violetpaw knew how much Twigpaw enjoyed the praise of older cats. *I guess that is just her way of fitting in.* Violetpaw understood her sister's need to be accepted. *Didn't I try to persuade ShadowClan to accept me as one of their own?* And the rogues. In the end, Needletail had been the only Shadow-Clan cat to treat her like kin. Violetpaw felt the familiar pang of grief. Needletail hadn't visited her since they'd reached the gorge. *She must be mad at me.*

Palepaw interrupted her thoughts. "Where is our new camp?"

Violetpaw stretched her nose toward the dark trees rising to one side of the lake. "Do you see those pines?"

Fringepaw climbed the verge beside the rabbit trail they

were following. "I see them!"

"Where?" Palepaw pushed alongside her sister.

"Over there!" Fringepaw mewed eagerly.

Gravelpaw frowned. "Is the camp in a *forest*?"

"It must be dark all the time." Palepaw glanced anxiously at Violetpaw.

"The camp's not far from the lakeshore," Violetpaw told her. "And living in a forest is great. It's sheltered and there's always prey."

"There was always prey by the gorge," Gravelpaw told her. "*And* there was a stream to drink from."

"There's a stream in the new camp," Violetpaw mewed.

Mintfur, who was a few tail-lengths ahead with Nettle-splash and Rabbitleap, glanced over her shoulder. "I hope it hasn't flooded."

Violetpaw's pelt prickled anxiously. What if it had? What if the camp had been washed away while they were gone?

Behind her, Hawkwing sniffed casually. "That stream will never flood." He was padding between Cloudmist and Cherrytail, while Molewhisker and Blossomheart flanked them. "The forest floor is too mossy. Rain can soak away easily. And there are channels that drain water toward the lake."

Gravelpaw's gaze was fixed on the horizon. "How long before we get there?"

"Two more sunups?" Hawkwing glanced questioningly at Molewhisker.

Molewhisker nodded. "We won't be there in time for tomorrow's full-moon gathering." He sounded unworried.

Violetpaw guessed that the ThunderClan tom had enjoyed his adventure with the SkyClan cats.

So what if they missed the Gathering? Wouldn't it be better to let their new Clanmates settle in before they met the other Clans? She remembered how overwhelmed she'd felt the first time she'd seen so many cats. And the other Clans would have more time to get used to the idea of SkyClan's new Clanmates. She wondered, with a twinge of unease, how ShadowClan would feel about SkyClan growing so fast. She guessed that it wasn't what they'd planned when they'd offered SkyClan part of their territory. But she pushed the thought away. Who cared how ShadowClan felt? She wasn't a ShadowClan cat anymore. Her new home was with Sky-Clan.

As the sun slipped below the horizon, Violetpaw felt a chill in her fur. Her belly growled with hunger.

"I'm tired," Fringepaw mewed.

"I'm hungry," Nectarpaw chimed in.

Mintfur pulled up and turned to the patrol. She looked at Hawkwing. "Should we make camp for the night?"

Violetpaw lifted her aching paws one at a time and shook them out, hoping he'd say yes.

Hawkwing scanned the hillside. He nodded to a dip where bushes gathered. A few trees circled it, promising shelter. "Let's try over there," he meowed. "That hollow looks like it might make a good camp."

Nettlesplash whisked his tail. "You check out the hollow. I'll take Gravelpaw and Nectarpaw hunting with Mintfur."

"I want to hunt too!" Palepaw mewed.

Hawkwing dipped his head. "Okay. We'll join you when we've had a look."

"I can make nests," Violetpaw offered. She could see a stretch of bracken farther downslope where she could gather fronds.

"I'll help," Fidgetpaw offered.

Frecklewish narrowed her gaze as she peered through the dying light. "I think I can see burdock. I'll dig up some roots. It will help with our aching paws."

Cloudmist blinked gratefully at the medicine cat. "It feels good to be part of a real Clan again."

Violetpaw's heart ached with sudden happiness. By the time the moon rose, she'd be settled into a fresh nest with a full belly, Clanmates at her side. She purred to herself. Clan life was better than she'd ever imagined before.

Violetpaw dreamed. Sunlight bathed a wide field. Ahead of her, a fat mouse scuttled through the grass. Licking her lips, she prepared to pounce. Something pricked at her pelt. *Go away.* She burrowed deeper into her dream. The mouse was moving sleepily in the sunshine. It would be an easy catch. Her pelt pricked more sharply. *Stop it!* Irritation tightened Violetpaw's belly. Something was trying to wake her. She grumbled in her sleep, trying to ignore the feeling that was pestering her.

It nagged harder, dragging her at last into wakefulness.

She opened her eyes.

Darkness shrouded the small hollow. She could hear the soft breathing of her sleeping companions.

What had woken her? Puzzled, she lifted her head and tasted the air.

The cool night air carried the scent of Needletail.

She came back! Quickly, Violetpaw scrambled out of her nest. She threaded her way between her Clanmates and padded out of the hollow. The hillside was drenched in moonlight. She scanned the rippling grass for Needletail. *Please be here.* A shadow moved near the bottom of the slope where heather crowded. As Violetpaw raced toward it, the shadow slipped into the heather. "Needletail!" she hissed desperately as she neared. "Stop!" She crashed through the bushes, spying Needletail's pelt moving between the branches.

"Wait!" Fury pounded in Violetpaw's chest. "Why do you wake me up just to run away?" Was this Needletail's revenge? "I'm sorry I left! You told me to, remember? I wanted to save you! I just felt like there was nothing I could do. If I'd stayed, Darktail would have killed me, and then he'd have killed all our Clanmates. Did you want that?"

Needletail's pelt swished between the bushes. Then there was silence. Had she left?

Violetpaw pushed her way through the heather until it opened into a small clearing. Needletail waited there, her green eyes glinting in the moonlight.

"Are you angry with me?" Violetpaw stared at her. "Is that why you keep appearing?"

Needletail nodded toward a tom, curled in a moss nest beneath a clump of heather.

Violetpaw froze, then hurried toward Needletail and

lowered her voice. "Who is he?"

Needletail blinked at her. "He's a cat I met many moons ago."

Violetpaw was so surprised to hear Needletail's voice again that she hardly heard the words. *Why now?* She forced herself to concentrate as Needletail went on.

"I knew him when I was alive. Now he's around every time I return."

"Return?" Violetpaw's thoughts were spinning. "Return from where? Are you with StarClan?"

Needletail looked down at her softly glowing pelt. No stars showed there. "Do I look like I'm with StarClan?"

Violetpaw stiffened. "The Dark Forest?" she asked anxiously.

"No." Needletail shifted her paws. "I don't know where I go. I only know that when I open my eyes, I'm near him."

"Can he see you?"

"Yes." Needletail flicked her ears. "He's the only one who can. Well, him and you."

"Is he dead too?" Violetpaw's pelt rippled nervously along her spine.

"No." Needletail looked at her as though she were a mouse-brain. "That's why I wanted to show him to you. I think he's important to the Clans. I think that's why I'm stuck here and why he's always near."

"What can I do to help?" Violetpaw was puzzled.

"Take him with you," Needletail ordered. "Take him to the Clans."

"Why?"

Needletail shrugged. "I don't know. All I know is that I can see him and I can see you. I think that I'm meant to make you two meet and that you're meant to take him to the Clans. If I help the Clans, then maybe I'll find StarClan."

Violetpaw gazed into Needletail's eyes, pity twisting her heart. *It must be so lonely here.* "I'll take him," she promised.

Needletail turned toward the heather.

"Are you leaving?" Violetpaw blinked at her.

"This is your quest now."

"Don't go!" One thought blazed in Violetpaw's mind. *Are you still angry with me?* Too scared to ask out loud, she stared imploringly at Needletail. Urgency flashed in her friend's eyes.

"Please," Needletail begged.

She needs me! Violetpaw's heart lifted, glad she could help. *But has she forgiven me?* "Wait—" Before she could finish, Needletail disappeared among the heather. As the breeze whisked away her scent, Violetpaw knew she was gone.

She heard moss stir beside her. The tom was waking. She backed away, her pelt bristling as he lifted his head and yawned.

He stiffened as he caught sight of her. "Who are you?" In a moment, he was on his paws, hackles high.

"Needletail brought me here," Violetpaw mewed quickly.

"Needletail?" The tom looked surprised. "Can *you* see her too?"

"Yes." Violetpaw didn't entirely trust this tom. She glanced toward a gap in the heather. She could dart away there if he turned nasty. "She was my friend, when she was alive."

"I met her when she was an apprentice." The tom narrowed his eyes. "I didn't see her again until after she died."

"Why do you keep following her?" Violetpaw asked.

The tom looked indignant. "*She* keeps following *me*." He glanced around the small clearing. "Is she here?"

"She just left." Violetpaw shifted her paws. "She brought me here to meet you."

The tom's eyes sparkled mischievously. "That was kind of her. Perhaps she thinks we're soul mates."

"Soul mates?" Violetpaw was confused.

"It *is* kind of romantic, don't you think? The moonlight? The heather?"

Romantic? Violetpaw bristled. "Do you flirt with every strange cat you meet?"

"Only the ones who appear in the middle of the night claiming a ghost brought them."

Violetpaw struggled for words. This tom was being impossible. "Stop it!" she snapped. "Needletail brought me to you for a reason." She saw his eyes flash with mischief again and pushed on quickly. "She thinks you might help the Clans."

The tom rolled his eyes. "You're a *Clan* cat." He sounded disappointed.

"So?" Violetpaw glared at him.

"There are two things I know about Clan cats." He climbed out of his nest. "They don't like strangers on their land, and they take everything *way* too seriously."

"I don't!" Violetpaw mewed indignantly.

The tom's ears twitched. "You seem to be taking this very seriously."

"That's because it *is* serious!" Violetpaw turned her tail on him, fuming, and began to march through the heather.

"Hey, wait!" He hurried after her. "I thought you and Needletail wanted me to help the Clans."

"I doubt that you've ever helped anyone but yourself." Violetpaw kept walking.

"That's not fair. You don't even know me." The tom wove ahead of her and blocked her way as she emerged onto the moonlit hillside.

She stared at him, not speaking.

"My name is Tree." He rounded his eyes apologetically. "I didn't mean to tease. I didn't realize it would upset you."

Violetpaw stared at her paws, annoyed that he'd been able to ruffle her fur so easily. "My name is Violetpaw," she mumbled.

"That's a pretty name."

She jerked up her muzzle. "Don't start flirting again!"

He stepped back. "I'm not. It's just a pretty name. Most of the cats I meet are called Rocky or Snake or something dumb like that. And my name's *Tree*."

Violetpaw narrowed her eyes suspiciously. "Are you a rogue?"

Tree shrugged. "I don't know what I am. I travel alone and I hunt and sleep where I like."

Violetpaw looked away and sniffed. "A loner."

"Is that what Clan cats call me?"

For the first time, she heard uncertainty in his mew. "I guess it's better than being a rogue," she conceded. She looked him over. He was muscular. His yellow pelt looked thick and well groomed. His amber eyes were bright and clear. *Take him with you.* Needletail's words rang in her mind. *Take him to the Clans.* Perhaps her friend was right. Perhaps the Clans needed him. And it might help Needletail find her way to StarClan.

"We're camped up there." She nodded toward the hollow.

"We?"

"Me and my Clanmates," Violetpaw explained. "We're heading home. You should come with us."

"Why?"

"Needletail thinks the Clans need you."

"Needletail's dead."

"Then she probably knows more than we do." Was this tom going to make everything difficult? "Come to the hollow at dawn. If you come now, you might alarm the others." She turned away, pausing when he didn't comment. "Will you come?"

"I guess."

Violetpaw shrugged, trying not to seem too eager. "It might be the only way to stop Needletail haunting you." She walked away, hoping that he would come. *I tried,* she told Needletail silently.

An angry yowl woke Violetpaw. She jerked her head up, blinking at the dawn light. Her companions' nests were empty. Hisses sounded from the edge of the hollow. *Tree!* She remembered at once and leaped up.

"Why are you here?" Hawkwing's growl sounded beyond the bushes.

"Violetpaw told me to come."

Violetpaw heard Tree's mew and pushed past the bushes. "He's right!" She stopped beside Hawkwing. "I did tell him to come."

Nettlesplash and Rabbitleap stood behind Tree, their hackles high. Mintfur and Blossomheart flanked him while Frecklewish stared at him through narrowed eyes and the apprentices hung back and watched. He was surrounded.

As he saw Violetpaw, relief flashed in his gaze. "You took your time." He smoothed his fur. "I was beginning to think you'd tricked me."

Hawkwing looked at Violetpaw, puzzled. "Who is he? Where did you meet him?"

"I found him last night," she mewed. "Needletail led me to him."

Hawkwing's eyes widened. "I thought Needletail was dead."

"She is." Violetpaw felt suddenly helpless. How was she going to explain?

Frecklewish nosed her way between her Clanmates. "Was Needletail from StarClan?"

Violetpaw looked at the medicine cat, hope pricking her paws. "She hasn't found StarClan yet, but she says she can't seem to escape this cat. She thinks he's important. She said that if we take him to the Clans, he might be able to help us. Then she'll be able to find her way to StarClan. I think we should let him come with us."

Nettlesplash stalked around Tree, sniffing him. "Does he *want* to come with us?"

"I don't have anything else to do," Tree sniffed. "And if you think I could help, I guess it can't do any harm."

Fidgetpaw padded from the bushes, a vole dangling from his jaws. He dropped it and stared at Tree. "Who's this?"

"This is Tree." Nettlesplash flicked his tail impatiently. "Violetpaw's dead friend found him. She thinks he might be important to the Clans. She wants him to travel home with us."

Gravelpaw shouldered his way past Mintfur. "Is he a rogue like Darktail?"

Tree sniffed. "Violetpaw says I'm a loner."

"A loner can't do any harm," Mintfur mewed.

"He seems friendly," Rabbitleap commented.

"Can he hunt?" Blossomheart asked.

Tree sat down and looked longingly at Fidgetpaw's vole. "While you discuss me, do you mind if I eat this?" He swiped his tongue around his lips. "I'm starving."

Fidgetpaw nudged it toward him. "Go ahead. There seems to be plenty of prey here."

"Thanks." Tree grabbed it and took a bite.

"I'm not sure Leafstar will be pleased if we bring back a loner," Blossomheart mewed.

Mintfur twitched her tail. "But what if Violetpaw is right?

What if he *is* important to the Clans? If we leave him here, we might never find him again."

"What if he's lying?" Gravelpaw's ear twitched uncertainly. "He might be a rogue. He might be like Darktail. There might be a whole gang of rogues waiting for us to show him the way to our new camp."

Tree poked the vole toward Violetpaw. "Have a bite," he meowed. "You must be hungry. You were up half the night."

She looked at him, wondering how he could be so relaxed.

"*Are* you a rogue?" Hawkwing nodded at Tree.

Tree looked at him. "I'm not sure what a rogue is. I told Violetpaw last night—I travel alone. I was born in the wild. My mother left me as soon as I was old enough to hunt. I've spent most of my life trying to stay away from Twolegs. They are obsessed with trying to tempt me into their nests with food, but I don't want to live in a Twoleg nest. Twolegs are noisy, and they smell weird."

Frecklewish let out a purr. "I know what you mean." Her gaze warmed as it met Tree's. "I've just escaped from a Twoleg *hive*."

"Really?" Tree looked shocked. "How long were you there?"

"Moons." Frecklewish nodded at Violetpaw. "Luckily, Violetpaw thought of a way for me to escape."

Tree winked at Violetpaw. "She's clearly got a talent for rescuing cats." He swallowed another mouthful and burped. "So?" He looked around the SkyClan cats. "Am I coming with you?"

Hawkwing and Frecklewish exchanged looks. Then Frecklewish nodded.

"Yes." Hawkwing dipped his head to the yellow tom. "If you'd like to."

Violetpaw glanced at the sky, wondering if StarClan was watching. *Does this mean you'll help Needletail find her way to you?* She looked at Tree, who was washing his vole-stained paws. If Needletail could find her way to StarClan, it would be worth putting up with this arrogant mouse-brain.

CHAPTER 19

For the first time in days, Twigpaw's fur felt dry. She relished the fresh breeze in her pelt as she followed Sparrowpelt and Sandynose along the ridge that led to the ThunderClan border. Leafstar had sent them to re-mark the scent line, washed away after days of rain.

Sandynose nodded toward the stretch of forest where pine gave way to oak. Twigpaw breathed the ThunderClan scents that rolled across the border, trying to ignore a pang of homesickness. She focused on Sandynose.

"Well-marked borders make good neighbors," he meowed. "When every cat is clear where their boundaries lie, there is no excuse for misunderstandings. And misunderstandings can lead to battles."

Twigpaw tried hard to look attentive. She pushed away a prickle of resentment. Was Sandynose trying to remind her that she hadn't reported seeing Dovewing and Tigerheart inside SkyClan territory? *He's just trying to be a good mentor,* she told herself sternly. She was determined to earn her warrior name. This wasn't just her Clan; it was Hawkwing's and Violetpaw's Clan too. When they returned, she wanted them to be proud of her.

"What did I say?" Sandynose was staring at her.

"Good borders make good neighbors," Twigpaw repeated, hoping he hadn't said anything else important while she'd been caught in her own thoughts.

"Good." He looked pleased.

She puffed out her chest, relieved.

Sparrowpelt marked the pines along the edge. "I can't wait until my kits are old enough to explore here." He glanced around the forest. "It's a good place to grow up." The lake was visible between the trees, sparkling in the bright leaf-fall sunshine. Needles crunched beneath his paws. Prey-scents hung on the air.

"Has Quailkit recovered from his sniffles?" Twigpaw asked.

"Yes." Sparrowpelt purred. "Leafpool gave him coltsfoot. This morning he felt so much better, he wanted to see if he could jump the stream. Sunnykit and Pigeonkit dared him to try."

Sandynose flicked his tail. "It sounds as though Tinycloud has her paws full with those three."

"They're a joy," Sparrowpelt meowed as he marked another tree. "Now I want the Clan to thrive, not just for my Clanmates, but for them."

"Kits can be a worry." Sandynose's gaze darkened thoughtfully. "We have so many hopes for them. And yet we can't protect them from every danger or disappointment." Twigpaw pricked her ears. Was he talking about Finpaw? She wandered farther along the border, sniffing for stale markers as he went on. "And they grow up so quickly, so sure they know everything, and so determined to make their own choices, even if they're wrong. We can only pray that StarClan guides their paws."

Twigpaw hurried ahead, following a weak scent line and refreshing it as she went. If he was complaining about Finpaw's friendship with her, she didn't want to hear.

"Well done!" Sandynose called to her through the trees. "You picked up that scent line well."

Was he actually praising her? She looked at him, puzzled. Perhaps he wasn't dropping hints about her friendship with Finpaw after all. *Stop being paranoid!*

"You seem to have a natural sense of where the border lies," Sandynose went on. Twigpaw didn't tell him that it used to be the old border with ShadowClan, and she'd marked the ThunderClan side many times with Ivypool. "Head toward the lake, and mark the border there," he told her. "Sparrowpelt and I will head toward the ditches."

He trusted her to work alone. Twigpaw lifted her tail. Had she won his confidence at last? Hope pricking in her pelt, she crossed the rise and followed a gully toward the lake, carefully marking each tree as she passed.

"Twigpaw!"

She froze as she heard Finpaw's mew. His pelt flashed behind a bramble, and he bounced out, excitedly, and stopped in front of her.

She glanced nervously between the trees. She could still see Sandynose and Sparrowpelt heading inland. "Aren't you supposed to be training with Bellaleaf?" she breathed.

Finpaw paced excitedly back and forth. "She said I'd done enough training this morning. I'm allowed to explore. So I thought I'd come and explore with you."

"I'm training." Twigpaw shifted uneasily.

"I thought you were marking borders," Finpaw mewed. "I can help."

Her pelt pricked guiltily. "I'm not meant to hang out with you," she mewed softly.

Finpaw frowned. "Why not?"

Twigpaw glanced toward Sandynose. He had disappeared behind some bracken. "Your father thinks you'll learn quicker if I'm not distracting you all the time."

"Sandynose said that?" Finpaw's eyes widened. "He must have bees in his brain. You've helped me so much!"

"Maybe you should just stick with Bellaleaf for now. You do have a lot of catching up to do." Twigpaw tried to smooth over the awkwardness. She didn't want to sour Finpaw's relationship with his father. "We can hang out when we're warriors."

"Yeah, right." Finpaw lashed his tail angrily. "Like you'll want to hang out with me once you're a great warrior and I'm just lumbering around like a clumsy badger because I've only got a half tail."

Twigpaw stared at him. "I'll always want to hang out with you."

"So you think I *will* be like a clumsy badger?"

"No!" Twigpaw's ears twitched uncomfortably. "Of course not. You're going to be a great warrior too, if you train hard."

Finpaw grunted crossly. "I'm never going to be the warrior

Sandynose hoped I would be. *He* knows it and I know it. It's probably why he doesn't want me hanging out with you. He probably thinks I'll hold you back."

Twigpaw stared at him. "That's not true."

"Then why does he want to keep us apart?"

Twigpaw shrugged. Should she tell him that she suspected Sandynose would only ever see her as a disloyal ThunderClan cat?

"It's not fair." Finpaw sat down. "I'm never going to be a great warrior, and now I'm not allowed to be friends with you."

"No one will ever stop us being friends." Twigpaw padded close. She stared at him until he returned her gaze. "You're special to me."

"I am?"

"Of course you are." Twigpaw nudged his cheek with her nose. "Once we're warriors, no one will be able to keep us apart. I don't care if it puts Sandynose's tail in a twist. You're going to prove to him that you're a great warrior and so am I. We'll be the best warriors in SkyClan, and he won't be able to stop us doing anything we want."

Finpaw lifted his muzzle, his eyes bright. "You're right. He might think he knows best now, but once we can outrun, out-hunt, and outfight him, he won't be able to tell us what to do."

"Exactly." Twigpaw's heart lurched as she glimpsed a brown pelt between the trees. Sandynose was watching them. "But you'd better go and find Bellaleaf now. I've got borders to mark before your father gets back."

"Okay." Finpaw stood up and flicked his half tail happily.

"I'll see you back at camp later." He trotted away, glancing over his shoulder as he went.

As he disappeared behind the brambles, Twigpaw turned toward Sandynose. Her mentor was heading toward her. She tried to read his gaze. Was he angry that she'd been talking to Finpaw?

"*He* came to talk to me," she mewed defensively.

"And you sent him away." Sandynose looked satisfied. "You did well. The harder each of you concentrates on your duties, the faster you'll earn your warrior names."

And the faster Finpaw will lose interest in a ThunderClan traitor. Twigpaw turned away. "I'll go and mark the rest of the border." She headed for the lake.

"We'll meet you on the shore when you're done," Sandynose called after her.

Twigpaw tried to keep her pelt smooth. She should be happy that she'd finally pleased Sandynose. But she couldn't help feeling that she'd been mouse-hearted. In ThunderClan, she'd be a warrior by now. She would never have let a SkyClan cat boss her around. Did she want to be a SkyClan cat so much that she was willing to roll over and act like prey whenever Sandynose ordered her to? Anxiety rippled through her pelt. Would she ever earn the respect she'd had in ThunderClan? Was this what it cost to stay with Hawkwing, Violetpaw, and Finpaw?

Twigpaw followed Sandynose and Sparrowpelt back to camp. As they neared the cedar grove, she stiffened.

ThunderClan scent. The familiar smells of Ivypool, Cinderheart, and Bumblestripe hung on the bracken that lined the path. She leaned down and sniffed the needle-strewn earth, and their scents bathed her nose. They had come this way recently.

She quickened her step, hurrying through the camp entrance.

The three ThunderClan warriors faced Leafstar, speaking in low mews. Bellaleaf and Sagenose listened as Finpaw moved restlessly behind them. Leafpool wove anxiously around her Clanmates. Violetpaw could see there was something wrong. Ivypool's pelt was unkempt. Bumblestripe's fur was streaked with mud. She could see swelling around Cinderheart's ears.

"There was no warning," Ivypool meowed.

"The camp is ruined." Bumblestripe's eyes were wide and dark.

"What's happened?" She hurried forward, cutting into the conversation.

Ivypool blinked at her solemnly. "There was a rockslide in the camp," she told her grimly.

Twigpaw tried to picture it, her belly tightening. "From the cliff?"

Bumblestripe nodded. "The rain loosened the earth up there. It brought down a great chunk of the cliff face."

"Is anyone hurt?" Twigpaw could hardly believe her ears.

"Everyone is battered and bruised," Ivypool told her. "But no one died."

"Snowbush is badly injured." Cinderheart's eyes sparkled with worry. "Alderheart hasn't left his side."

Twigpaw's throat tightened. "Is Lilyheart okay?" Lilyheart had been almost a mother to her.

"She's fine," Cinderheart told her. "But she's worried about Snowbush. We all are."

Sparrowpelt padded closer. "Did Blossomfall's kits escape?"

"We got them out before the worst of it," Ivypool reported.

Leafpool looked at Leafstar. "Perhaps I should return to ThunderClan to help with the injuries."

"It's okay," Ivypool assured her. "Alderheart and Jayfeather are managing."

"But you said the medicine den is full of mud and stone." Leafpool's fur rippled along her spine.

"That's why we came," Ivypool told her. "We rescued some of the herbs. But we lost most of them. We were hoping you could spare some of yours."

"Of course." Leafpool glanced toward her den, as though working out what she could give from her store.

"We can gather more herbs for you," Leafstar offered.

"I know what they look like. I can help," Twigpaw volunteered. Her early moons as a kit had been spent shadowing Alderheart while he'd been a medicine-cat apprentice.

Sandynose swished his tail. "You're supposed to be training," he told her.

She stared at him. "But this is an emergency."

"It's ThunderClan's emergency, not ours."

Twigpaw could hardly believe her ears. After all Thunder-Clan had done for SkyClan. How could he begrudge them help at a time like this?

Leafstar glanced around the camp. Fallowfern, Harry-brook and Plumwillow were watching from beside the stream. "I don't have many cats, but I'll be glad to spare them," she told Ivypool. "And of course Twigpaw can help." She looked sternly at Sandynose. "I'm sure her training can wait."

Ivypool's ears twitched. "I'm surprised there's anything left for her to learn," she mewed. "But we appreciate your help. ThunderClan is camped on the shore until we can shift the earth and stones away from the dens. Patrols have been working day and night since the rain stopped. We're making good progress. But we need herbs for the injured."

Leafstar nodded to Twigpaw. "If Leafpool tells you what herbs you need to gather, can you lead a patrol to find them?"

Twigpaw nodded eagerly.

"They'll need thyme, comfrey, and marigold," Leafpool told her. "Goldenrod if you can find it, nettles if you can't."

Leafstar signaled with her tail. "Take Fallowfern, Harrybrook and Plumwillow with you," she told Twigpaw. She turned to Ivypool. "Bellaleaf and Finpaw can escort you back to camp. Make use of them."

Sandynose's pelt ruffled. "Who's going to protect our camp with so many cats gone?" He looked toward the nursery, where Tinycloud was peering from the entrance.

"I'm sure we'll be safe enough until sundown," Leafstar told him. She nodded Twigpaw away with her nose. "The sooner you start, the more herbs you'll find."

Twigpaw headed for the entrance, pleased that she could help.

Sandynose followed her. He blocked her path and leaned close to her ear as Fallowfern and Harrybrook hurried toward her. "You can't live with a paw in two camps," he hissed.

She stepped away, blinking at him. "Are you accusing me of being disloyal?"

"No." His gaze was cold. "You will make a great warrior one day. But first you need to decide which Clan you want to fight for."

His words cut like thorns. She stared as he stalked away. And yet she couldn't feel angry with him. Guiltily, she recognized the truth. Shame scorched her pelt. Sandynose had seen something she didn't want to admit even to herself. Her heart lay as much with ThunderClan as with SkyClan. If staying here meant turning her back on her old Clan, was it a decision she could ever live with?

CHAPTER 20

Alderheart dipped his pad into the dried oak he'd chewed into ointment and ran it gently over the cut on Sorrelstripe's leg. She winced a little.

"How sore is it?" He checked for warmth and swelling at the edges of the broken skin, relieved when he found none.

"It just stings," she told him.

"It should heal in a few days," Alderheart assured her. He leaned back and looked around the makeshift camp. Nests crowded beneath the birch branches that overhung the shore. The swollen lake lapped the pebbles nearby. They'd built the camp hurriedly, and nests were unraveling, sticks and twigs dangling from them already, and moss scattered around their edges.

Bramblestar had reported that their camp in the hollow would be habitable soon, but it would be a long time before all the stone and earth would be completely cleared. Some of the fallen rocks were too big to move and would always remain in the clearing, a reminder of the disaster.

No cat died. Alderheart looked at the nest where Snowbush lay. *Not yet, at least.* The tom hadn't moved since he'd collapsed into it. Alderheart and Jayfeather had bound his broken leg and eased honey and nettles into his mouth to fight the fever that had gripped him. Lilyheart had hardly left his side. She was with him now, resting her front paws on the side of his nest. Her eyes glittered with worry. Alderheart wished he could tell her that Snowbush would recover soon, but the infection was lingering, and he could tell from the quiet way Jayfeather moved around him that the blind medicine cat didn't hold out much hope for the white tom.

As Sorrelstripe limped away, weariness dragged at Alderheart's bones. He'd hardly slept since the rockslide. There were too many cats to take care of. The falling stones had left the whole Clan cut and bruised. Perhaps now, though, he could nap. The Gathering was tonight. He wanted to be alert. What if one of the leaders brought a clue about the six-toed cat? *Or more evidence of the coming storm.*

He reasoned with himself, looking at the blue sky, reflected in the still lake. *The rain has stopped.* He wanted to believe the worst was over. But until StarClan's prophecy had been fulfilled and the six-toed cat had been found, how could there be anything but darkness waiting?

He crouched and rested his chin on his paws, allowing his eyes to close. Pebbles crunched as his Clanmates came and went around him. Fresh-kill scents drifted on the air. Eaglekit and Stemkit squeaked excitedly among the trees. *We are still here.* Alderheart comforted himself as sleep blurred the edges of his thoughts.

"Alderheart!" Lilyheart's panicked mew jerked him awake.

He jumped to his paws as Lilyheart shook Snowbush. The white tom's head lolled back, the whites of his eyes showing. Alderheart leaped across the pebbles and skidded to a halt beside the nest. "Jayfeather!" His wail echoed along the shore. Where had he gone?

He touched his paws to Snowbush's chest. The white tom jerked suddenly beneath them. Heat burned through Alderheart's pads. "We have to cool him down!" He ripped a wad of moss from the nest and shoved it toward Lilyheart. "Soak this in the lake and bring it back." Lilyheart snatched it between her jaws and raced for the water's edge.

Snowbush jerked again, flapping from one side of his nest to the other, his eyes staring blindly. Foam frothed at the corners of his mouth. "Help me hold him still," Alderheart yowled desperately.

Poppyfrost leaped to help, throwing herself over Snowbush's hind legs. Bumblestripe hurried to the nest and pushed his paws against Snowbush's chest. Alderheart tried to hold Snowbush's head still, but the tom was thrashing too wildly. His thoughts spun. Was there an herb that would stop this? He tried to think as Snowbush struggled in his paws. Had Jayfeather ever mentioned one?

"What's wrong with him?" Poppyfrost wailed, her eyes glittering with fear.

"The fever." Alderheart glanced at Snowbush's broken leg, flailing while Poppyfrost tried to pin it down. Could Snowbush feel the pain? Was he aware of anything? Desperation showed in the tom's frantic gaze. Spit dribbled from his mouth.

Suddenly, the tom fell still. Alderheart slumped with relief. The fit was over. Then he saw Snowbush's eyes. They were dull. Grief stabbed Alderheart's chest as he recognized death in them.

Pebbles swished as Lilyheart reached him. She dropped dripping moss beside the nest. "Is he okay now?" She gazed at Snowbush.

Alderheart dragged his gaze from the tom to the small, dark tabby she-cat. "He's dead," he croaked.

"Dead?" Lilyheart backed away. "But he survived the rock-slide. His leg was broken, that was all." She blinked in disbelief.

"We couldn't cure the infection." Alderheart gazed at her. He felt helpless. "It was inside. We couldn't reach it."

As he spoke, Jayfeather hurried toward him, weaving past Poppyfrost and Bumblestripe, who were staring in horror at Snowbush. The blind medicine cat reached the nest and touched his nose to Snowbush's throat. With a sigh, he gently closed the tom's eyes with his paw. "StarClan will protect him now."

Lilyheart's eyes flashed with anger. "Why didn't they protect him before?"

Jayfeather bowed his head wordlessly.

Alderheart searched for something to say that might comfort the she-cat, but her question rang in his mind like the plaintive cry of an owl. *Why didn't they protect him before?*

The journey to the island was slow. Alderheart's paws felt as heavy as his heart. Back in the makeshift camp, Millie and

Graystripe were sitting vigil, to be joined by the rest of the Clan when the Gathering was over. His Clanmates moved silently around him, as though drained of words by the horror of the past few days. Jayfeather had also stayed behind for the vigil.

Sparkpelt padded beside Alderheart, her pelt brushing his. He felt her looking at him from time to time, but she didn't speak; neither did he.

Bramblestar led the way over the tree-bridge and into the clearing. WindClan was already waiting beneath the Great Oak, their pelts rippling with anticipation. RiverClan wasn't here. Had Alderheart secretly hoped they would come? Perhaps. But he knew his hope had been empty.

SkyClan paced near the center. They seemed different from the lost Clan that had followed ThunderClan to the island a moon ago. This time they met the gazes of Wind-Clan and ShadowClan cats without apology. They walked with their heads up, purpose in their steps.

ShadowClan kept to the edge. Rowanstar sat in the shadows, away from his Clanmates. Had something happened? He remembered the tension he'd seen in their camp when he'd visited with Willowshine. Alderheart tried to catch the gazes of Puddleshine and then Tawnypelt, but it was like trying to catch butterflies in the wind. His belly tightened.

Alderheart took his place beside Kestrelflight and Leaf-pool. Puddleshine joined them but still avoided Alderheart's eye.

"How's Snowbush?" Leafpool asked.

Alderheart blinked at her, wishing there were a way to break the news more gently. "He died this afternoon." He still could hardly believe it.

Her eyes clouded. "The infection?"

"We couldn't stop it spreading." Guilt pricked at Alderheart's pelt.

Puddleshine shifted beside him. "I'm sorry," he meowed. "I didn't realize."

He noticed Puddleshine glancing at Rowanstar. "Are you okay?" he asked.

"I'm fine." Puddleshine shifted his paws uneasily.

Alderheart glanced questioningly at Kestrelflight.

Kestrelflight shrugged but didn't comment on Puddleshine's nervousness. Instead he returned the conversation to ThunderClan. "What caused Snowbush's infection?" he asked.

"A mudslide destroyed our camp during the storm," Alderheart told him. "Snowbush was crushed by falling rock."

Kestrelflight's eyes widened. "Do you think it's the prophecy?"

Alderheart returned his gaze. "I don't know," he mewed. "But I hope we find the six-toed cat soon. If the dark skies brought this, then what else will they bring?"

Puddleshine looked away quickly, as though hiding his thoughts.

Bramblestar leaped onto the lowest branch of the Great Oak, moving so that Harespring and Leafstar could take their places beside him. Rowanstar crossed the clearing wearily and jumped up beside them.

"It feels strange without Willowshine and Mothwing," Kestrelflight whispered, glancing at the empty space beside them.

Alderheart suddenly realized how many cats were missing. Not just RiverClan, but Dovewing and Snowbush. He glanced to the place where the deputies usually sat. The she-cat was alone beside Crowfeather. He guessed that Hawkwing had not yet returned from his quest to find SkyClan's missing Clanmates. But where was Tigerheart?

Bramblestar's mew interrupted his thoughts.

"We are here tonight with StarClan's blessing," he meowed. "The rains, which have battered every Clan, have brought special tragedy to ThunderClan. A mudslide pulled down part of the cliff that has always protected our camp. Snowbush died today of his injuries." Shocked whispers rippled through the Clans as Bramblestar went on. "Our camp will take a long time to clear. But the rest of the Clan suffered only minor injuries." He nodded to Leafstar. "SkyClan has kindly helped us by providing much-needed herbs."

"It was the least we could do," Leafstar dipped her head. "SkyClan is sorry for your tragedy. We will always be grateful that you have let Leafpool live with us while we are without our own medicine cat. Because of her, Tinycloud has brought three healthy kits into our Clan. Our camp is nearly finished, and we are enjoying our new territory. We hope to have more Clanmates soon. Hawkwing's patrol is expected back any day, and I feel certain he will bring with him old friends left behind at the gorge." She lifted her muzzle. "SkyClan will be a whole Clan once more."

"WindClan has also thrived, despite the weather," Harespring announced. He bowed to Bramblestar. "I am sorry for your loss. If there are any moorland herbs you need, Alderheart and Jayfeather are welcome to gather them. StarClan has blessed WindClan. The rains left us unscathed. Indeed, they have kept Twolegs and their dogs away. We have been able to hunt in peace and safety."

Alderheart felt a glimmer of hope. Perhaps he'd been too focused on ThunderClan's tragedy. WindClan and SkyClan seemed to be thriving. There were new kits in the Clans. ThunderClan had suffered in the mudslide, but the camp could be repaired. Snowbush's loss was heartbreaking, but the past moons had been filled with so many deaths; perhaps the loss of a single cat this moon was a sign the storms that had beset them were easing. Had the Clans avoided disaster without realizing it?

He puffed out his chest, ignoring the worry still gnawing in his belly, as Rowanstar shifted in the Great Oak. The ShadowClan leader looked hollow-eyed as he lifted his muzzle. His pelt clung to his frame, showing his ribs.

"You may have noticed," he began, "that Tigerheart is not present tonight."

Squirrelflight fidgeted uneasily as the Clans looked at the empty spot beside her.

"He went missing a few days ago."

Alderheart's pelt prickled along his spine. He glanced at

Ivypool. Her ears were twitching nervously. Brackenfur whispered in Cinderheart's ear. Bumblestripe and Honeyfur exchanged glances, and Ambermoon looked at her paws. They had all seen Tigerheart and Dovewing share prey when Tigerheart had lived with ThunderClan. Knowing looks had been exchanged when the two warriors had volunteered a little too eagerly for the same hunting patrol. Whispers had filled the elders' den and nursery when Dovewing had sat beside Tigerheart during Clan meetings.

When Dovewing had gone missing, the Clan had been worried, but beneath the worry there had been a sense of suspicion, which no cat had voiced under the defensive glare of Ivypool.

Now Ivypool seemed to shrink beneath her pelt. Tigerheart's disappearance was too much to be a coincidence. Could Dovewing really have deserted her Clan to be with the ShadowClan deputy?

Rowanstar went on. "We have sent out search parties, but he clearly took pains to cover his trail. There's been no sign of him. He gave no clue about where he was going or why he left."

Fernsong lifted his muzzle. "Perhaps he went in search of the six-toed cat."

Crowfeather scowled. "Tigerheart would love to be remembered as the cat who saved the Clans."

Alderheart wanted to believe the story. Setting off on his own quest to fulfil a StarClan prophecy might be the sort of thing Tigerheart would do. Perhaps Dovewing was helping him. Perhaps their only intention was to protect their Clans.

Rowanstar gazed darkly out at the gathered cats. "If Tigerheart wanted to save the Clans, he should have stayed where he was most needed."

There was an ominous ring in his mew. Alderheart suddenly felt the leaf-fall chill through his pelt.

"I have been struggling to hold ShadowClan together." Rowanstar's gaze was hard. "I had hoped, with a strong deputy like Tigerheart, that we could overcome the betrayals that have split the Clan over the past moons. But Tigerheart has left us." Anger flashed in his gaze as it swept around his Clanmates. "I could not hold the faith of my Clan before the rogues split us in two. I do not have the strength to repair the wounds that have been inflicted since then."

Alderheart's belly tightened as he saw ShadowClan stare back at their leader, their eyes reflecting the cold light of the moon. Was there no shred of loyalty left?

"I can no longer lead ShadowClan," Rowanstar meowed.

Alderheart's breath caught in his throat. WindClan, ThunderClan, and SkyClan watched silently as ShadowClan shifted, exchanging glances. Had they known Rowanstar would do this?

Scorchfur stared at Rowanstar, his gaze unreadable. Juniperclaw leaned close to Strikestone and whispered in his ear. Only Whorlpaw, Flowerpaw, and Snakepaw looked alarmed.

Rowanstar went on. "Leafstar." He dipped his head. "I give our territory to you in exchange for a home. Let me, and whatever Clanmates I have left, join SkyClan."

Scorchfur lashed his tail. "You can't give our land away!"

Grassheart turned on the dark gray tom. "He wouldn't have to if your sharp tongue hadn't cut the Clan into shreds."

"Don't blame me!" Scorchfur looked outraged.

"Scorchfur wasn't alone in wanting a stronger leader than Rowanstar," Juniperclaw snarled.

Tawnypelt's fur bristled. "No leader could have been strong enough to deal with so much treachery!"

Whorlpaw, Flowerpaw, and Snakepaw backed away from their Clanmates, their eyes wide with fear. As Stonewing and Grassheart bunched around their kits, Puddleshine pushed his way through the crowd.

The ShadowClan medicine cat blinked up at Leafstar. "Rowanstar is making the wisest decision. Without Tigerheart, we are no more than a bickering mob of starlings. We need the security of a Clan and the safety of Clanmates who hold the warrior code close to their hearts."

Scorchfur narrowed his eyes. "I've always stayed true to the warrior code."

"Then obey it now and support your leader in his decision." Puddleshine glared at him.

"He wants to give up our territory!" Juniperclaw spat.

"He wants his Clan to be safe." Puddleshine lifted his chin.

Stonewing blinked slowly. "There aren't enough cats left in ShadowClan to patrol our borders. If we join SkyClan, at least we can train our apprentices so that they can become better warriors than we have been."

Alderheart watched the shocked silence, hardly daring to

breathe. ShadowClan was disappearing. How could a Clan simply cease to exist? He looked at Leafstar.

"We will welcome any ShadowClan warriors who wish to join us," the SkyClan leader meowed calmly. "We will be honored to have them. But those who do not join must leave the territory. I will not have outcasts living on the land Rowanstar has given us."

Anxious mews sounded from among the other Clans.

Nightcloud's ears twitched anxiously. "SkyClan must not replace ShadowClan!"

"That's not what StarClan meant when they led them here," Leafpool called.

Passion surged in Alderheart's chest. "There must be five Clans!"

He saw Sparkpelt lean forward to speak. Was she going to agree with him this time? "It didn't take long for SkyClan to claim more territory!" She stared accusingly at the SkyClan cats. "I knew they shouldn't have come here."

"We didn't claim territory!" Sandynose yowled back. "We have taken nothing that wasn't given to us freely."

"The lake Clans were falling apart when we arrived," Sagenose added. "It's not our fault."

The words struck Alderheart like a blow. Sagenose was right. The rogues had torn ShadowClan apart. They'd driven RiverClan to hide within their borders like loners. *Five Clans was supposed to be our destiny, and now we are three.* The ground seemed to shift beneath Alderheart's paws. *This is the storm.* Bringing SkyClan back was supposed to have made the Clans stronger, but instead it had brought about the end of Shadow-Clan.

He stared desperately at Leafpool. "This is all wrong!" he breathed.

She gazed at him, her eyes like dark pools. "There is nothing we can do but listen for StarClan."

StarClan! Anger choked Alderheart. StarClan's meddling had caused this storm. Why should he believe that they would fix it?

CHAPTER 21

❧

Wind blustered across the lake, whipping small waves into whitecaps. The sun lifted into a vivid blue sky. Violetpaw breathed in the musty scents of the leaf-fall forest. She smelled the peaty tang of moorland and looked toward the heather-covered hill, wondering if WindClan cats were watching her patrol's progress around the shore.

Her paws ached. She glanced back at Cloudmist and Cherrytail. Their paws must be raw from the journey. They weren't used to such traveling and looked weary and anxious.

Cloudmist looked nervously from water to forest. "Where does SkyClan live?"

Hawkwing, padding beside her, nodded to the halfbridge and the pine trees beyond. "Our land is there."

Tree narrowed his eyes. "Last time I was here, warriors chased me off."

"They won't chase you off this time," Hawkwing promised.

Cherrytail tasted the air as they neared the trees, her pelt suddenly rippling excitedly. "I can smell SkyClan scent!"

Fidgetpaw and Frecklewish lifted their noses, their eyes brightening as they smelled it too.

Gravelpaw glanced at his littermates. "It doesn't smell like our scent," he grunted.

"Yes it does," Fringepaw argued. "It's just a bit muskier, that's all."

Violetpaw flicked her tail happily. "Your scent will smell the same once you've eaten forest prey for a moon."

Gravelpaw huffed. "I don't *want* to smell different."

Mintfur padded closer to her kit, brushing beside him. "Change can be hard," she mewed sympathetically. "But you'll be among Clanmates."

"I was already among Clanmates at the gorge," Gravelpaw grumbled.

Violetpaw fell in beside him. "Wait till you meet Twig-paw. She's great. So is Finpaw. And Reedpaw and Dewpaw. They're really nice."

Behind them, Molewhisker halted. "I should leave you here." He glanced toward the oak forest at the top of the shore. They were crossing ThunderClan territory.

Hawkwing faced the brown-and-cream tom. "Thank you for your help." He dipped his head formally, then touched his muzzle to Molewhisker's shoulder. "If you ever need help, SkyClan is in your debt."

Molewhisker blinked at him warmly. "It's been fun." He glanced at Frecklewish. "And I'm always happy to help rescue a Clan cat from Twolegs."

Frecklewish purred. She'd relished the journey more than anyone, running ahead to see what lay over the next rise and scrambling up hills to feel fresh wind in her fur. Clearly she was delighted to be free of her Twoleg prison.

Violetpaw blinked gratefully at Molewhisker as the ThunderClan tom headed toward the oaks. "Good-bye!" she called. "Thanks!"

He flicked his tail in reply before disappearing among the undergrowth.

Hawkwing picked up the pace as they neared the half bridge, turning inland and heading toward the pines. Violetpaw's heart quickened. How was Twigpaw? Had she missed them? She couldn't wait to share her adventures with her sister.

As Hawkwing led the way up the short steep bank, Rabbitleap's pelt began to prickle uneasily.

Violetpaw glanced at him. "Are you okay?"

Blossomheart wrinkled her nose. "Can you smell that?"

The patrol slowed behind Hawkwing as they padded into the pine forest.

Violetpaw tasted the air. What had spooked her Clanmates? A sour tang touched her tongue. "Is that ShadowClan scent?"

"Yes." Hawkwing stopped and scanned the trees. His hackles lifted.

Rabbitleap stretched his muzzle to sniff a bramble.

Blossomheart padded forward and sniffed the ground. "It's everywhere. And it's fresh."

Cloudmist's eyes widened in alarm. "Are you sure we're on SkyClan territory?"

"Of course." Hawkwing's fur was bristling. He padded forward.

Violetpaw unsheathed her claws. Had ShadowClan taken back their land while the patrol had been gone?

"Let's check the camp," Rabbitleap suggested.

With a nod, Hawkwing hurried past the brambles, onto the track that led to the cedar grove.

Violetpaw followed, her Clanmates bunched close around her. The ShadowClan smell strengthened as they neared the camp. Violetpaw's mouth grew dry. Had ShadowClan driven SkyClan out? She tasted the air again, confused as she smelled recent SkyClan scents. The familiar smell rolled from the fern walls of the camp, visible now between the trees.

Hawkwing was frowning, clearly puzzled. Violetpaw pricked her ears for the sound of conflict, but as they neared the entrance, she heard the cheerful mew of Finpaw.

"We're going to need lots more moss!"

"And ferns." Twigpaw answered him.

"I'll take Whorlpaw and Flowerpaw into the forest to collect some." Finpaw sounded excited. "You stay here with Dewpaw and Snakepaw and finish the nests we've already started."

Whorlpaw, Flowerpaw, and Snakepaw? Weren't they *ShadowClan* apprentices? Why were they helping Twigpaw build nests?

She caught Rabbitleap's eye. Her mentor looked bewildered. The stench of ShadowClan was so strong as they neared the camp entrance that Violetpaw closed her mouth. "What's going on?"

As she spoke, Finpaw hurtled from the camp entrance,

Whorlpaw and Flowerpaw at his tail. He skidded to a halt as he saw the patrol. His eyes widened in surprise, and then happiness. "You're back!" His gaze flitted to the cats following Hawkwing and Blossomheart. "And you found our Clanmates!"

Hawkwing stared at Whorlpaw and Flowerpaw. "What's going on here?"

Finpaw glanced at the ShadowClan apprentices. "Leafstar will explain." He mewed quickly. "We need to fetch ferns and moss." His gaze flickered over Gravelpaw, Fringepaw, Palepaw, and Nectarpaw. "It looks like the apprentices' den is going to be very full!"

Without explaining, he hared away into the forest, Whorlpaw and Flowerpaw racing after him.

Violetpaw was pleased to see that his tail had healed and he seemed happy. But she didn't understand why he was so excited to be collecting supplies with ShadowClan apprentices.

Hawkwing fluffed out his pelt. "Come on," he growled. "Let's find out what's happened." He marched into camp.

As Violetpaw followed him through the fern tunnel, she blinked in surprise. The half-built camp they had left had been transformed. The walls of the dens were neatly woven. Lichen and brambles padded the medicine den. Ferns had been cleared to leave a wide, open space around the stream.

And cats were everywhere. She stared at Sandynose and Plumwillow lazing in a patch of grass while Tinycloud rolled on her back beside them, letting Quailkit, Pigeonkit, and

Sunnykit scramble over her belly. On the other side of camp, ShadowClan warriors were pushing pawfuls of moss through the entrance of the warriors' den. Inside, Sparrowpelt was giving orders. "There's enough space for five more nests, but I think we'll have to build a second den if every cat's going to stay warm through leaf-bare."

Stonewing surveyed the bramble walls from outside. "There's room here to extend the walls." He glanced at the low branches of the cedar, hanging overhead. "This tree will make a natural roof."

"We can fetch supplies from our old camp," Grassheart meowed.

Hawkwing stared, his mouth open. "What in StarClan is going on here?"

At his mew, Leafstar nosed her way through the lichen that covered the entrance to her den in the hollow of the old cedar. Her eyes lit up as she saw the patrol. "You're back!" Tail high, she scrambled down the twisted roots and hurried to meet her Clanmates. She wove between Cherrytail and Cloudmist, touching noses with Nettlesplash and Mintfur before stopping in front of Frecklewish. "You're safe." Eyes glistening, she pressed her cheek to the medicine cat's.

Leafpool and Puddleshine padded from the medicine den and watched the returning cats curiously.

Tree backed away as Plumwillow and Sandynose leaped to their paws and bustled around their old Clanmates.

"How was the journey?"

"Are you well?"

They peppered them with questions while Fallowfern, Bellaleaf, and Sagenose hurried to join them.

Violetpaw looked past them to Twigpaw.

Twigpaw gazed at her, eyes shining, for a moment, before racing from the apprentices' den to greet her. Purring loudly, she rubbed her muzzle along Violetpaw's jaw, then turned to press her cheek to Hawkwing's nose. "You're safe." Her words came as a happy sigh. She blinked at the rest of the patrol. "And you found so many."

"We're glad to be home," Hawkwing told her. "How have you been?"

"Great!"

Violetpaw thought she saw hesitation flash in Twigpaw's gaze. Had she really been fine?

Twigpaw didn't give her a chance to wonder. "How was the journey? Was it hard finding our Clanmates? Were there dogs? Foxes?" She was breathless with excitement.

"We'll tell you about it later." Hawkwing sounded distracted. His gaze kept flitting to Rowanstar, who was crouched stiffly beside Tawnypelt while his Clanmates watched Sky-Clan's reunion. "First we need to know what's going on here." He padded to Leafstar, interrupting her conversation with Frecklewish and Fidgetpaw. "Why are there ShadowClan warriors in our camp?" he asked bluntly.

Silence spread among the SkyClan cats. ShadowClan moved closer together. Rowanstar narrowed his eyes.

Only Snakepaw carried on chattering. "I hope Finpaw brings back plenty of ferns. We're going to need even more nests than we thought. I've never seen so many—" She stopped as she looked around, as though suddenly aware that she was the only cat talking.

Leafstar met Hawkwing's gaze. "Rowanstar disbanded ShadowClan at the Gathering last night. He asked for sanctuary here for himself and his Clan."

"Sanctuary?" Hawkwing looked around. "From what? Are the rogues back?"

"No." Leafstar glanced at the ShadowClan leader and lowered her voice. "I think he wanted sanctuary from his own Clanmates," she whispered.

Hawkwing's eyes narrowed. "But they're here, with him."

"They are SkyClan now," Leafstar told him. "And, unlike Rowanstar, I will not tolerate disloyalty or arguments between Clanmates."

Violetpaw shifted her paws uneasily. She looked at the ShadowClan leader, hunched at the edge of the camp; she could understand why his Clanmates had lost respect for him. He seemed defeated in a way Leafstar could never be.

Blossomheart frowned. "So ShadowClan is part of SkyClan now?"

"Yes," Leafstar meowed. "Rowanstar gave us their land. And without land, a Clan can't survive."

"We did," Hawkwing reminded her.

"Only just." Leafstar looked around at her returned Clanmates. "But now we are together once more, and we have our own territory." She began purring. "You must be hungry. I will organize hunting patrols."

Violetpaw realized that her belly was hollow. The stale mouse she'd eaten that morning had done little to satisfy the hunger of traveling for so long.

"Bellaleaf." Leafstar nodded to the pale orange she-cat. "Take Sandynose and two ShadowClan warriors and hunt near ShadowClan's old camp. Plumwillow, take Sagenose—"

Sandynose cut in. He was staring at Tree. "Who's he?"

The loner shifted nervously a tail-length outside the group. "I'm Tree," he murmured.

Leafstar blinked at Nettlesplash. "Did you recruit him at the gorge?"

Nettlesplash shook his head.

Violetpaw stepped forward. "I found him," she mewed. "He was on his own. I thought he should come with us."

"Needletail led Violetpaw to him," Hawkwing explained.

Leafstar looked puzzled. "I thought Needletail was dead."

"She is," Hawkwing told her. "She visited Violetpaw and told her that Tree was important to the Clans."

Tawnypelt padded forward, staring at Tree through narrowed eyes. "He looks familiar," she mewed. "I think I saw him with Needletail many moons ago." She paced around the loner, inspecting him. "But having Needletail as a friend is no recommendation." Her gaze flicked sharply to Violetpaw.

"That's not fair!" Violetpaw bristled. "Needletail gave her life to save the Clans!"

"After she betrayed them," Tawnypelt growled.

Hawkwing moved closer to Violetpaw. "Violetpaw trusts Needletail, and I trust Violetpaw."

"Violetpaw is young. The young make mistakes." Leaf-star's hard gaze flitted from Violetpaw to Rowanstar. "We have seen for ourselves what happens to a Clan that lets strangers in."

Violetpaw's heart sank. *She's going to send him away!* "But he might be important!" She had to stop Leafstar from making the wrong choice.

Leafstar looked unconvinced. "If he were important, *StarClan* would have led you to him, not Needletail. She can't be truste—"

"Wait!" Puddleshine cut her off. The medicine cat was staring at Tree's paws. He pushed his way through the crowd of SkyClan cats and nudged Tawnypelt out of the way. "Look at his hind paw!" His pelt was prickling excitedly.

Leafpool hurried after him, following his gaze. "Six toes," she breathed. She stared at Leafstar. "There really is a six-toed cat. This is the cat StarClan told us about!"

Hawkwing frowned, puzzled. "StarClan told you about Tree?"

"They sent a vision to Willowshine," Puddleshine told him. "They showed her a cat with six toes on its hind paw and said, 'To fend off a storm, you will need an extra claw.'" The medicine cat's eyes shone with relief. "And now we've found him."

Leafpool's gaze trailed thoughtfully over Tree. "We need to figure out what's special about him."

"And how he can help us." Puddleshine paced excitedly around the loner.

Leafstar's tail twitched. "I suppose that if StarClan has

prophesied it, then we must accept you." She padded closer to Tree, wariness in her gaze. "For now."

Relief flooded through Violetpaw. She wondered if Needletail could see this. Was she on her way to StarClan?

"Bellaleaf! Plumwillow!" Leafstar beckoned to the two warriors. "Take those hunting patrols out. We have mouths to feed."

The Clans broke from the stillness that had held them. Violetpaw blinked as warriors moved around her. It felt strange to be home and surrounded by so many cats. She glanced toward the apprentices' den.

Twigpaw's pelt brushed her side. "Finpaw and I have been building nests since you went. But we didn't realize we'd need so many." She glanced toward Fringepaw and her littermates. "I'm not sure the apprentices' den will be big enough."

Leafstar padded toward them, her muzzle high. "You two won't need nests." She caught Violetpaw's eye. "It's time you and your sister moved to the warriors' den."

Excitement welled in Violetpaw's chest. "Really?" She could hardly believe her ears.

Leafstar dipped her head. "Twigpaw has learned enough about SkyClan's ways, and you have traveled beyond the horizon to bring your Clanmates home. You have both earned warrior names."

Violetpaw turned to Twigpaw, her heart almost bursting with joy. At last they would be warriors together, fighting and hunting for the same Clan. With a purr, she touched Twigpaw's cheek. Everything was finally as it should be.

CHAPTER 22

❧

Twigpaw felt Violetpaw's breath on her cheek. They were going to be warriors. She waited for happiness to well in her chest, but nothing stirred.

Hawkwing's rich purr throbbed in her ears. "I'm proud of you both," he rumbled. "You'll be great SkyClan warriors."

Fringepaw, Reedpaw, and Dewpaw crowded around them. Twigpaw blinked numbly, wondering why she felt so far away.

"You're going to get your warrior name!" Dewpaw thrust his muzzle against hers. "Congratulations." His eyes widened. "I have to fetch Finpaw. He'll want to watch the ceremony."

Twigpaw didn't move as the tom raced out of camp.

"Twigpaw!" Violetpaw's mew jolted her from her daze.

"What?" She blinked at her sister.

"Aren't you pleased?" Violetpaw was staring at her anxiously.

Twigpaw shook out her fur. "Of course I'm pleased." She forced a purr. "I've wanted this for so long." *I'm going to be a warrior.* She was aware of cats moving around her. *A SkyClan warrior.* The camp seemed suddenly crowded. ShadowClan fussed over the warriors' den. SkyClan chattered eagerly.

282

Twigpaw could barely breathe. "I have to get out of here."

Violetpaw didn't seem to hear. She was focused on Hawk-wing. "I wonder what my warrior name will be. I hope it's nice. Do you think Twigpaw will get a nice name? She'll prob-ably get a fierce one. She's so practical."

Twigpaw backed away.

Hawkwing caught her eye. "Where are you going?"

"I just need some air," she mewed.

"Don't be long." Hawkwing's eyes sparkled brightly. "Leaf-star will want to get on with the ceremony."

"I'll be back." Twigpaw turned and wove between Sky-Clan and ShadowClan, quickening her step as she neared the entrance before racing out of camp.

She swerved from the track, crashing through bracken, running as fast as she could, running anywhere she could be alone. She reached a slope, where fallen trees crisscrossed the ground, leaving open sky ahead. She pulled up, then stood panting. *What's wrong with me?* Why was panic scorching beneath her pelt? *This is everything I wanted.*

"Twigpaw?" Finpaw's mew took her by surprise. She turned and saw him at the head of the slope, looking down at her. "I thought I recognized your pelt. Where are you going? Dew-paw says you're about to have your naming ceremony. He's taking Whorlpaw and Flowerpaw back to camp to watch it." He stared at her, puzzled. "Why are you out here?"

"I needed some air." The run had left her fur ruffled. Heat pulsed from her pelt.

Finpaw padded toward her, his eyes round. "Are you okay?"

"Yes." Twigpaw pretended to be happy. "Leafstar's announcement took me by surprise, that's all. And the camp is so crowded. I just needed some space."

"I guess it's a big thing," he mewed. "Getting your warrior name."

"Yeah." She gazed at him. His yellow eyes sparkled. His thick pelt rippled. "Violetpaw's so excited." Finpaw looked more like a warrior than an apprentice. "You'll probably get your name soon."

"I still have lots to learn." He was staring at her warily, as though he'd guessed she was making small talk to hide something more serious.

"I should be getting back to camp," Twigpaw mewed. "The ceremony will start any moment. Violetpaw will never forgive me if I'm late."

"It must mean a lot, sharing a naming ceremony with her after being apart for so long," Finpaw guessed.

"Yes," Twigpaw padded past him. "It's what we've both always dreamed of." Her heart twisted. *But I always thought we'd be together in ThunderClan.* She thought of Alderheart and Lilyheart. They wouldn't be there to see her receive her warrior name. And Ivypool. *She taught me most. And she always supported me.* She wondered what they were doing. Were they rebuilding the camp? She hadn't had the chance to tell Lilyheart how sorry she was about Snowbush. At the Gathering, she'd watched the cats she'd grown up among, bruised and battered by the rockslide, unable to speak to them because Sandynose was watching her, waiting for her to prove she was a traitor.

Finpaw fell in beside her. "You don't seem very excited," he mewed softly.

Twigpaw lifted her muzzle. "I am." *And I will be.* She pushed thoughts of ThunderClan from her mind. *This is what I chose.* "It's going to be the best day ever." Hurrying, she followed the route she had come, pushing through the bracken and padding into camp.

Her Clanmates had formed a circle beside the stream. ShadowClan had joined them. Her sister was standing beside Hawkwing at one end, while Leafstar paced in the middle.

"You're here!" Violetpaw beckoned urgently with her tail. As Twigpaw crossed the ring, Finpaw padded around the outside of the circle and slid in beside Dewpaw. "Where have you been?" Violetpaw hissed.

"I told you," Twigpaw whispered back. "I went to get some air."

Hawkwing lapped the fur between her ears. Violetpaw fussed around her, smoothing her ruffled pelt with a paw. "You have to look neat." Her eyes were wide. She looked nervous. "I'm so excited. I hope I say the right thing."

"Just do what Leafstar tells you and answer when she asks you something," Hawkwing advised.

"There are questions?" Violetpaw blinked nervously. "What if I don't know the answers?"

"You will." Hawkwing touched his muzzle to her cheek, then nudged her toward Leafstar.

"Violetpaw." The SkyClan leader puffed out her chest as Violetpaw crossed the clearing to meet her. She touched her nose softly to Violetpaw's head.

Twigpaw's belly churned. *I'm next.*

"I, Leafstar of SkyClan, call upon our warrior ancestors to look down on this apprentice. She has trained hard, and learned the warrior code. I commend her to you as a warrior in her turn." She held Violetpaw's gaze as the apprentice looked eagerly into her eyes. "Violetpaw, do you promise to uphold the warrior code and protect and defend this Clan, even at the cost of your life?"

"I do." Violetpaw's mew was thick with emotion.

"Then, by the powers of StarClan, I give you your warrior name." Leafstar's eyes glistened with pride. "Violetpaw, from this moment you will be known as Violetshine, in memory of your mother and because of the brightness of your spirit. StarClan honors your bravery and your loyalty, and we welcome you as a full warrior of SkyClan." She rested her muzzle on Violetpaw's bowed head.

"Violetshine! Violetshine!" Yowls of celebration rang around the camp as the other SkyClan cats began cheering Violetshine's warrior name. Stonewing joined in, then Grassheart. Juniperclaw, Snowbird, and Strikestone followed. Even Rowanstar moved his lips. Scorchfur glanced angrily at his Clanmates, but then began to cheer beside them.

"Violetshine!" Twigpaw heard her own voice ringing among the others. *I can do this,* she told herself. *I only have to say* I do.

Hawkwing's mew choked. His eyes were clouded, his chest out. *He's so proud of her.* Claws seemed to embed themselves in Twigpaw's heart. *I want him to be that proud of me.*

She padded forward, crossing the grass to where Leafstar and Violetshine waited for her. Each paw step felt heavier than the last, slowing until she stopped. She blinked at Leafstar, feeling sick.

She couldn't do this. She felt like she was suffocating, like she couldn't get enough air. *This isn't right. I'm not SkyClan. . . .*

The words tumbled from her mouth before she could think about them. "I am ThunderClan," she rasped. "I'm so sorry. I need to go back to them."

Leafstar's eyes widened in shock.

The cheering of the Clans faltered into silence. Twigpaw did not dare meet Violetshine's eyes. She tried not to imagine the expression on Hawkwing's face.

She fixed her gaze on Leafstar. "I wish I felt like a SkyClan cat." She wanted to run from the camp. She wanted to race through the forest and burst into ThunderClan's camp and tell them she was coming home. She wanted to see their eyes light up and to hear them break into joyful purrs. But life was never that simple. What Clan would want a cat who couldn't make up her mind? *I can make up my mind! This time I know I'm doing the right thing.* But would anyone believe her? "I belong with ThunderClan."

Anger flashed in Leafstar's gaze. "You should have said something earlier." Her pelt ruffled. "This is not the right time to change your mind."

Trembling, Twigpaw held her gaze. "It's better than changing it after the ceremony."

Sandynose padded forward. Twigpaw braced herself for his

harsh words, but his expression was gentle. He stood beside her, his pelt touching hers. "Twigpaw has not made this decision lightly. I've seen her struggling to do the right thing. Her heart has been torn in two directions since she came." He looked at Leafstar. "I'm proud she found the courage to decide."

Leafstar grunted. "She's wasted our time."

"She's found where her true loyalty lies. That is not a waste of anyone's time," Sandynose meowed. "If she'd stayed here, with half her heart in ThunderClan, what use would she have been?"

Twigpaw padded forward. "I'm sorry." Shame crawled beneath her pelt. She glanced at Finpaw. He was staring at her, disappointment in his wide yellow gaze.

Leafstar turned away, flicking her tail. "The ceremony is over," she meowed, dismissing the watching cats.

Hawkwing hurried to Twigpaw's side. "Sandynose is right," he meowed. "You've been brave."

The claws in Twigpaw's heart curled deeper as she saw sadness flashing through his eyes. "I wanted to be with you and Violetshine," she mewed plaintively. "But ever since I came here, I've felt guilty for leaving ThunderClan." She dropped her gaze. "And I've missed them."

A growl sounded behind her. She turned.

Violetshine glared at her. "You're abandoning me again!"

"No, I'm not," Twigpaw stiffened with shock. "I'm still your sister. Nothing will change that."

Violetshine wasn't listening. "You left me when we were

in ShadowClan. And you're leaving me now. All for your precious ThunderClan! What's so special about them? They're just a bunch of meddling know-it-alls. Why do you want to be with them instead of me?"

Twigpaw could hear the pain in her sister's anger. She wished she could fix it. She wished she could pretend that her heart lay with SkyClan and stay here with Violetshine and Hawkwing. "I'll never be happy if I stay here."

"I don't care!" Violetshine hissed. "I don't care if you're not happy! What about me? Why am *I* never allowed to be happy?" Her eyes rounded as though she realized what she'd said. Her body shook. She dropped her gaze. "I'm sorry," she mumbled. "I just believed that everything was finally going to be the way I dreamed it would be."

Twigpaw thrust her muzzle against Violetshine's. "I will always love you. And Hawkwing. And the time I've spent with you will always be a special memory."

Hawkwing pressed against them, soothing Violetshine with a gentle stroke of his tail. "Twigpaw is right," he meowed softly. "We will always be kin. We'll miss Twigpaw, but isn't it better to know she's found where she belongs than to live with her knowing she wishes she were somewhere else?"

Violetshine lifted her glistening gaze. "I just wish she wanted to be with us," she mewed thickly.

Guilt throbbed in Twigpaw's chest.

Leafstar cleared her throat behind them. "Twigpaw, if you're not a SkyClan cat," she mewed, her voice gentle but clear, "perhaps you should return to ThunderClan." She turned her gaze toward the camp entrance.

Twigpaw stared at the SkyClan leader. Leafstar wouldn't look back. *I've disappointed her.* "I'll go," she mewed. "Thank you for all you've done for me."

Leafstar nodded without looking back and walked away.

Twigpaw touched her nose to Violetshine's cheek, and then Hawkwing's. "Take care of each other."

Hawkwing blinked at her sadly. Violetshine turned away.

Her heart felt like it was breaking as she padded toward the fern entrance. She felt the eyes of her Clanmates on her and heard them murmuring in hushed mews.

"ThunderClan!"

"She was never really happy here."

"Then why did she come in the first place?"

Would SkyClan ever forgive her?

At the entrance, paw steps sounded behind her. "Twigpaw!" Finpaw caught up to her.

She looked at him, bracing herself for more pain. Saying good-bye to Finpaw would hurt more than unsheathed claws. "I'm sorry," she began.

"Why?"

"For leaving you," she mewed. "I will miss you."

"You don't have to miss me." He stared at her steadily.

Was he asking her to stay?

"I'm coming with you." He lifted his muzzle stubbornly. "And no one can stop me."

"But this is your Clan!" Twigpaw could hardly believe her ears.

"ThunderClan can be my Clan from now on."

Did he really mean it? "What about Sandynose and Plum-willow, Reedpaw and Dewpaw?"

"They can manage without me." Finpaw fluffed out his pelt. "I don't care if I'm ThunderClan or SkyClan or even ShadowClan. Just as long as I'm with you."

Twigpaw stared at him, unable to find words. She nodded to him and padded out of camp. Her heart struggled from beneath the weight of grief, and seemed to sing with the birds twittering in the branches overhead as, purring, he followed her.

CHAPTER 23

❧

"Why did she ask us to meet *here?"* Alderheart's breath billowed in the cold night air. He paced the lakeshore, pebbles crunching beneath his paws. This was SkyClan land now, but it still carried the scent of ShadowClan. A few tail-lengths away lay the RiverClan border.

"I don't know. She said we were to get as close to River-Clan's shoreline as we could." Kestrelflight peered over the border. "I guess she'll tell us when she comes."

Leafpool had arrived at ThunderClan's camp that morning, promising she'd be home soon but that first, all the medicine cats must meet beside the lake at moonhigh. Then she'd left, hurrying away to give the same message to WindClan.

Now the waning moon hung in the crow-black sky. Stars glittered over the lake. Alderheart fluffed out his pelt against the chill and glanced at Jayfeather.

It surprised him that the blind medicine cat wasn't complaining. He sat silently now, blinking into the darkness.

"Are you warm enough?" Alderheart asked.

Jayfeather sniffed. "What does it matter? I'm here and I'm staying whether I'm cold or not."

Alderheart felt reassured. Jayfeather would always be Jayfeather. Leafpool's secretiveness had unnerved him. It wasn't like her. He'd tried to read her gaze while she'd told him about the meeting. But it gave nothing away. Was she planning to break more bad news? Was there worse to come than ShadowClan's collapse?

One spark of hope had lit the gloom that had hung around Alderheart since the Gathering two nights ago. Twigpaw had arrived at the ThunderClan camp with Finpaw. She'd begged Bramblestar to take them in, and had told him that when she'd followed her kin to SkyClan, she hadn't realized how deep her loyalty to ThunderClan reached.

Bramblestar hadn't said yes yet. He was worried about Twigpaw's fickleness and wasn't yet sure he trusted Finpaw. According to Bramblestar, the SkyClan tom had left his own Clan too easily. But he had promised to consider their request if they could prove their loyalty, and Alderheart secretly felt sure that his father couldn't turn them away when they had nowhere left to go.

"Look!" Kestrelflight lifted his tail excitedly.

An owl was swooping across the lake. The water was so still it reflected the great outstretched wings along with the moonlight. The owl glided above the water for the length of the lake before sweeping into the air and circling around the island. Its cry echoed around the hills as it disappeared among the trees.

"Was that a sign from StarClan?" Kestrelflight gasped. "Owls rarely go near the water."

Jayfeather pulled his paws in tighter. "What do you think

they're trying to tell us?" he grunted. "That an owl will save us?"

Kestrelflight turned on him crossly. "Why wouldn't it be a sign?"

"We've had plenty of signs already," Jayfeather gazed at him blindly. "We don't need any more."

Alderheart padded between them. "I would like to solve one prophecy before we get another one," he conceded. He felt frustrated that he'd made no progress on finding the six-toed cat—if it even *was* a six-toed cat they were meant to find. The rockslide had left him little time to search beyond Clan borders.

The undergrowth at the top of the shore shivered. Four shadows moved in the moonlight.

"Leafpool!" Alderheart recognized her scent before he could make her out clearly. Puddleshine was with her, and two more cats he'd never seen before.

They padded down the shore and stopped in front of him.

Leafpool dipped her head. "Thank you for coming."

Jayfeather's nose twitched. "Who are *they*?" His blind blue gaze pointed straight at the two cats standing behind Leafpool.

Puddleshine whisked his tail happily. "They are SkyClan's medicine cats."

The mottled brown she-cat padded forward, her eyes shining. "I'm Frecklewish." She nodded to the black-and-white tom behind her. "This is my apprentice, Fidgetpaw."

"Hello." Fidgetpaw sounded nervous.

"SkyClan has three medicine cats now!" Kestrelflight sounded surprised. "WindClan is the only Clan left with one. I think it's time I found myself an apprentice."

Alderheart caught Puddleshine's eye. Kestrelflight had included the ShadowClan tom among SkyClan's medicine cats. How could he concede so easily that ShadowClan no longer existed? He looked away quickly. "Twigpaw said that the patrol had returned, but she didn't say they'd brought back your medicine cats."

Jayfeather flicked his tail toward Leafpool. "You can come home now that SkyClan no longer needs you."

"I will," she promised. "As soon as Frecklewish and Fidgetpaw have settled in, and I've shown them where the best herbs can be gathered."

"Let's worry about herbs later!" Frecklewish shifted impatiently. "There's more to tell. Hawkwing's patrol brought back more than just Clanmates."

There was excitement in her mew. Alderheart blinked at her.

Kestrelflight pricked his ears. "What else did they bring?"

Leafpool turned her muzzle toward the forest. A fifth shadow emerged from the undergrowth.

Jayfeather's nose wrinkled. "A loner?"

Alderheart detected the scent of a tom, and stiffened nervously. The loner looked sleek and well-muscled, his yellow pelt glowing in the moonlight as he padded toward them.

As he reached Leafpool, he dipped his head to the medicine cats. "I'm Tree."

Jayfeather's gaze narrowed. "You're the six-toed cat."

"How did you guess?" Alderheart turned to the blind medicine cat in surprise.

Jayfeather padded forward and sniffed the tom. "Why else would Leafpool make so much drama out of bringing us out?"

Leafpool sniffed. "There's another reason I asked you here. Didn't you think it was strange I wanted to meet on this stretch of shore?"

"I thought you wanted to save us the trek to the Moonpool," Jayfeather grunted.

Alderheart wasn't listening. He was staring at Tree's paws. Which one had six toes? It was hard to see in the moonlight. Suddenly, he saw it—an extra claw among the toes on his hind leg, just as StarClan had predicted. He wished Willowshine could be here to see it for herself.

Kestrelflight blinked at Leafpool. "Is there something special about this place?"

Frecklewish and Leafpool exchanged glances.

"Yes." Frecklewish answered. "We've had a chance to talk with Tree. He has a power that might help us."

"I hope he does," Jayfeather sniffed. "Why else would StarClan ask us to find him?"

Kestrelflight flicked his tail. "What is it?"

"How's it connected to this piece of shore?" Alderheart's ears twitched. How was the six-toed cat going to help?

Paw steps sounded at the edge of the forest. Cats were padding from the trees, slinking onto the shore. The scents of

ShadowClan filled the air. Scorchfur and Juniperclaw led their Clanmates across the pebbles. Tawnypelt walked beside Rowanstar. The ShadowClan leader gazed ahead blankly as Tawnypelt guided him forward. Violetshine followed behind. She looked nervous, as though she was self-conscious about being the only SkyClan cat.

Jayfeather bristled. "Why are *they* here?" he demanded.

Kestrelflight blinked at Puddleshine. "Did you know they were coming?"

"They have to be here," Puddleshine explained. "They need to see what Tree can show us."

Alderheart's thoughts swam. What was the six-toed cat going to show them? And what did ShadowClan have to do with it? His heart quickened. Did Tree know how to keep ShadowClan from disappearing?

"Is this close to the place?" Leafpool gazed at Violetshine as the young warrior neared the water's edge.

Violetshine's eyes flashed with fear as she gazed across the border. "Close enough," she breathed.

Jayfeather lashed his tail. "What's going on?"

"We have to be close to where Needletail died," Leafpool meowed softly.

"*And* the others." Juniperclaw padded forward, his eyes dark. His Clanmates shifted nervously around him.

"Tree has the power to bring dead cats from the darkness so we can see them," Leafpool explained.

See the dead? Alderheart's pelt prickled uneasily. "How?"

Leafpool blinked at him. "I don't know. Nor does he. It

was a gift he was born with."

Tree padded to the border. "The dead are all around us, all the time," he meowed. "I can sense them, and sometimes I can make them appear."

Alderheart glanced over his shoulder, shivering. Unease wormed beneath his pelt. *Are we being watched by more than StarClan?* Was Needletail ever close by when he was missing her?

"I can't make *all* dead cats appear," Tree went on. "Needletail told me about StarClan. I've never seen a StarClan cat. I think I can only sense cats who are still tied to the living. They've stuck close to us. They can't move on until they've done what they feel they need to do. Like Needletail." The loner glanced at Violetshine. "She will only find her way to StarClan when she has finished what she started here."

Violetshine's eyes glistened with emotion as Tree went on.

Puddleshine's eyes were wide with excitement. "He says he might be able to make our lost Clanmates appear," he mewed breathlessly. "So many are gone. And we don't know whether they died or got lost or left with the rogues."

Jayfeather fur ruffled. "Is that all you want to know? Which of your Clanmates are dead?"

Kestrelflight padded closer to the loner and followed his gaze across the border. "How will seeing the dead help fend off a storm? That's what the six-toed cat was for, right?"

Leafpool exchanged glances with Puddleshine and Frecklewish. "We don't know. But that is his power. Let him use it." She turned to Tree as though signaling to him to begin.

Alderheart felt silence rise like a flood around him,

swallowing every breath of wind. The cats were as still as ice as they watched Tree gaze over the water. Hardly daring to breathe, Alderheart strained to see movement, but nothing appeared on the wide, flat expanse. Disappointment tugged at his belly.

"What are we doing here?" Rowanstar's explosive mew shattered the peace. "There's nothing to see. This is crazy! That loner has bees in his brain. He's mocking us!"

"Hush." Tawnypelt soothed him.

Violetshine padded closer to Tree. She was staring at him with complete trust. Once more, Alderheart turned his gaze to the lake. His heart lurched as he saw movement. In the breathless air, the water began to stir. Ripples moved across it as figures emerged through the surface.

Cats waded from the depths, emerging dry and wide-eyed onto the shore. Light glowed softly beneath their pelts.

"Beenose!" Scorchfur hurried forward to touch noses with his kit.

His Clanmates streamed around him, rushing to greet the dead.

"Mistcloud!"

"Lioneye!"

"Dawnpelt!"

They called their names, joy and grief choking their mews in equal measure.

Puddleshine's ears twitched anxiously. "Where are Cloverfoot and Slatefur?"

"Where's Berryheart and Yarrowleaf?" Scorchfur asked Beenose.

"And Sleekwhisker?" Juniperclaw scanned the dead cats for his littermate.

"If they're not with us, or in StarClan, they must still be alive," Beenose murmured.

"Alive?" Juniperclaw blinked.

"Where?" Stonewing mewed.

"Why have they stayed away from their Clan?" Grassheart's eyes rounded questioningly.

Alderheart blinked, as shocked as ShadowClan to hear that so many of their Clanmates might still be out there, alive somewhere. His attention was snatched away as he recognized a ghostly pelt. His heart seemed to skip. "Needletail." He stared at her as she padded from the water, her pelt dry as bone and glowing as though she were lit from the inside. Grief choked him.

She stopped in front of him, her eyes flashing in the teasing way they used to when she was still alive. "Did you miss me?"

"Of course." Alderheart's mew caught in his throat. She hadn't changed. Even her scent was the same. He felt her breath on his cheek as she turned her muzzle.

"Violetpaw." Needletail's eyes glowed with affection as she saw her friend.

"I'm Violetshine now." She raced to meet Needletail, a purr rumbling in her chest. She stopped short and blinked, as though a thought had just struck her. "You're not with StarClan."

"Not yet," Needletail told her. "But I am with Clanmates now, thanks to you and Tree. And we will not go far until you are all safe."

"You're not angry with me anymore?" Violetshine blinked at her anxiously.

"I never was," Needletail murmured. "You were the best friend I ever had. We will always be sisters."

Rowanstar stood as though his paws had become part of the shore, staring wordlessly.

Tawnypelt hurried from his side and brushed her muzzle against the cheek of first Birchbark and then Lioneye. "It's good to see you once more."

"We never left you," Lioneye mewed.

"We couldn't," Birchbark told her. "Not until we'd seen the wrongs put right."

Beenose slid between them and faced Tawnypelt. "You must save ShadowClan."

"How?" Rowanstar pushed past his Clanmates, growling, and faced the dead cats. "There's nothing left!"

Beenose stared at him, her eyes glittering in the moonlight. "There is you, and there is still hope. You must fight for your Clan, Rowanstar."

"You must find your missing Clanmates," Lioneye told him.

Rowanstar lashed his tail. "Don't look to me for leadership!" he snarled. "I failed my Clan. I failed my kin." Pain crossed his face. Was he thinking of Tigerheart? "I'm not worthy of being their leader."

Panic fluttered in Alderheart's belly. He was giving up! "Rowanstar." He faced the ginger tom. "You can try. You can—"

Rowanstar cut him off with a hiss. "Don't call me Rowanstar! I have no right to that name."

"But StarClan gave it to you!" How could he deny the gift given by his ancestors? Did he doubt their wisdom?

"StarClan was wrong." Rowanstar's green gaze burned with rage. "From now on I am Rowan*claw*."

As he spoke, the ghostly cats began to fade.

"No!" Alderheart's darted forward, trying to reach Needletail as she began to shimmer into the cold, night air.

Puddleshine stared desperately at his fading Clanmates. "Don't leave!"

"We have questions to ask!" Tawnypelt wailed.

Needletail's eyes burned for a moment longer. She threw Alderheart a knowing look and disappeared.

"I'm sorry." Tree broke the startled silence. "It's hard to hold them here long." He looked hopefully at the distraught cats. "They delivered their message, right?"

Leafpool padded to Tree's side. "Yes," she told him gently. "Thank you for bringing them here."

Tree blinked at her anxiously. "So everything's going to be okay now? You can save the Clans?"

The loner waited for an answer, but no cat spoke.

Alderheart gazed at him, wondering at Tree's simple faith. Didn't he realize that the dead cats hadn't delivered a message of hope? They'd delivered a warning.

All the prophecies StarClan had sent since he had become a medicine cat had told him to do one thing: bring the five Clans together to keep them strong. And now StarClan had gone to extraordinary measures to bring them this message—they must save ShadowClan. But ShadowClan couldn't survive without a savior, and if Rowanclaw wasn't up to the job, who would be?

He stared into the lake where the ghost cats had disappeared and felt a chill to his very bones.

What is left of ShadowClan? And how long before it's too late to save them?

CHAPTER 1

"Look at this tree!" Finpaw exclaimed. "It's *huge*! Do you think there are squirrels up there?"

Twigpaw halted, suppressing a sigh of exasperation as she watched Finpaw scamper over to a massive oak tree and balance precariously on a thick, gnarled root. Her paws were tingling with anxiety and anticipation. She didn't want to stop *again*; she wanted to be at ThunderClan's camp.

What if they don't want us?

"I wouldn't be surprised," Twigpaw responded, firmly pushing her nervousness away. "But we're not hunting now. Remember, we have to reach the ThunderClan camp before it gets dark."

Already the sun was starting to go down, flooding the forest floor with scarlet light, barred with the long, dark shadows of trees. Twigpaw and Finpaw had spent most of the afternoon traveling from the SkyClan camp, slowed down by Finpaw's irrepressible urge to explore.

"I can't wait!" Finpaw leaped off the root and raced across the grass to rejoin Twigpaw. She had to step back abruptly to save herself from being knocked over. Finpaw's tail flipped into her face.

"Hey, watch it!" she exclaimed with a glare.

"Sorry." Finpaw veered in front of Twigpaw, and she almost fell over her own paws trying to avoid him. "Do you think they'll be pleased to see us?"

A flutter of anticipation woke inside Twigpaw's belly at the thought of meeting her old Clanmates again. *I tried so hard to be a SkyClan warrior,* she thought. *But my heart is in ThunderClan. I'm so glad I made the decision to come back . . . and even happier that Finpaw decided to come with me. Surely they'll welcome us. ThunderClan is my home.*

"I'm sure they will," she replied to Finpaw.

"Is it true what they say about ThunderClan?" Finpaw asked as the two young cats walked on side by side. He stretched his jaws into an enormous yawn. "Are they really so bossy, always telling other cats what to do?"

Twigpaw wasn't sure how to reply. She knew that was exactly the way the other Clans sometimes viewed Bramblestar's cats, but she had lived with ThunderClan for many moons, and she knew there was no simple answer.

Besides, she had more important things on her mind. Even though she had told Finpaw she was sure ThunderClan would be pleased to see them, she couldn't help wondering how they would really react when she and her friend walked into their camp. *They will be happy, right? Surely they've missed me since I chose to go with my father?*

Twigpaw's father, Hawkwing, was the deputy of SkyClan,

and every cat had expected she would stay in the newly settled Clan with him and her sister, Violetshine.

But I wasn't raised there, she told herself. *It took me a while to realize how big a part ThunderClan has played in my life, right from when I was a kit.*

As they rounded a bramble thicket, a familiar scent drifted over Twigpaw; she opened her jaws to taste the air more carefully.

"What is it?" Finpaw asked. "Is it prey? I'm starving!"

"No," Twigpaw replied. "It's the ThunderClan border scent markers. We're almost home! Come on!"

She bounded forward, with Finpaw pelting along enthusiastically at her side. The ThunderClan scent grew stronger as they approached the border, and as they reached the line of scent markers, Twigpaw began to distinguish another familiar scent, this one of a single cat.

"That's Sparkpelt!" she exclaimed. "You must have met her when SkyClan was living in the ThunderClan camp. She's Alderheart's sister. She must be somewhere around here. Sparkpelt!" she yowled, leaping up onto a small boulder that lay on the border line. "Hey, Sparkpelt!"

A clump of ferns rustled, and the fronds parted as Sparkpelt charged into the open. To Twigpaw's amazement, her orange tabby pelt was bristling, and when she halted at the border, she arched her back and slid out her claws as if she was facing an enemy.

"Twigpaw! What's going on here?" she demanded. "Why are you so far away from your camp, without your mentors?

Has SkyClan been attacked? Is it more rogues?"

"No, no, everything's fine," Twigpaw meowed reassuringly, feeling almost amused at Sparkpelt's urgent questions. "There's no trouble in SkyClan."

Sparkpelt relaxed slightly, her fluffed-out fur lying flat once more. But her eyes narrowed in suspicion as she glanced from Twigpaw to Finpaw and back again. "So what *are* you doing here?" she asked.

Once again Twigpaw felt the enormity of what she was doing, like a huge cloud gathering over her head, ready to release a storm. *There's no going back,* she thought. *Leafstar would never take me in again, after this. What will happen if ThunderClan sends me away?*

"I've come home," she replied, leaping down from her boulder. It was hard to form the words, as if her mouth were full of prey that she couldn't spit out. "I want to be part of Thunder-Clan again."

"And I've come with her," Finpaw added cheerfully.

Sparkpelt's ears twitched. "Just like that?" she meowed scornfully. "Cats can't just defect to whichever Clan they feel like, whenever they want. That isn't how it works. You made your decision, Twigpaw, and now you have to stick to it. And this SkyClan cat—he has no relationship to ThunderClan, so what does he think he's doing here?"

Pain slashed deep inside Twigpaw like a massive claw. Whatever she had expected, it wasn't this outright rejection. *I thought Sparkpelt was my friend!* Her head drooped, and she struggled to keep her voice steady as she responded.

"I know I must have hurt and upset some of you when I chose to go with my kin to SkyClan," she began, praying that she would find the right words. "It was a huge mistake, and I shouldn't have left the way I did. But surely you can understand that I was mixed up at the time?"

Sparkpelt made no reply, but the tip of her tail twitched once, then back again.

"Living with SkyClan showed me that I really *am* a ThunderClan cat," Twigpaw went on desperately. "This is where I belong."

"I'm not sure Bramblestar will see it that way," Sparkpelt growled.

"I need to talk to him," Twigpaw assured her. "I just want the chance to tell him how I feel. If Bramblestar doesn't allow me back, then I'll accept his decision."

But what in StarClan will I do if that happens? she asked herself.

"There's no way Bramblestar will turn away a cat like Twigpaw!" Finpaw mewed, bright and full of spirit as he always was. "Twigpaw is great!"

Sparkpelt fixed the small brown tom with a glare. "And who are you again, and what exactly are you doing here?"

"I'm Finpaw." Sparkpelt's aggressive stance didn't seem to bother him at all; he faced the ThunderClan warrior with his head raised and his short tail stuck in the air. "We met when SkyClan first came to the lake—remember?"

"Now I do." Sparkpelt's eyes narrowed again. "That still doesn't tell me why you're here."

"I'm here to be part of ThunderClan with Twigpaw,"

Finpaw asserted confidently. "All the cats in ThunderClan are heroes—every cat around the lake knows that. You're the best! I want to join you and have adventures!"

Sparkpelt seemed unmoved by Finpaw's praise. "Well, all right," she meowed, flicking her ears irritably. "I'll take you to our camp. Walk a tail-length ahead of me, so I can keep an eye on you. And don't think of putting a single *whisker* out of line."

"We're not enemies!" Twigpaw's pelt bristled indignantly. "What do you think we're going to do?"

"Keep your fur on!" Sparkpelt retorted. "I'm just taking the proper precautions."

And hedgehogs fly! Twigpaw thought resentfully.

With Finpaw at her side, she crossed the border and headed in the familiar direction of the stone hollow, feeling awkward under Sparkpelt's suspicious gaze. She was trying hard to ignore the growing heaviness in her belly, but Sparkpelt's hostility had come as a nasty shock.

It'll be fine once we get to the camp, she reassured herself. *Bramblestar will understand. He* has *to!*

The sun had gone down by the time the cats reached the thorn barrier that stretched across the entrance to the hollow, and twilight brought the chill of early leaf-fall. Sparkpelt pushed past the apprentices to lead the way down the tunnel.

"Follow me," she mewed curtly.

When Twigpaw emerged into the stone hollow, the whole of ThunderClan seemed to be there. Her heart warmed as she saw so many familiar faces: Cherryfall and Molewhisker sharing a piece of prey beside the fresh-kill pile; Blossomfall sitting with Cinderheart at the entrance to the nursery while their kits frisked and play wrestled around their paws; Graystripe and Millie stretched out drowsily side by side in front of the hazel bush where they slept; Leafpool and Jayfeather earnestly discussing something beside the bramble screen that shielded their den.

With a swish of her tail Sparkpelt beckoned the two apprentices a few paces farther into the camp, then signaled for them to halt. "Wait here," she ordered.

Twigpaw watched her as she bounded across the hollow and scrambled up the tumbled rocks to the Highledge, where she disappeared into Bramblestar's den.

"I hope everything's going to be okay," Twigpaw murmured.

"Of course it will." Finpaw nuzzled her shoulder briefly. "Bramblestar would have to have bees in his brain not to want you in his Clan."

Before Twigpaw could reply, Sorrelstripe slid out of the warriors' den and headed toward the thorn tunnel, only to come to an abrupt stop as she spotted Twigpaw and Finpaw.

"Hey!" she exclaimed. "Twigpaw's here!"

Her surprised yowl alerted every cat in the camp. Cats in the open sprang to their paws, while more pushed their way out of the warriors' den. All of them crowded around Twigpaw and Finpaw, until Twigpaw felt that she could hardly breathe in the midst of so many bright, questioning eyes and twitching whiskers.

"I thought I caught a familiar scent." Brackenfur gave Twigpaw a friendly nod. "It's good to see you, Twigpaw."

"Why are you here?" Fernsong asked.

"Is there trouble in SkyClan?" Lionblaze slid out his claws. "Do you need our help?"

Twigpaw swallowed hard, her pelt prickling with nervousness. Every cat was looking at her expectantly. "No, SkyClan is fine," Twigpaw replied. "But I've left them. I've come home to live in ThunderClan."

Utter silence greeted her announcement for a couple of heartbeats, followed by an outbreak of astonished yowling.

"Coming *home*? Your home is in SkyClan now."

"What about your kin?"

"Who is this SkyClan cat with you?"

Berrynose, at the front of the crowd, looked down at Twigpaw with a disdainful twitch of his whiskers. "You chose to leave, and now you want back in?" he demanded. "Can we ever trust you again?"

Murmurs of agreement came from several other cats.

Twigpaw wished that the ground would open up and swallow her, until she spotted movement from the medicine cats' den. With a gasp of relief she recognized Alderheart pushing his way through the cluster of cats to stand at her side.

Thank StarClan! Alderheart practically raised me. He'll understand.

"Of course we can trust her," Alderheart meowed, his dark ginger pelt beginning to bristle as he faced Berrynose. "Of course we want her back! She was raised in ThunderClan, so she's one of us." His amber eyes were warm and supportive as he gazed at her.

Twigpaw felt as if the sun had just come out from behind a cloud when she heard Alderheart call her "one of us." Aware that some of her former Clanmates were still hostile, she tried to hide her sudden happiness by bowing her head and studying her paws. But Alderheart's praise made her feel warm from her ears to her tail-tip.

I've missed Alderheart so much since I left ThunderClan!

"Twigpaw!"

A commanding yowl rang out across the camp. Twigpaw looked up to see Bramblestar standing on the Highledge with Sparkpelt by his side. He beckoned Twigpaw with his tail. "Come up here," he ordered. "You and I must talk."

Twigpaw exchanged an uncertain glance with Finpaw. *Will he be okay if I leave him here by himself?*

Then Alderheart gave her a gentle push. "Go on," he meowed. "I'll look after Finpaw. Let's find you some prey," he added to the young tom. "You must be hungry."

"Starving!" Finpaw agreed fervently.

Reassured, Twigpaw hurried across the camp and began to climb the tumbled rocks. Sparkpelt passed her heading downward; she said nothing, but gave Twigpaw an unfriendly stare.

"Come into my den," Bramblestar invited Twigpaw when she reached the Highledge.

Following him inside, Twigpaw felt uncomfortable, almost unworthy, to be having a private conversation with the

ThunderClan leader. To her relief, Bramblestar didn't seem angry, but there was concern in his eyes as he stood looking down at her.

"Sparkpelt reported to me that you say you want to rejoin ThunderClan," he said. "You must realize, Twigpaw, that it's not usual for a cat to be so confused about where they belong."

Something in his words woke a spark of defiance inside Twigpaw. "How many cats have grown up the way I did?" she challenged Bramblestar. "Has any other cat lost her parents and her entire Clan, been separated from her sister, and then found a father she thought was dead? I admit I was confused, but I know where I belong now. Haven't I proved my loyalty to ThunderClan by coming back? I'm ready to become a ThunderClan warrior."

Bramblestar's voice was quiet as he responded. "I don't doubt that loyalty to ThunderClan is in your heart today," he mewed. "But it's not always that simple. The warrior code requires us to be loyal to *one* Clan. If you're moving back and forth between Clans, where does your heart really lie?"

Pausing, he settled himself in his nest and motioned with one paw for Twigpaw to sit opposite him.

"I remember when I was an apprentice, back in the old forest," he began. "Something similar happened: Graystripe left ThunderClan for RiverClan because he had kits with a River-Clan cat named Silverstream. She died, and when RiverClan claimed the kits, Graystripe thought it was his duty to go with them and raise them."

"Graystripe . . . ," Twigpaw breathed out, hardly able to

imagine that the sturdy, loyal elder would ever have mated with a cat from another Clan.

Bramblestar nodded. "Then, when RiverClan invaded and tried to take Sunningrocks from ThunderClan, Graystripe couldn't fight for them against us. RiverClan drove him into exile. Bluestar, who was leader then, took him back, but it was a tense and confusing time, and no cat knew who could be trusted."

"But it worked out in the end, right?" Twigpaw pointed out. "Every cat trusts Graystripe now. Besides," she added, her neck fur beginning to bristle in spite of her efforts to stay calm, "SkyClan isn't going to *attack* us! That's mouse-brained!"

The words were hardly out before Twigpaw realized that a mere apprentice shouldn't call her Clan leader mouse-brained. *I've probably ruined my chances of getting back in!*

But Bramblestar's only response was to twitch his ears. "I know they won't—but when you get so indignant at the very idea, it shows that you still hold some loyalty to your kin's Clan. SkyClan is in your blood."

"But I've already tried SkyClan!" Twigpaw protested. "Now I *know* I don't belong there."

Bramblestar hesitated, letting out a thoughtful sigh. "I can see you really mean it," he mewed at last. "And I would be happy to welcome you back into ThunderClan, but . . ." His voice trailed off.

Twigpaw's sudden flash of optimism at the Clan leader's first words faded into uncertainty. "But?"

"This is where your story is different from Graystripe's,"

Bramblestar told her. "He was a grown *warrior* when he switched Clans, not an apprentice. You chose to leave ThunderClan right before your warrior ceremony rather than become a ThunderClan warrior. Twigpaw, I want to believe that you will be loyal to ThunderClan, but I think it will be the right thing for you to complete a short apprenticeship here . . . a kind of probation, to make sure you really want to be a ThunderClan warrior."

At first Twigpaw felt hot anger gathering in her belly. She had already completed a ThunderClan apprenticeship, and then another after she left to join SkyClan. She had assumed that Bramblestar would make her a warrior right away.

More apprentice work? she thought. *I bet that no cat who ever lived has ever shifted as many ticks off the elders' pelts!*

But Twigpaw knew she had to control her anger. She was too grateful for the chance that the Clan leader was offering her, and she knew that she had no choice. Leafstar would never welcome her back.

Besides, she reflected, *what's a few more moons of apprenticeship, compared to the whole of the rest of my life in ThunderClan?*

"Okay, Bramblestar," she agreed. "It'll be good to work with Ivypool again." Relief was spreading through her—even if she had to be an apprentice again, at least Bramblestar wasn't going to send her away.

"Oh, no, Ivypool can't be your mentor," Bramblestar meowed. "She's in the nursery now, about to have the kits she's expecting with Fernsong. No, I'll have to find a different cat for you. . . ."

Twigpaw waited, her paws itching with impatience. *Cherryfall might be a good mentor. Or maybe Whitewing . . .*

"Yes . . ." Bramblestar let out a purr of satisfaction. "I think you'll do very well with Sparkpelt."

Oh, StarClan, no! Twigpaw barely stopped herself from speaking the words aloud. *I know Sparkpelt doesn't want me here.* Then she realized that Bramblestar might already be testing her. "Fine," she mewed, trying to sound enthusiastic. "I promise I'll try my hardest."

"Good." Bramblestar rose to his paws and beckoned with his tail for Twigpaw to follow him out onto the Highledge and down the tumbled rocks into the camp. Most of the Clan was still waiting, and a murmur of anticipation rose from them as their leader appeared with Twigpaw behind him. They gathered around in a wide circle with Bramblestar and Twigpaw at the center; then Bramblestar called for Finpaw to join them.

"Cats of ThunderClan," their leader began. "As you can see, Twigpaw has returned to us. I have decided that she should continue her apprenticeship here in ThunderClan."

Glancing around, Twigpaw was relieved to see that most of her Clanmates looked happy to welcome her back, though she could see uncertainty in the eyes of some of them.

"She'll still be an apprentice?" Dewnose muttered.

Meanwhile, Bramblestar turned to Finpaw. "What are we to do with you, Finpaw?" he asked, half to himself.

Twigpaw realized guiltily that she hadn't even asked Bramblestar about Finpaw. *But surely Bramblestar won't send him away?*

Finpaw stood boldly in front of the Clan leader and met his gaze. "I want to be a ThunderClan warrior," he declared. "I've heard so many tales about Firestar, and how brave and honorable you all are. This is the best Clan in the forest, and I can't wait to be part of it." He gave an excited little jump. "*Please* let me join!"

Twigpaw could hear murmurs of appreciation at the young tom's enthusiastic words.

"Let him in, Bramblestar," Graystripe called out. "We need eager young cats like him."

"Yes, we can't afford to turn any promising cat away," Squirrelflight added; her green gaze rested on Finpaw, half amused and half admiring.

"I don't know . . ." Thornclaw looked doubtful. "Should we really be taking in just any cat? Not every cat is right for ThunderClan, after all."

"True," Cloudtail meowed with a flick of his tail. "Look at what's been happening since the Clans started taking in every cat that happens to stroll into camp."

Listening to the senior warrior, Twigpaw couldn't help thinking about the destruction Darktail and his rogues had caused—but also the chaos *she* had caused when she'd led the remains of SkyClan into the ThunderClan camp. She wondered whether Cloudtail was aiming the sly remark at her, though the white tom's gaze was firmly fixed on his leader.

"Maybe SkyClan cats don't understand that they can't just jump from one Clan to another," Brightheart said sternly. "Finpaw, you have to be sure."

Finpaw's eyes widened. "I *am* sure," he said earnestly. "I want to be part of ThunderClan."

"These are unusual times," Bramblestar said thoughtfully. "With so many changes in the Clans, we have to consider making changes as well. It's possible that StarClan has some reason to want us to welcome Finpaw to ThunderClan... And he does seem convinced that this is where he belongs."

"We should keep him for now." Cherryfall spoke up. "Let's give him a trial and see if he shapes up."

"Oh, I will!" Finpaw's eyes stretched wide as his confident gaze swept around the group of cats. "I promise!"

Bramblestar nodded. "Very well. Finpaw, we'll welcome you as an apprentice for now, but you must show loyalty to ThunderClan. Can you do that?"

Too overwhelmed to speak, Finpaw nodded eagerly.

"Then, Finpaw, from this time forward you will be a ThunderClan apprentice," Bramblestar announced. "Larksong, you are a loyal and committed cat. You will be his mentor and pass on your skills and experience to him."

The young black tom, looking stunned at his leader's praise and the honor of being chosen as a mentor, took a pace forward and dipped his head respectfully. "I won't let you down, Bramblestar."

Finpaw skipped across the circle of cats to stand in front of Larksong, and reached up to touch noses with him. "This is going to be *great*!" he announced.

"Finpaw! Finpaw!" the ThunderClan cats acclaimed him. Twigpaw could see that he was going to be popular, and she couldn't repress a tiny twinge of jealousy. *Are they more excited to have Finpaw join the Clan than they are to have me back?*

Her heart lurched as Bramblestar turned to her. "Do I need a ceremony?" she asked him. "I mean, what's the point. I've already had one. Twice," she added, the last word under her breath.

"You should do as you're told," Sparkpelt snapped at her from where she stood a couple of tail-lengths away.

Uh-oh, Twigpaw thought. *She's not going to be pleased when she finds out what Bramblestar has in mind.*

"Yes, you had a ceremony with Ivypool," Bramblestar meowed, his voice even. "And now you need one with your new mentor."

"It's so exciting!" Finpaw piped up. "We'll be apprentices together."

"Sure we will," Twigpaw responded, wishing she could share her friend's enthusiasm. She turned and nodded to Bramblestar, wishing too that she hadn't protested in the first place. *I don't want to start out by being difficult.*

"Then from this time forward," Bramblestar began, "Twigpaw will be a ThunderClan apprentice. Sparkpelt," Bramblestar continued, "you are a brave and loyal Thunder-Clan cat, and I know that you will pass on all you have learned to Twigpaw."

"What?" Sparkpelt's eyes widened and her neck fur began to fluff up as she gazed at Twigpaw. But she had enough sense not to protest her Clan leader's decision, even though he was her father. "I'll do my best, Bramblestar," she added with a sigh.

Twigpaw padded over to Sparkpelt and made herself touch noses with her as she met her new mentor's irritated gaze. *I'll show you!* she resolved. *I'll be the best apprentice any cat ever had.*

Once the ceremony was over, Bramblestar returned to his den, and the rest of the Clan began to disperse. Most of them headed for the warriors' den to settle into their nests for the night.

Twigpaw found herself alone in the middle of the camp, suddenly feeling a little lost, as if she didn't belong there after all.

I'm sure I made the right decision to come back, she insisted to herself. *But I never thought it would be like this. I thought it would be better. . . .*

A few tail-lengths away, Larksong was talking to Finpaw, making arrangements to take him on a tour of the territory the following day. Finpaw was bouncing up and down, hardly able to contain his excitement.

Somehow her friend's enthusiasm made Twigpaw feel even more uncertain. Staring at him, she waited for the swell of excitement to come back to her. Instead she felt strangely flat.

Oh, StarClan! This is my home now. So why don't I feel happier to be back among my Clan?

ERIN HUNTER

is inspired by a fascination with the ferocity of the natural world. As well as having great respect for nature in all its forms, Erin enjoys creating rich, mythical explanations for animal behavior. She is also the author of the Survivors, Seekers, and Bravelands series.

Download the free Warriors app at www.warriorcats.com.

WARRIORS: THE PROPHECIES BEGIN

In the first series, sinister perils threaten the four warrior Clans. Into the midst of this turmoil comes Rusty, an ordinary housecat, who may just be the bravest of them all.

Also available as audiobooks!

WARRIORS: THE NEW PROPHECY

In the second series, follow the next generation of heroic cats as they set off on a quest to save the Clans from destruction.

WARRIORS: POWER OF THREE

In the third series, Firestar's grandchildren begin their training as warrior cats. Prophecy foretells that they will hold more power than any cats before them.

HARPER
An Imprint of HarperCollins Publishers

www.warriorcats.com

WARRIORS: SUPER EDITIONS

These extra-long, stand-alone adventures will take
you deep inside each of the Clans with thrilling tales
featuring the most legendary warrior cats.

HARPER
An Imprint of HarperCollinsPublishers

www.warriorcats.com

READ EVERY
SEEKERS
BOOK

Seekers: The Original Series

Three young bears . . . one destiny.
Discover the fate that awaits them on their adventure.

Seekers: Return to the Wild

The stakes are higher than ever as the bears search for a way home.

Seekers: Manga

The bears come to life in manga!

HARPER
An Imprint of HarperCollinsPublishers

www.seekerbears.com